Dear Reader

Now that my work on *The Immortals* series is done—the books are all written, and the ones that haven't yet been released are in various stages of production—I'm often asked which of the six presented the most challenge to write, and the answer is: all of them—though each in their own unique way.

When I started writing *Evermore*, I was so focused on telling that particular story that I didn't see it as the start of a series. I was just doing what I always did—attempting to make sense of my own life experiences under the guise of fiction. Ever's grief over losing her family was directly channeled from my own grief over losing my loved ones, and as I began to find my way out of the darkness, Ever did too. It wasn't until I'd reached the end of the story that I realized it was really just the beginning, she had a much bigger journey ahead of her, there was so much more still to tell.

In book two, *Blue Moon*, Ever faces a heart-wrenching decision between the past and the present, and to be honest, I wasn't entirely sure which path she'd choose until I stood on the precipice right alongside her. It was also around that point that I realized the true scope of her journey—the sacrifices she'd be required to make—and exactly how the series would end.

Shadowland, the third book, provides a major turning point for the series. Not only are the stakes raised to a whole new level, but events that seem simple on the surface—the arrival of Jude, the flip-side of immortality—ultimately bear powerful repercussions that'll reverberate in later books.

With *Dark Flame* I made a conscious effort to take Ever's journey in a much . . . well, *darker* direction. It's her struggle with the dark side of herself that allows her to locate the light in the person she once considered her enemy. It's a powerful moment for Ever, one that redefines everything she once thought she knew about herself.

A lot happens in the penultimate book in the series, *Night Star* (coming to the UK in March)—relationships change, serious decisions are made, and everything is put into motion for the grand finale to come. While getting all those pieces lined up sometimes felt like a very tricky game of chess, at it's heart, *Night Star* is a story of friendships—or, more accurately, the fragile nature of friendships. How they can shift and change into something wholly unrecognizable—and how their dissolution can be just as devastating as any romantic break-up.

As for *Everlasting* . . . well, as it's not yet been released, there's not a lot I can say except that it was a very bittersweet moment when I typed "The End." I'd lived with these characters for the last few years, and probably spent more time talking to them than I did my own husband. They became almost real to me— like imaginary playmates—and I have to admit that saying good- bye was no easy task. Even now, as I continue my work on the spin-off series featuring Ever's younger sister, Riley, as well as my upcoming YA series, *Soul Seekers*, I occasionally find myself thinking about Ever and Damen, and Miles and Haven, and Ava and the twins, and Roman and yes, even Drina—wondering where they are, what they're doing, and if they're happy with the ending I gave them. Mostly, I hope that they're happy.

Alyson Noël

EVERLASTING
THE IMMORTALS

Alyson Noël is the author of many books for teens, including the bestselling The Immortals series. Her books have been published in thirty-five countries and have sold millions of copies around the world. She lives in California, where she's busy working on her next novel, but her favourite city is Paris. If Alyson could travel back in time she'd visit Renaissance Florence, but only if she could take her modern-day grooming habits! Alyson is an eternal optimist, who always believes in silver linings.

EVER LASTING

THE IMMORTALS

Alyson Noël

MACMILLAN

First published in the US 2011 by St. Martin's Press

This edition published in the UK 2011 by Macmillan Children's Books
a division of Macmillan Publishers Limited
20 New Wharf Road, London N1 9RR
Basingstoke and Oxford
Associated companies throughout the world
www.panmacmillan.com

ISBN 978-0-330-52812-2

1 3 5 7 9 8 6 4 2

A CIP catalogue record for this book is available from
the British Library.

Printed and bound in the UK by CPI Mackays, Chatham ME5 8TD

FOR MY READERS:

THANK YOU FOR SHARING EVER AND DAMEN'S JOURNEY WITH ME—MY GRATITUDE FOR YOUR ENTHUSIASM, GENEROSITY, KINDNESS, AND SUPPORT KNOWS NO BOUNDS! YOU ARE AMAZING, AND AWESOME, AND I COULDN'T HAVE DONE IT WITHOUT YOU!

AURA COLOR CHART

RED: Energy, strength, anger, sexuality, passion, fear, ego

ORANGE: Self-control, ambition, courage, thoughtfulness, lack of will, apathetic

YELLOW: Optimistic, happy, intellectual, friendly, indecisive, easily led

GREEN: Peaceful, healing, compassion, deceitful, jealous

BLUE: Spiritual, loyal, creative, sensitive, kind, moody

VIOLET: Highly spiritual, wisdom, intuition

INDIGO: Benevolence, highly intuitive, seeker

PINK: Love, sincerity, friendship

GRAY: Depression, sadness, exhaustion, low energy, skepticism

BROWN: Greed, self-involvement, opinionated

BLACK: Lacking energy, illness, imminent death

WHITE: Perfect balance

KNOW, THEREFORE, THAT FROM THE GREATER SILENCE I SHALL RETURN . . . FORGET NOT THAT I SHALL COME BACK TO YOU . . . A LITTLE WHILE, A MOMENT OF REST UPON THE WIND, AND ANOTHER WOMAN SHALL BEAR ME.

KAHLIL GIBRAN

ONE

"Ever—wait!"

Damen reaches toward me, grasping my shoulder, hoping to slow me, to bring me back to him, but I keep moving forward, can't afford the delay. Not when we're so close, almost there.

The worry streaming off him like rain from a windshield, not dimming in the least when he picks up the pace, matches my stride, and laces his fingers with mine.

"We should head back. This can't be the place. Nothing about it looks remotely the same." His gaze travels the distance from the disturbing landscape to my face.

"You're right. Nothing about it *is* remotely the same." I hover at the perimeter, my breath coming too quick, my heart beginning to race. Taking a moment to survey my surroundings before I hazard a step forward again. One small stride followed by another, until my feet sink so deep into the mud-laden earth, the tops of them vanish completely. "I knew it," I whisper, the words barely audible, though I don't need to speak for Damen to hear me, it's just as easy to communicate telepathically. "It's exactly like the dream. It's . . ."

He looks at me. Waiting.

"Well, it's just as I expected." I glance to the side, my blue eyes meeting his dark ones, holding the look, wanting him to see what I see. "All of this, everything you see here, it's like . . . it's like it's all changed because of *me*."

He kneels beside me, fingers splayed on my back, running his palm in slow circles up and down the path of my spine. Wanting to soothe, to refute everything I just said, but choosing to swallow the words instead. No matter what he says—no matter how good and solid an argument he may wage—he knows better. Knows all too well that I will not be swayed.

I heard the old woman. He heard her too. Saw the way her finger pointed, the way her eyes stared accusingly—listened to the haunting tune of her creepy song with its cryptic lyrics and lingering melody.

The warning intended solely for me.

And now *this*.

I sigh as I gaze upon it—Haven's grave—so to speak. The spot where just a few weeks before I dug deep into the earth to bury her belongings—all that was left of her—the clothes she wore when I sent her soul into the Shadowland. A spot I held sacred, hallowed—now transmuted, transformed. The once rich earth turned to a wet, soggy mush with no sign of the flowers I'd manifested, no life of any kind. The air no longer shimmering, no longer glistening, virtually indistinguishable from the dark part of Summerland I'd stumbled upon earlier. So bleak, so foreboding in both its feel and appearance, Damen and I are the only creatures willing to venture anywhere near it.

The birds keeping to the perimeter—the carpet of nearby

grass shrinking back on itself—providing all the evidence I need to know it's changed because of me.

Like fertilizer sprinkled onto a small patch of weeds—each immortal soul I've sent to the Shadowland has tainted and infected the Summerland. Creating its opposite, its shadow-self— an unwelcome yin to Summerland's yang. A place so dark, so dreary, and so contrary, magick and manifesting cannot exist.

"I don't like this." Damen's voice is edgy, as his eyes dart, eager to leave.

And while I don't like it either, while I'm just as ready to turn around and never look back, it's not quite as simple as that.

It's only been a few days since my last visit, and despite knowing that I did what I had to, that I was left with no choice but to kill Haven, my former best friend, I can't seem to keep myself from returning, from asking forgiveness—forgiveness for my actions as well as hers. And that short amount of time is all it took to go from light to dark—to grow murky, muddy, and barren—which means it's up to me to do something to stop it from spreading even further.

From getting any worse.

"What exactly did you see in the dream?" Damen's voice softens as his eyes pore over me.

I take a deep breath and sink my heels deeper, the pockets of my old worn jeans dipping into the mud, but not really caring. I can manifest a clean, new pair just as soon as we're out of here. My clothes are the least of my concerns in the face of all this.

"It's not a new dream." I turn and meet his gaze, seeing the flash of surprise that crosses his face. "I've had it before. A long time ago. Just before you decided to leave me on my own, so I could decide between you and Jude." He swallows hard, flinches ever so slightly at the unpleasant memory, which makes me feel bad, it wasn't the point I was trying to make. "Back then, I was sure Riley had sent it. I mean, she appeared in it, and she seemed so vibrant and . . . *alive.*" I shake my head. "And, well, maybe it was her, maybe it was just wishful thinking, a result of my missing her. But, just after she'd gotten my attention, I realized it was *you* she wanted me to see. You were the point of the dream."

His eyes widen. "And . . ." he prompts, jaw tightening, poised for the worst.

"*And* . . . it's like you were trapped in this tall, glass, rectangular prison, and you were fighting like hell to escape. But no matter how hard you fought, you couldn't break free. Even though I tried to help, tried to get your attention so we could work together, it's like . . . like you couldn't see me. I was right there on the other side, with only the glass between us, and yet, I may as well have been invisible to you—you had no sense of my presence. Couldn't see what was right there in front of you . . ."

He nods. Nods in a way that tells me his logical side, the side that likes tidy explanations and easy solutions, is raring to take over. "Classic dreamscape scenario," he says, brow slanted with relief. "Seriously. Sounds to me like you think I'm not paying you enough attention—that I don't really listen—or maybe even—"

But before he can go any further, I cut it right there. "Trust me, it wasn't the kind of dream that can be found in some Dream Interpretation One-oh-one book. In tonight's dream, just like the dream I had before, when you realized you couldn't fight it, when you realized you were trapped forever, well, you gave up. You just dropped your fists, closed your eyes, and slipped away. Slipped into the Shadowland."

He swallows hard, tries to take it in stride, but it's no use. He's clearly as shaken as I was when I dreamed it.

"And then, just after that, everything disappeared. And by *everything* I mean you, the glass prison, the stage—*all of it*. The only thing left was this gloomy, damp patch of earth, a lot like the one we're in now." I rub my lips together, seeing the scene so clearly in my head it's as though I'm immersed in it. "But that last part was new. I mean, it wasn't in the original dream. Still, the second I woke I *knew* that not only were the two dreams connected, but that they were connected to this place as well. I *knew* I had to come here. Had to see for myself. See if I was right. I'm just sorry I dragged you along for the ride."

My eyes graze over him, taking in his bed-ruffled hair, the soft, wrinkled T-shirt, the worn-in jeans—clothes gathered in a hurry, in haste, just seconds before I manifested the golden veil of light that led us both here. Feeling his strong, capable arms sliding around me, the warmth of them reminding me of just a few hours earlier when we slid between the sheets, tucked our bodies tightly together, and settled in for the night.

Back when our only immediate concern was that of Sabine and how she would handle the second week in a row that I'd failed to go home.

How she'd handle the fact that I took her at her word when she warned me not to come back until I sought the kind of help she's convinced that I need.

And while I've no doubt I need help, especially in light of all that's before me, unfortunately it's not the kind of help Sabine meant. It's not the kind of help that can be found in a prescription, a psychiatrist's couch, or even the latest self-help book.

It requires something much greater than that.

We linger, the two of us gazing upon Haven's grave. Damen's

thoughts carefully melding with mine, reminding me that no matter the consequences, no matter what lies ahead, he's there for me. I had no choice but to do what I did.

By killing Haven, I saved Miles. Saved myself. She couldn't handle the power, pushed every last limit. My making her immortal brought out a whole new side of her—one that we didn't expect.

But that's where Damen and I differ. I'm more inclined to believe what Miles said just shortly after I'd spared him from her. That there was nothing new or surprising about Haven's dark side, it'd always been there, she exhibited signs all along. But, as her friends, we fought to ignore it—chose to look past it, to see only the light. And when I looked into her eyes that night, saw the way they gleamed with victory when she tossed Roman's shirt—my last remaining hope of getting the antidote that will allow Damen and me to be together—into the flames, well, there was no doubt in my mind that her dark side had completely extinguished the better part of her.

And as far as Drina's death is concerned, well, it was either kill or be killed. It's as simple as that. Roman's the unfortunate one—but still an accident pure and simple. A misunderstanding of the most tragic kind, I'm sure of that now. I know in my heart that Jude's disastrous interference was an act he committed solely in my best interest. His intentions were good.

I saw it unfold in his head.

We rise to our feet, slowly, solemnly, all too aware that the answers we seek won't be found here, that our best bet is to start at the Great Halls of Learning and see where that leads. And we're just about to go there, when we hear it. The tune that causes us to freeze:

From the mud it shall rise
Lifting upward toward vast dreamy skies
Just as you—you—you shall rise too . . .

Damen grasps my hand tighter, pulls me closer, as we turn to face her together. Taking in the long wisps of hair that, having escaped the confines of the braid that trails down her back, float freely around her crumpled, ancient face, making for an eerie silvery halo effect, while her rheumy, cataract-clumped eyes settle on mine.

From the deep and dark depths
It struggles toward the light
Desiring only one thing
The truth!
The truth of its being
But will you let it?
Will you let it rise and blossom and grow?
Or will you damn it to the depths?
Will you banish its worn and weary soul?

She repeats the tune, emphasizing the end of each verse. Her voice rising as she sings, *"Rise—skies—too—depths—light— thing—truth—being—it—grow—depths—soul—soul—soul—"* repeating the last part again and again, her eyes moving over me, analyzing, observing, even though they appear to be sightless, as her gnarled, bumpy old hands lift before her—cupping, rising— her fingers slowly unfolding as a spray of ash spews forth from her palms.

Damen's grip tightens, flashing her a harsh meaningful

glare as he warns, "Stay back." Maneuvering in front of me, when he adds, "Stop right there. Don't come any closer." His voice level, sure, containing an underlying threat that's impossible to miss.

But if she heard, she pays him no notice. Her feet keep moving, shuffling forward, while her eyes keep staring and her lips continue to utter the tune. Stopping just shy of us, poised right at the very edge of the perimeter—the place where the grass ends and the mud begins—her voice suddenly changing, lowering, when she says, "We've been waiting for you." She bows low before me, bending with a surprising amount of agility and grace for someone so aged, so . . . *antiquated*.

"So you've said," I reply, much to Damen's dismay.

Don't engage her! he mentally warns. *Just follow my lead. I'll get us out of here.*

Words I'm sure she overheard when her gaze switches to him. The sun-bleached blue of her clumpy old irises practically rolling in their sockets when she says, "Damen."

The sound of it causing him to stiffen, as he mentally and physically prepares for just about anything—anything except what comes next.

"Damen. Augustus. *Notte.* Esposito. You're the reason." Her wispy hair lifts and twirls in a manifested breeze that swirls all around. "And Adelina, the cure." She presses her palms together as her gaze pleads with mine.

I glance between them, unable to decide which is more disturbing: the fact that she knows his name—his *full* name, including one I've never heard before, along with one pronounced in a way I've never heard before, or the way Damen's face blanched and his body stilled the moment she blamed him.

Not to mention, who the heck is *Adelina*?

But the replies that swirl through his mind die long before they can reach his lips, halted by the lilt of her voice, saying, "Eight. Eight. Thirteen. Oh. Eight. It's the key. The key that you need."

I glance between the two of them, noting the way his eyes narrow, his jaw grinds, muttering a string of undecipherable words under his breath as he grips my hand tighter and attempts to heave us both out of the mud, away from her.

But despite his warning me not to look back, I do anyway. Glancing over my shoulder and staring right into those rheumy old eyes, her skin so fragile, so translucent, it appears to be lit from within, her lips softly yielding as she sings, *"Eight—eight—thirteen—oh—eight.* That's the beginning. The beginning of the end. Only you can unlock it. Only you—you— you—*Adelina* . . ."

The words lingering, haunting, taunting—chasing us all the way out of Summerland.

All the way back to the earth plane.

TWO

"We can't just ignore it." I turn, peering right at him, knowing I'm right just as sure as I know he won't see it that way.

"Sure we can. In fact, I already am." His words coming much gruffer than he intended, prompting the apology that soon blooms in his hand—a single red tulip with a curving green stem.

He offers it to me and I'm quick to receive it, bringing it to my nose, allowing its soft petals to brush against my lips as I inhale the barely perceptible scent he placed there for me. Watching as he paces the wide space between the bed and the window, his bare feet traversing the stone floors, to the plush rug, to the stone floors, and back. Aware of the conflict that plays in his head, knowing I need to make my case quickly before he has a chance to build one of his own.

"You can't just turn your back on something because it's *weird*, or *foreign*, or, in this case, *grossly unpleasant*. Damen, seriously, trust me when I say that I'm just as creeped out by her as you are. And yet, I refuse to believe that her finding us over and over again is some meaningless, random event. There's no such thing as coincidence and you know it. She's been trying to tell me something for weeks. What with the song, and the pointing, and the . . ." My body twitches in an involuntary shudder I'd prefer he not see, prompting me to sink onto the bed and rub my hands over my arms, chasing the goose bumps away. "Anyway, it's clear that she's trying to tell us something, give us a clue of some kind. And, well, I think we should at least try to determine what that might be—don't you?" I pause, giving him a chance to respond, but all I get is the stubborn slant of his shoulders, the firm tilt of his head, and a long, lingering silence as he stares out the window with his back turned to me. The sight of it practically begging me to add, "I mean, what could it hurt to try to figure it out? If she turns out to be as old and crazy and senile as you think, then, fine. Whatever. No harm done. It's like, why bother worrying about a few days of wasted time when we're staring down an eternity? Then again, if it turns out she's *not* crazy, well—"

Not getting a chance to finish before he turns, his face wearing an expression so dark and stormy I can't help but flinch. "What could it *hurt*?" His mouth goes grim as his eyes fix on mine. "After all that we've been through—did you really mean to ask that?"

I kick my toe against the rug, feeling far more serious than he realizes, far more serious than I'm prepared to let on. Instinctively knowing deep down inside that the scene we just witnessed bore way more meaning than he'd care to admit. The universe is not at all random. There's a definite reason for everything. And I've no doubt in my heart, in my soul, that that seemingly crazy, blind old lady is offering a clue to something I really need to know.

Though I have no idea how to convince Damen of that.

"Is this really how you want to spend our winter break? Sleuthing after some demented old woman's riddle? Trying to track down a deeper meaning that, in my humble opinion, does *not* exist?"

Better than the alternative, I think, though I restrict the words to my head. Remembering Sabine's face the night after I'd finally returned home in the wee hours of the morning—just after sending my former best friend to the Shadowland and the impromptu memorial that followed in Summerland. The way she looked at me, her robe cinched tightly around her, her lips colorless and grim. But her eyes were the worst—the normally bright blue irises eclipsed by the deep lavender circles that spread just beneath. Staring at me with a horrible combination of anger and fear, her voice harsh, the words measured, well rehearsed, when she gave me the choice between getting the help she's convinced that I need or finding another place to live. Sure I was just being obstinate when I nodded, circled back, and made my way out the door.

Made my way over to Damen's, where I've been ever since.

I clear the thought from my head, tucking it away to a place I'll later revisit. Knowing that at some point I'll have to deal with our issues head-on, but for now, this situation with the dark side of Summerland clearly takes precedence.

I can't allow for distractions, not when I still have one more good point to make. Something I know he'd hoped would go unmentioned the moment I notice the flash of trouble that crosses his face.

"She knew your name," I say, dismayed by the way he casually lifts his shoulders, tries to wave it away.

"She hangs out in Summerland, a place where knowledge is

plentiful. There for the taking." He quirks a brow as his mouth tugs up at the side. "I'm sure it's all there in the Great Halls of Learning for just about anyone to find."

"Not just *anyone*," I state. "Only the worthy." Having experienced its opposite firsthand, remembering the not-so-long-ago time when I was counted among the *un*worthy, when the Great Halls of Learning barred me from entering until I pulled myself together, and got my *good mojo*—as Jude would say—back on track again. A terrible time I hope to never revisit.

Damen looks at me, and while it's clear he has no immediate plans to surrender, it's also clear he's all for finding a compromise. This sort of defensiveness and evasiveness is getting us nowhere. We need action. We need to form a plan.

"She knew you were called *Esposito*." I eyeball him carefully, wondering how he'll try to squirm out of that. "Your *orphan* name," I add, referring to the name that was imposed on him back when he was mortal, just after his parents were murdered and he, left alone with no one to care for him, became a ward of the church.

And though he's quick to reply, saying, "Again, more information that's available to anyone who seeks it. Amounting to no more than an unhappy memory of a long-ago past I prefer not to dwell on." He chases it with a sigh, a sure sign that the fight's seeping out of him along with his breath.

"She also called you by another name. *Notte*?" I look at him, my gaze making it clear that while he may prefer to brush it off and move on to other subjects, I'm not quite through with this one. I need answers. Real and solid answers. A shrug and quirked eyebrow don't begin to qualify.

He turns away, but only for a moment, before he's back to facing me. And the way his shoulders slope, the way his hands sink deep into his pockets, the way his jaw softens in silent resignation—well, it makes me feel bad for pushing it like this. Though the feeling doesn't last long, it's soon overruled by curiosity, as I cross all my limbs and wait for his reply.

"*Notte.*" He nods, giving the name a beautiful, Italian twist I couldn't manage if I'd tried. "One of my names. One of the many, *many* surnames I went by."

I look at him, not allowing myself to blink, not wanting to miss a thing.

Watching the path of his long lean body as he swallows, rubs his chin, crosses his legs at the ankle, and settles back against the window ledge. Taking a moment to mess with the shutters, gaze out at the pool, the moonlit ocean beyond, before snapping it shut and turning to me. "She called me Augustus too, which was my second name—my middle name. My mother insisted on one, though they weren't so common at the time. And, since you and I first met in August, on August eighth to be exact, well, I later adopted it as a last name, changing it a bit to match the month, thinking there was some kind of deeper meaning behind it. That it somehow connected me to *you.*"

I swallow hard, my fingers fiddling with the crystal horseshoe bracelet he gave me that day at the track, a little overwhelmed by a sentiment I didn't expect.

"But, you have to understand, Ever, I've been around for a *very* long time. I had no choice but to change my identity every now and again. I couldn't afford for anyone to catch on to my abnormally long life span, as well as the truth of . . . *what I am.*"

I nod, everything he's said so far makes perfect sense, but there's more, much more, and he knows it. "So how far back does the name *Notte* go, anyway?" I ask.

He shutters his eyes, rubs the lids. Keeping them closed

when he says, *"All* the way back. Back to the very beginning. It's my family name. My true surname."

I steady my breath, determined not to overreact. My mind swimming with so many questions, the most prominent being: *How the hell did the old lady know that?* Soon followed by: *How the hell did the old lady know that when I didn't even know that?*

"There was no reason to mention it." He addresses the thought in my mind. "The past is just that—*past.* Over. There's no reason to revisit. I much prefer to concentrate on the present, right *now,* this moment in time." His face lifts a little, as his dark eyes light upon mine. Glinting with the promise of a brand new idea, he makes a move in my direction, hoping I'll agree to the distraction.

His progress soon halted when I say, "You don't seem to mind revisiting the past when we go to the pavilion." And when I see the way he flinches, I chide myself for not being fair.

The pavilion, the beautiful gift he manifested for my seventeenth birthday, is the only place where we can truly be together—well, keeping within the confines of the events of the time. But still, it's the only place where we can truly enjoy skin-on-skin contact, free of the fear of him dying, free of any worries of invoking the DNA curse that keeps us separated here on the earth plane. We just choose a scene from one of our past lives, merge into it, and enjoy getting swept away by the lush, romantic moment. And I fully admit to loving it every bit as much as he does.

"I'm sorry," I start. "I didn't mean—"

But he just waves it away. Having reclaimed his position at the windowsill when he says, "So what is it you'd have me do, Ever?" His gaze making up in kindness what the words seemed to lack. "Just where would you have me take it from here? I'm willing to tell you anything you want to know about my past. I'll gladly draw up a timeline of every name I was ever known by, including the reason I chose it. We don't need some crazy old lady for that. It's not my intention to hide anything from you, or deceive you in any way. The only reason we haven't gone over it before is because it just seemed so unnecessary. I much prefer to look forward than back."

The silence that follows has him rubbing his eyes and stifling a yawn, and a quick peek at his bedside clock reveals why—it's still deep into the middle of the night. I've kept him from sleep.

I reach out, offering my hand as I pull him close to me, toward the bed. Smiling at the way his eyes light up for the first time since he awoke to me thrashing and kicking my way out of a horrible nightmare. Quickly overcome by the swarm of his warmth, the tingle and heat only he can provide. His arms sliding around me as he pushes me back—back onto the blankets, the rumpled pillows and sheets, his lips sweeping the ridge of my collarbone before dusting my neck.

Mine at his ear, nipping, tugging the lobe, voice barely a whisper, I say, "You're right. This can wait until morning. For now, I just want to be *here*."

THREE

After two solid weeks of waking up in Damen's bed, wrapped in Damen's arms, you'd think I'd have grown used to it by now.

But nope.

Not even close.

Though I *could* get used to it.

I'd *like* to get used to it.

Used to the solid assurance of his body snuggled tightly around mine, the warmth of his breath at my ear . . .

But as of now, I'm nowhere near.

I'm always a little disoriented at first. Requiring a handful of moments to piece it together, take stock of this new set of circumstances. Determine my location, my situation, and just how I came to find myself here.

And it's always that last part, that how-I-got-here part, that never fails to deflate me.

Which is never a good way to greet a new day.

"Buon giorno," Damen whispers, his voice a little scratchy,

unused. Choosing to start each morning with one of the many languages he speaks, today settling on his native Italian, pushing his face into the curtain of long blond hair that spills down my neck, while inhaling deeply.

"*Buon giorno,* yourself," I say, the words muffled, spoken straight into the plush, down-filled pillow my face is burrowed into.

"How'd you sleep?"

I roll onto my back, push my hair out of my eyes, and enjoy a nice, long moment of simply admiring him. Realizing that's yet another thing that I'm still not quite used to—the look of him. The pure and startling beauty of him. It's a pretty awe-inducing sight.

"Okay." I shrug, stealing a moment to close my eyes so I can manifest some minty fresh breath before I continue, "I mean, I don't remember it, so that must be a good sign, right?"

He lifts himself off the sheet, settling his weight onto his elbow while resting his head against his palm to better see me. "You don't remember it? *None* of it?" he asks in a voice that's ridiculously hopeful.

"Well, let's see . . ." I fake ponder, index finger tapping my chin. "I remember you turning off the lights and sliding in beside me . . ." I sneak a peek at him. "I remember your hands . . . or at least the *almost* feel of your hands . . ." His gaze blurs ever so slightly, a sure sign he's remembering too. "And I seem to *vaguely* remember the *almost* feel of your lips . . . but, like I said, the memory's pretty vague so I can't be too sure . . ."

"*Vague?*" He grins, eyes flashing in a way that makes it all too clear just how willing he is to refresh my memory.

I return the smile, though it soon fades when I say, "Oh, and yeah, I seem to remember something about a late-night/early-morning impromptu visit to Summerland, and the crazy old lady where we buried Haven's belongings, and how you, somewhat reluctantly, agreed to help me uncover the meaning of her crazy, cryptic message. . . ." I meet his gaze again, and yep, it's just as I thought. He looks as though I'd opened a spigot and dumped a load of cold water right onto his head.

He turns on his back and stares at the ceiling, engaging in a moment of deep, thoughtful silence, before he sits up, swings his legs over the side, and fights to untangle the sheet from his knee.

"Damen—" I start, unsure of what follows, but it's not like it matters, he's quick to fill in the blanks.

"I was hoping we could spend our winter break doing *other* things." He moves toward the window where he stops, looks at me.

"What kind of things?" I narrow my gaze, wondering what other things there could possibly be.

"Well, for starters, don't you think it's time we settled this whole thing with Sabine?"

I grab the pillow from his side, and plop it right over my face. A move I recognize as being incredibly ineffective, not to mention immature, but at the moment, I don't care. I mean, if I don't even want to *think* about Sabine, then I think it's safe to say that I really don't want to *talk* about Sabine either. But there he is, attempting to chat about my number-one, off-limits, completely taboo—or at least for the moment anyway—subject.

"Ever . . ." He plucks at the pillow, but I just grip it tighter. "You can't leave it like this. It's not right. You have to go back there eventually." He tugs one more time before sighing and retreating to his place by the window.

"You kicking me out?" I lower the pillow to my belly, turn

on my side, and wrap my arms around it, as though it'll shield me from whatever comes next.

"No!" He's quick to shake his head. Fingers raking through his tangle of hair, making sense of it, pushing it back into place. Gazing at me with a look of outright astonishment when he says, "Why would I do *that*?" His hand returns to his side, settles by his leg. "I love going to bed with you, just as much as I love waking up with you. I thought you knew that?"

"Are you sure?" I venture, reading the dismay in his gaze. "I mean, it's not too frustrating? You know, the two of us sleeping with each other, without being able to really and truly *sleep* with each other?" I press my lips together, feeling the heat rise to my cheeks.

"The only thing I find frustrating is you trying to hide under a pillow in order to avoid talking about Sabine."

I close my eyes, allowing my fingers to mindlessly pick at the pillowcase seam, aware of my mood shifting, changing, slipping to the opposite side of his, and hoping I can stop it before it goes too far, divides us too much.

"There's nothing to say. She thinks I'm crazy. I think I'm not. Or at least not in the way that she thinks." I peer at him, trying to insert a little levity, but it slides right past him. He's taking this far too seriously. "Anyway, she's so entirely sold on her opinion that my only real choice is to agree with it, or go away. That's the choice she presented me with. And yeah, while I freely admit that it hurts, hurts in a way that goes pretty dang deep, there's still this part of me that can't help but think maybe it's for the better. You know?"

His eyes narrow, thinking, weighing, before he folds his arms across his chest, causing his muscles to twitch and then settle. "No, I don't know. Why don't you explain it to me?"

"Well, it's like you always say: I'll have to say my good-byes eventually—sooner rather than later. I mean, according to you, that's pretty much a given, right? So what's the point of making peace, of insisting on hanging around for a few more months, when I'll have to split soon anyway? You said so yourself; it won't be long before she catches on—before everyone catches on. She'll see that neither one of us has aged, not even a day. And since there's no logical way to explain something like that, and since Sabine's a person who expects nothing less than absolute black-and-white logic, well, there's really not much more to say on the subject, is there?"

We exchange a look, and although I've hit all the points, including the ones that originally came from him, it's clear he needs more. He's still not convinced of why I shouldn't get out of bed, march myself over there, and try to make peace. Which means he's either being incredibly stubborn, or I've failed to make my case, or both.

"It's like, why delay the inevitable?" I swallow hard and hug the pillow again. "I mean, maybe this whole thing happened for a reason. You know how I've been dreading the good-bye, and so, now that this has happened, maybe it'll just make it easier—maybe this is just the solution I've been looking for all this time—*maybe this is like a gift from the universe?*" The words coming so quickly, I pause to catch my breath, though one look in his eyes makes it clear he's still not riding tandem with me. So I decide to switch gears, try another approach, hoping this one might work a little better. "Tell me, Damen, tell me for reals, in all of your years, with all of your arrivals and departures, so to speak, did you never once pick a fight, or even use a fight as a reason to leave?"

"Of course I did." He averts his gaze, fingers picking at the waistband of his black cotton briefs. "On more than one occasion, I assure you. But that doesn't mean it was the right thing to do."

I fall quiet, having nothing more to add. Squinting as he turns to adjust the shutters, welcoming a dull slant of light from what appears to be a very gray, sunless, mid-December day.

"Maybe you're right." He studies the scenery. "Maybe this will make for the cleanest break. It's not like you can tell her the truth. It'd be like fuel to her fire. She wouldn't accept it. And if by some miracle she did, well, then, she'd be quick to condemn it. And the worst part is, she'd be right. What I've done—what I've made you—it's unnatural. It goes against *every* law of nature." He pauses, turns back to me, a look of true regret marring his gaze. "If there's one thing I'm sure of, it's that we are not living the life that was intended. Our bodies are immortal, true, but our souls clearly are not. Our lives flaunt the most fundamental laws of nature. We are the opposite of what we were meant to be."

I start to speak up, start to say something, if for no other reason than the fact that I hate to see him this way. But he won't let me. He's far from finished. Still got a few more points he's determined to make.

"If nothing else, the Shadowland has assured me of that. You were there, Ever, twice if I remember—the first time, through me, and more recently, because of Haven. So tell me, can you deny what I've said? Can you deny that it's true?"

I take a deep breath, thinking about that horrible day when Haven slammed her fist right into my throat. Right into the sweet spot—my fifth chakra—the center for a lack of discernment, misuse of information, and trusting all the wrong people. One solid punch was all it took to kill me, to end me, to send me crashing, reeling, spinning into that horrible dark oblivion. The abyss. The home for immortals' souls. Remembering how I'd swirled through the blackness, lost in the void, taunted by a never-ending stream of images of all my past lives. Forced to relive the mistakes that I'd made, all the misguided decisions, the wrongs I'd committed—feeling others' pain as intensely as my own. Finding my way out only when the truth was finally revealed. Spared from an eternity of deep isolation when I was left with no doubt in my mind that Damen was The One.

My soul mate.

My one and only for all of eternity.

The sudden revelation along with my complete and total declaration, acknowledging the truth of Damen and me, of our love, is the only thing that healed me, absolved me.

The only thing that freed me of the burden of my weak chakra.

The only reason I'm sitting here now.

I nod, having nothing to add. He knows what I saw, what I experienced, just as clearly as if he were there.

"It's just you and me, Ever. We have only each other. A prospect that may be more appealing to me than you, but only because I've grown used to a lone wolf existence."

"We have Miles," I say, quick to remind Damen how he's now in on our immortal secret. "And Jude." My breath stalls, still feeling a little weird about mentioning him in Damen's presence, despite them recently deciding to bury the past and start fresh. "So, it's not like we're totally without friends, right?"

But he just shrugs, reflecting on the part I failed to mention, the part that's too painful to utter. The fact that someday, Miles and Jude will be old and gray-haired, eating early-bird dinners and looking forward to a rousing game of shuffleboard, while Damen and I will be exactly the same, completely unchanged.

"I guess I just hate to see you and Sabine end it this way," he finally says, gaze like an unexpressed sigh. "But maybe you're right, maybe it's as good a way as any. Seeing that it's inevitable and all."

I toss the pillow aside and reach for him. I hate when he goes dark like this, when his thoughts turn inward and he starts blaming himself. I'll do anything to change the subject, to erase it completely. But he's already turned, missing the gesture, so I drop my arm back to my side and pick at the comforter.

"Okay, so, barring a sit-down powwow with Sabine, what else did you have in mind? You know, for our winter break?" I ask, hoping to chase this dark cloud away.

It takes him a moment to respond, to lift himself above the despair. But when he does, it's so worth it. The smile that lights up his face instantly brightens what once had the makings of a dark, dreary day.

"Well, I was thinking we could do something spontaneous, maybe even a little bit crazy. I was thinking we could actually try having a little *fun* for a change. You remember fun, don't you?"

"Vaguely." I nod, a willing player in this particular game.

"I thought we could take a vacation somewhere . . ." He shoots me a sly, mysterious look before padding toward the cream-colored leather chaise at the opposite side of the room. Reaching for the dark silk robe he'd abandoned along the arm sometime last night and quickly slipping it on. His body moving so fluidly it's as though he melted right into it.

I study him carefully, wondering if he'd sincerely been planning something like that all along, or if he's just trying to entice me with a plan he made up on the fly.

"But . . ." He pauses, securing the sash in a way that leaves it dipping low against his hips, the robe hanging open and loose, allowing for a wide swath of bare chest and defined abs to remain on display.

I slide my back up the headboard while lifting the sheet to my chin—his state of near nakedness making me extremely aware of my own. Still not used to living as a couple, living so intimately, the morning always leaves me feeling more than a little shy and inhibited.

"Ever, I know how eager you are to get right to the bottom of all the things that are bothering you. And, like I said last night, I'm willing to help . . ."

I look at him, bracing myself for the full-on brunt of his honed and polished negotiation skills. I can practically *see* the case he builds in his eyes.

"So, I'm willing to give it one week. I'll give you one full week of my nonstop, undivided, crazy-old-lady-code-cracking attention, and then, when that week is up, if we haven't gotten anywhere, well, all I ask is that you accept the defeat graciously so we can move on to my much better, much brighter, much *funner* plan. What do you say?"

I gnaw at the inside of my cheek, taking a moment to gather my reply. "Well, I say that depends."

He looks at me, shifting in a way that loosens the robe ever so slightly. Expanding the view. Not playing fair.

"Depends on this *plan* of yours." I keep my gaze fixed on his eyes. "I need to know what I'm getting into—where you're planning to take me. I can't just blindly agree to any ol' thing. I have my standards, you know." I look away, look down at my hands, refusing the sight of him, the whole glorious bounty of him, and choose to focus on my cuticles instead.

Hearing him laugh in reply, the sound of it like a deep, joyous roar that fills up the room, fills up my heart. Happy to know that the dark moment from a moment ago is forgotten for now.

Turning and making his way into the bath, the words drifting over his shoulder when he says, "A vacation. Just you and me and some glorious exotic location. A right and proper vacation, Ever. Far from everyone, and everything. A vacation in a place of my choosing. That's all you need to agree to. Leave the details to me."

I smile to myself, loving the sound of that and the images it spurs in my mind, but I'm not about to reveal that, so to him I just say, "We'll see." The words drowned out by the sound of gushing water coming from his oversized shower. "We'll see about that," I whisper, tempted to join him, knowing that's exactly what he wants, but with only a week to crack the code, I head for his laptop instead.

FOUR

"Find anything?" Damen rubs a towel against his wet hair, ridding it of excess water before tossing it aside in favor of a quick comb-through with his fingers.

I push away from his desk and swivel a few inches toward him, rolling the chair back and forth and from side to side as I say, "I ran several searches—ran those numbers she mentioned, thinking it might be a date, or a code, or a link to an important passage, or hymn, or a psalm, or a poem, or . . . something." I shrug. "I even ran that name she mentioned, *Adelina*. But nothing came up. So then I ran a search on the numbers and the name together, but still nothing. Or at least nothing that seems even remotely connected to us, anyway."

He nods, disappears into his walk-in closet for a moment, then reappears wearing a clean pair of jeans and a black wool sweater. While I opt for the far easier, somewhat lazy approach of manifesting my own set of clothes, which turn out to be pretty similar.

Except that my sweater is blue. He likes me in blue. Brings out the blue in my eyes, he says.

"So, where do we start?" He lowers himself onto the chaise and slides on some shoes—black TOMS slip-ons, one of the few things he actually buys anymore—but only because part of the proceeds go to charity.

Gone are the handcrafted Italian leather motorcycle boots he wore when we met. It's now cheap rubber flip-flops in the summer, TOMS in the winter. Aside from his opulent, over-sized, multimillion-dollar mansion, and the shiny, black, fully loaded BMW M6 Coupe that sits in the garage (a car I pretty much forced him to re-manifest and keep), his somewhat recent vow to live simpler, less flamboyantly, more conscientiously, and less materialistically appears to be one he plans to keep.

"For the next week, I'm all yours." He rises to his feet, taking a moment to shake out each leg and settle the hems of his jeans.

"Only for the next week?" I stand before the framed full-length mirror that leans against the wall, trying to convince my hair to do something other than just lie flat against my head. But after manifesting some curls and waves that don't really do it for me, I return it to the way it was and settle on a low loose ponytail.

"While you and I have no expiration date, this little project of yours does—as you clearly agreed. So, tell me, where do we start?" He looks at me, awaits further instruction on how to proceed.

I check out my profile, smoothing my hands over the stray wisps of hair that insist on springing out from the sides, thinking I should try something else, that I'm not quite pleased with the reflection that stares back, when I take a deep breath and force myself to accept it.

Whenever I look at me, all I see are things I'd like to change.

Whenever Damen looks at me, all he sees is a glorious gift from the universe.

Somewhere in the middle lies the truth.

"C'mon." I turn away from me in favor of him, knowing we have no time to waste, that a busy week, a week like I've planned, can feel like only a minute or two when it's all said and done.

Grasping his hand in mine, we stand side by side, the two of us envisioning that soft golden veil of shimmering light, the one that leads us to Summerland.

We skip the vast fragrant field of glistening flowers and pulsating trees, choosing to land at the foot of the broad swath of steps that leads right up to the Great Halls of Learning. Pausing a moment, our thoughts silenced, eyes wide, looking upon it with such awe our breath halts right in our throats.

Taking in its beautiful elaborate carvings, its grand sloping roof, its imposing columns, its impressive front doors—all of its vast and varied parts rapidly shifting, conjuring images of the Great Pyramids of Giza morphing into the Lotus Temple, which transforms into the Taj Mahal, and so on. The building reshaping, reforming, until the world's greatest wonders are represented in its ever-changing façade. Admitting only those who can see it for what it truly is—an awe-inspiring place created of love, and knowledge, and everything good.

The doors spring open before us, and we hurry up the stairs and into the large spacious entry filled with the most brilliant warm light—a luminous showering radiance that, like the rest of Summerland, permeates every nook and cranny, every corner, every space, allowing for no shadows or dark spots (except for the ones of my making) and doesn't seem to emanate from any one place.

We move among white marble columns that appear to have been lifted right out of ancient Greek times, along multiple rows of long, carved wooden tables and benches crowded with priests, rabbis, shamans, seekers of every kind, including: *Jude?*

The moment his name appears in my mind, he lifts his head and looks right at me. Thoughts are things, consisting of energy of the purest kind, and here in Summerland they can be heard by just about anybody.

"Ever . . ." He lifts a hand to his forehead, smoothing the area just above his spliced brow before moving to the tangle of long bronze dreadlocks he pushes away from his face. "And Damen . . ." His expression remains inscrutable, unreadable, though it's clear he's working pretty hard to keep it that way.

He rises from his seat, a little reluctantly to my eye. But when Damen moves toward him with a grin that lights up his face, Jude does his best to match it with one of his own, allowing his dimples to spring into place.

I stay put, watching the two of them engage in the usual palm-smacking, back-slapping, male-greeting ritual. Trying to read the meaning behind Jude's reddened cheeks, not to mention the flash of chagrin in his aqua-green gaze.

I mean, even though he and Damen have called a truce, even though he's now in on pretty much all of our biggest secrets and has no plans to spill them, even though I'm absolutely certain that his uncanny ability to thwart all my best plans is not at all calculated on his part, but that something else, some higher force, is driving him to do it, to always interfere at the absolute worst time possible—I can't stop from hesitating, can't overcome my reluctance to greet him.

But it only takes a moment for me to recognize that hesitation for what it really is.

Guilt.

Good old-fashioned guilt.

No more, no less.

The kind of guilt that comes from sharing a long, somewhat convoluted, and at times quite romantic past with someone, and yet, in the end, always choosing someone else.

No matter how hard Jude tried, I always chose Damen over him. And just very recently, I've done so again.

Yet despite my knowing I made the best choice, the right choice, the *only* choice, despite my instinctively knowing there's someone else out there, someone who's much better suited for him than me, Jude doesn't quite see it that way.

He glances back and forth between us, his gaze ultimately settling on mine in a way that causes an unmistakable wave of cool, languid calm to flow through my body—a phenomenon I've experienced only with him, in this life as well as the others before it. And try as he might to stay distant and neutral, it's impossible to miss the flash of longing that plays in his gaze—a small seed of hope he still isn't free of. Even though it's over in a second, even though he's quick to replace it with something else, something containing far less ache, something far more benign, I take a moment to manifest a bright shining night star over his head, wishing once again that he'll soon find the one person in the universe who's meant just for him, who's far better suited than I could ever be.

Then I make it disappear before they can see it.

"What brings you here?" I force a smile onto my face and keep it there until it starts to feel real.

He shuffles, rocks back and forth on his heels as his hands

fumble at the loops of his jeans. Sorting through his thoughts, carefully weighing his options, deciding between complete or partial honesty, and going with complete when he says, "I just like it here. I can't help it. Though Ava warns me not to overdo it, I just can't seem to stay away."

"Summerland is like that." Damen nods, as though he completely understands, as though he's actually struggled with the same temptation himself. And who knows, maybe he has and we just haven't gotten around to covering that. "The lure is pretty great," he adds. "It's a chore to ignore."

"Are you researching anything in particular?" I strive to keep my voice light, conversational, despite rising up on my toes trying to get a glimpse of the tablet he was studying when we came in. But he's too smart for that, and is quick to erase it the moment he sees what I'm doing.

Which is why I'm so shocked when he says, "Honestly, I was doing a little research on *you*." His eyes burn on mine, causing Damen's to narrow, trying to determine just what that meant. I glance back and forth between them, scrambling for something to say, but Jude beats me to it. "I was trying to figure out why I always seem to get in your way."

I pause, my throat gone suddenly dry, forcing me to clear it before I can speak. "And did you come to any conclusions?" I ask, pretty much everything about me, my voice, my stance, my expression, my demeanor, projecting loud and clear that my interest in this subject knows virtually no limits.

He shakes his head, his face wearing an apology words can't express. "No, or at least nothing concrete," he says.

My shoulders sink, as a sigh escapes my lips, and I can't help but think how nice it would've been if Jude could've done all of my homework for me, but it's never that easy.

"Though there was something . . ."

He's got my full attention again, Damen's too from what I can tell.

"It's not anything that I *saw* per se, it was more a thought that kept coming to me. One I couldn't chase away."

"That's how Summerland works." I nod, a little too vigorously. "Or at least the Great Halls anyway. It's not always concrete, you know. It's not always something you read or experience. Sometimes it's just a persistent thought that refuses to leave until you pay it some notice."

He nods, curls his thumbs around his belt loops and glances toward Damen and me. "Anyway, while I know this'll probably sound judgmental, I think you know by now that I don't really mean it that way, but, well, I can't help thinking that all of your problems, all of your . . . *obstacles* . . . well . . . I can't help but think they all stem from your immortality."

He sneaks a quick peek at Damen, and I do the same. Both of us knowing Damen's responsible for the state that we're in—both of us knowing he's all too aware of that.

"What I mean is, your whole thing with the elixir, and, well, whatever else is required, it's not like I'm up on the details, but still, my point is, it's just not natural, you know? We're not supposed to reach *physical* immortality—that's what the soul is for. The *soul* is the immortal part of us. It recycles, over and over again from what I've seen, but it *never* dies. We're meant to strive beyond the physical world, not . . . not settle for it and *only* it . . ." He winces, but now that he's started, he knows he has no choice but to finish. Besides, it's not like we can't hear it in his head, hear the words reeling toward us as he says, "You're not supposed to embrace the physical world as though it's the last stop—as though that's all there is."

I fall quiet. Damen does too. Both of us marveling at how Jude's words provide an all-too-familiar, somewhat eerie echo of what Damen said a little earlier back in his room.

And I can't help but wonder if there's a reason for that—if I'm meant to hear it. I mean really and truly hear it, and maybe even do something about it.

Maybe I'm meant to pay it some serious notice. As opposed to waving it away like I'm most inclined to do.

Jude squinches his face, reducing his eyes to two narrow slits of the most brilliant blue-green—a sliver of tempting tropical sea that'd be so easy to wade into. "And I think . . . maybe . . . well, I think the karma you've accumulated from making *that* choice is keeping you from experiencing . . ." He shuffles, fumbles, finally pulling it together enough to say, "Well, I think it's keeping you from experiencing *true happiness. Real bliss.* If you know what I mean."

Oh, I think I know what you mean.

I sigh. Damen sighs too. The two of us sounding like a chorus of frustrated discontent.

"So, anything else?" I lift my brow, realizing the words sounded far brusquer than intended and trying to soften the tone when I add, "I mean, any insight on how to get around all of that?"

Jude's mouth grows grim in a way that fades his normally brown skin to an edge of white that outlines his lips—lips I've kissed once—twice—I can't be too sure, there've been so many lives the three of us have all shared. His face full of sincerity when he says, "Sorry. That's all I got. So . . . anyway, I'll leave you guys to it and . . ."

He starts to move away, clearly eager to wrap it up and move on with his day. And while Damen's still lost in thought, lost in a dark cloud of blame, I reach out, fingers catching Jude's bicep as I pull him back to me in a show of brute strength, a pleading look in my eye, and a hastily released thought I took absolutely no time to consider, no time to edit.

Damen looks at me, having been yanked right out of his own thoughts to focus on mine. The distinct, somewhat alarming, more than a little embarrassing sound of: *No, don't go!* that swirled through my head, swirled through the room, before I could stop it.

"Um, what I mean is, you don't have to leave on *our* account . . ."

Damen squints, regarding me with great interest. The same goes for Jude. Resulting in two sets of lifted brows, one spliced, one perfect in every conceivable way, while the eyes that lie beneath are centered on me.

Knowing I need to finish the thought before they both come to some horrible conclusion, one that'll bring us full circle again, I say, "What I meant was, do you really have to leave? Now?" Ugh. I roll my eyes at myself. What the heck is wrong with me? Bad to worse doesn't even begin to describe it, and, unfortunately, Jude seems to agree.

"Well, I thought I'd leave you to your privacy, maybe explore a bit, meet up with Romy, Rayne, and Ava." He shrugs, the gesture showing the full state of discomfort I've put him in.

"They're here?" I glance all around though I don't expect to find them. It's more an attempt to get ahold of myself than anything else.

Jude shoots me an odd look, though he's quick to chase it with: "No, they're back on the earth plane, why?" His brow drops, his mouth flattens. "Ever—what's this about?"

Damen's energy radiates beside me, and I know he's thinking

the same thing. So I take a deep breath, take a moment to carefully meet each of their gazes as I force the words from my lips. "Listen, I've got a little . . . *research project* I'm working on. And, since I've only got one week to get to the bottom of it," I shoot Damen a pointed look, "I thought, well, if you don't mind, I, I mean, *we*—" My gaze holds onto Damen's, pretty much begging him to trust me on this. "Well, in light of the time constraints and the insights you shared, I thought we could really use your help. I think your perspective could come in really, really handy. But of course, it's up to you . . ."

Jude glances at us, weighing, considering, choosing to address his words to me when he says, "Fine. I'm in. It's the least I can do for bungling the whole thing with Haven and just about everything else where you're concerned. So tell me, where do we begin?"

FIVE

I slide in beside Damen, my left knee pressed snugly against his right. The sight of it shielded by the thick wooden tabletop, sparing Jude from the view. No need to rub his nose in it. Make him feel any worse than he already does.

Still, it's not long before he rises from his place just across from us, mumbling something about a new tact he'd like to try, something that just sprang to mind. Though despite the excuse, it's pretty clear he's looking for escape, longing to go somewhere else, somewhere offering less proximity to Damen and me.

I peer at the large crystal globe that hovers before Damen, trying to make out the images it unfolds. But from this angle all I get is a colorful blur. To really see it, you need to sit directly in front of it. Still, I can tell by the way Damen observes it, shoulders slumped, head bent forward ever so slightly, breath coming steady and slow, that whatever he's watching, it's nothing of interest, nothing that'll lead us to the info we need. In fact, if anything, it appears to be lulling him to sleep.

Frowning at the tablet before me that's providing about as much hope as Damen's globe, I push it away in disgust and glance all around. Desperate for a little help, from someone, or something—I'm not at all picky, I'll take what I can get at this point, but no help appears. Everyone remains immersed in their business, their own personal quest, paying no notice of me. And despite my closing my eyes, despite the stream of questions that flows from my mind, despite my obvious plea for assistance that rings loud and clear, the Great Halls make no attempt to address it, no attempt to whisk me away to just the right room like it's done so many times before.

Other than granting admittance, the Great Halls of Learning seem to be ignoring me today.

I try to sit still, try to concentrate, meditate, go to that nice quiet space—but I'm too restless, too agitated, and I can't seem to focus. My mind storming with the kind of thoughts that make it impossible to find any peace. I mean, how am I supposed to relax and concentrate on the flow of each passing breath, when I'm all too aware of the ticking clock that practically hangs over my head? A constant reminder of just how rapidly my one-week deadline is shrinking, inching closer to the end.

Peeking once again at Damen's globe spinning before him, I can't help but feel glum, defeated, allowing my mind to travel to a place I'd prefer that it didn't.

A place of doubt.

Second-guessing.

Extreme reservation.

The part that wants to believe, quickly overruled by the question of which would be worse: to be right about my hunch—or totally wrong in every way?

Would it be better to be solely responsible for the appearance of the murky part of Summerland—to be the object of the crazy old lady's hope as well as her scorn?

Or is it better to be way off base about it all, dead wrong in every sense? Which, in essence, would lighten my load and free me of the burden, the huge responsibility of it all.

What if that old lady really is just some demented Summerland interloper like Damen claims?

What if the dream I was sure Riley sent bears no greater meaning than the one Damen's already convinced of—a pathetic cry from my subconscious for more attention from him?

What if I'm just wasting our time? Misusing a week that could be much better spent?

And, even worse, what if I'm acting just selfish enough to drag Jude into it too, when it's so painfully obvious how uncomfortable it is for him to be around Damen and me?

I swallow hard and glance at Damen, knowing it's time to cry uncle, time to manifest a duffle bag stuffed with all the usual vacation essentials so that we can scram out of here and head off to whatever destination he wants. Just because we have an eternity together doesn't mean I should so willingly waste even a few days of it. But first, there's just one last thing I want to try, and I'll need to go to the pavilion to do it.

He meets my gaze, those dark, heavily lashed, almond-shaped eyes staring right into mine, his lips parting in a way that prompts me to lean toward him, placing my hand on his arm when I say, "Damen, I have an idea."

His globe halts, vanishes, and by the look in his eye, he's clearly relieved to be free of it.

"Why don't you go find Jude and tell him to quit looking,

that I changed my mind, I don't want him to waste any more time, while I head for the pavilion and wait there for you."

"The pavilion?" He smiles, eyes shining with promise.

I nod, taking a moment to kiss his forehead, his nose, his lips, before pulling away and saying, "And hurry!"

SIX

He definitely hurried.

I can tell just by looking.

Usually he's so everything-in-its-place perfect—the poster boy for ultimate cool, calm, and complete and total collectedness no matter the occasion. But, standing before me now, with his face slightly flushed, his hair falling into his eyes, his clothes the slightest bit disheveled, well, on anyone else it would hardly be worth noticing, but on Damen, it's a sure sign of eager anticipation.

"Well this was unexpected. Welcome. In fact, *more* than welcome, don't get me wrong, but still unexpected."

I haul myself up from my slunked-down position on the big, white, *marshmallowy* couch. Clearing my face of disappointment, I struggle to replace it with an eagerness to match Damen's own—an act that proves to be no easy feat after just having failed at my last-ditch idea.

Still, it's time to move on, I'm sure of that now, so I force a smile onto my face, one that starts to feel real the moment I see the freshly picked tulip Damen holds in his hand. His face lights up with a grin that grows in intensity as he moves closer to me, covering the distance in less than a handful of steps, his body appearing like a rapid dark blur until the next thing I know he's placing the tulip onto my lap, settling in beside me, and glimpsing the remote I still grasp.

"Did you find Jude?" I ask, wanting to cover the serious aspects before we get too distracted by our pasts.

He nods, scooches closer, allows his arm to slide around me.

"*And?* Did he find anything?"

Damen looks at me, the slight shake of his head the only answer I need.

But even though it leaves me feeling somewhat deflated (okay, maybe more than *somewhat*), I don't sigh or groan or anything of the sort. In fact, I don't do much of anything to let on just how the news affects me.

Part of me knowing it's all for the best—just when Damen and I are doing so well, fully committed to each other like never before—just when he's ready to whisk me away on some wonderful, exotic, romantic (still undetermined) vacation—well, the last thing I need is to throw a wrench into our current state of bliss—especially after all that we went through to find ourselves here.

The last thing we need is for me to lead us all off on some crazy wild-goose chase, steadfastly ignoring the obvious, the glaring, impossible-to-ignore fact that all signs clearly point to me being wrong. Well aware that this is one of those times when it's best to be wrong, that being right would only end in a batch of extreme unpleasantness.

Yep, part of me knows exactly that.

And, as for the other part, well, it's just gonna have to learn to cry uncle.

"So, which one will it be?" Damen asks, wasting no time in stealing the remote.

I narrow my eyes, frowning at him in a playful way. Remembering the last time he didn't swipe it in time, allowing me to push a series of buttons that revealed a tragic yet ultimately hopeful slave life he'd hoped to keep hidden.

"It's not because of that," he says, misreading the frown and trying to hand it right back. Wanting me to know, in no uncertain terms, that I really, truly have seen it all, witnessed all of my lives, no matter how bad.

But I'm quick to wave it away, everything I've tried so far has failed, so I'm happy to let him take over from here.

My gaze level on his, unable to keep the flush from rising to my cheeks when I say, "How about London?" I blush. I can't help it. No matter how frivolous and shallow I might've been, I'm really quite fond of the life I once lived as the beautiful, dark-haired, spoiled daughter of a British land baron. I guess because I was so untroubled back then, so free of burdens. My untimely demise at Drina's hands was the only dark spot on that entire horizon.

Damen squints, fingers poised over the buttons. "Are you sure? London? Not Amsterdam?" He looks at me with an irresistible puppy dog gaze.

My lips quirk in response, knowing exactly why Damen always wants to revisit Amsterdam, despite his claim that it's because he gets to paint (art being a love that trails second to me), I know better. I know it's because he gets to paint me as a barely clothed, very flirtatious, completely immodest, Titian-haired artist's muse.

I nod my consent, thinking it's the least I can do after all that time I spent boring him to death in the Great Halls of Learning. And it's just a matter of seconds until the screen flashes before us and he grabs hold of my hand, rising from the couch as he quickly leads me to it.

But just like I usually do, I skid to a stop right before it. From where I stand, it appears to be a hard, heavy, foreboding slab—the kind that would gladly reward you with a major concussion for being foolish enough to even try to merge into it. Giving no visible sign that it's something that yields enough for one to slip into.

And, just like he usually does, Damen looks at me and says, *"Believe."*

So I do. Taking a deep breath and closing my eyes as though I'm about to dive into a very deep pool, I press my body against it, continuing to push until we're clear on the other side—until we're one with the scene.

The first thing I do is bury my hands deep into my hair. Threading my fingers through the strands and smiling at the soft silky feel of it. I love this hair. I know it's vain, but I can't help it, I do. Its color consisting of the most beautiful blazing red, like a riotous sunset with just a hint of gold traipsing through. And when I gaze down at my dress, or, more accurately, the barely there slip of flesh-colored silk that drapes and swirls all around me, precariously held together by a loose knot tied at the back of my neck, well, I'm always newly amazed by the amount of confidence it takes to wear something like this. When I'm here, dressed as her, I don't feel the slightest bit shy.

But then I'm no longer seventeen-year-old Ever—she's been replaced by nineteen-year-old Fleur—a beautiful Dutch girl with no doubt of her beauty, no doubt of herself.

No doubt of the bottomless love shining in the eyes of the darkly handsome artist who stands at his easel and paints her.

I move through the field of tulips, gracefully, easily, enjoying the feel of the soft, silky petals and stems brushing against me, stopping in just the right spot and turning toward him, holding the pose he's asked me to keep.

My gaze moving among the flowers to the cloud-streaked sky, pretending to be preoccupied, captivated by the bounty of nature that surrounds me, when really I'm just waiting for the inevitable moment when he'll abandon the painting for me.

I allow my eyes to light onto his, permitting only a ghost of a smile when I see the way his brush trembles—a sure sign that it's just a matter of seconds before he ditches the pleasure of capturing me on canvas for the pleasure of capturing me in his arms. I can see the hunger, the smoldering blaze of desire that flares in his gaze.

And it's not long before he sets his brush aside and makes his way toward me. His gait slow, controlled, but completely deliberate, the fire in his eyes heating to where I can feel their warmth from where I stand. Pretending to be so absorbed in the pose I've yet to notice his nearness, the tingle and heat that flows through me, into me, all around me—a flirtatious game we both like to play.

But instead of taking me into his arms, he stops just before me, face uncertain, fingers quivering as he reaches into his pocket for the small silver flask. The one containing the strange, red, opalescent brew he often drinks. His eyes continuing to burn into mine, though along with the usual blur of need, there's something new lurking behind it—something as impossible to read as it is to deny.

His fingers shake as he grasps the flask, lifts it in offering. His body urging me to take it, to taste it, as his tormented gaze tells a whole other story. Belying a secret battle that wages within, until finally, overruled by an unnamed fear, his expression changes to one of a bitter resolution so brutal, he returns the flask, and reaches for me instead.

His arms circling, clasping me tightly to his chest, his body emitting such love, such reverence, I close my eyes and sink into him. Sink into the feel of his touch, of his lips meeting mine—lost in the wonderful, floaty, weightless feeling of being with him. Like skimming through clouds, surfing over rainbows—we are gravity defying, boundless. The two of us locked in the kind of deeply lingering soulful kiss we can no longer manage back home on the earth plane.

Kissing in a way that, while much better than what we're capable of back home, also bears the restrictions of what transpired before.

His fingers creep upward, slipping into the flimsy silk knot at my neck. Just about to release it, release me, when I (she!) make a small sound of protest and push him away. And, well, at that moment, I can't help but curse her.

Stupid Fleur.

Stupid girl I used to be.

I mean, if she was so dang confident—so carefree and sure of herself—then why did she stop him just when they got to the good part, just when they were about to . . .

Overcome with annoyance that the decisions I made then continue to haunt me today—determining what we're capable of, just how far we're permitted to go—my frustration grows so great, the next thing I know I'm hurled right out of the scene.

Right out of character.

Right out of being Fleur, and back to being me, Ever.

I stand there, eyes wide, gasping for breath. Amazed to find myself still part of the scenery, able to observe all that goes on before me, though no longer claiming one of the starring roles.

I had no idea I could do this. No idea I could willfully reduce myself to an onlooker. Had no idea such a thing was even possible.

But while I'm standing here gawking at the wonder of it all, Damen remains completely oblivious. Too caught up to notice. Too immersed in the moment to realize that the girl he tries his best to unwrap is now, well, *unoccupied*, for lack of a better word.

"Damen," I whisper, though he fails to turn, fails to realize she's just an empty, soulless shell. "Damen," I repeat, a bit harsher this time, but sheesh, enough already. It's like watching your boyfriend make out with someone else, even though that someone else used to be you. But still, it's too weird for comfort. It's freaking me out.

He pulls away grudgingly, reluctantly, turning to me with a look that can only be described as complete and utter confusion. A deep crimson creeping from his neck to his cheeks when he realizes he's just spent the last several seconds engaged in the Summerland equivalent of a pre-teen girl practicing kissing on a pillow.

His eyes dart between us—between the moving, living, breathing, real version of *me* standing before him, and the unoccupied and therefore somewhat translucent version of Fleur at his side. And while she's still about as alluring as it gets, her current state of suspended animation with her eyes all squinty, lips all puckered, hair all askew, well, I can't help but laugh, realizing he doesn't see it quite in the way that I do when he fails to laugh too.

"What's going on?" Damen frowns, readjusting the loose cotton shirt he wore in that time.

"I'm sorry—I just . . ." I look around, doing my best to smother the laugh, knowing he's embarrassed enough as it is. "I guess I just . . ." I shrug and start again. "Well, I'm not exactly sure what happened. It's like, one minute I was going through the motions and the next I was so frustrated with her for pushing you away my frustration propelled me right out of the scene, right out of *her*."

"And how long ago was that? How long have you been standing there watching?" he asks, when what he's really wondering is just how embarrassed he should be.

"Not long. Really." I nod vigorously in hopes he'll believe me.

He nods too, obviously relieved, his color returning to normal as he reaches for me.

"I'm sorry, Ever. I really, truly am. Everything I've tried so far has failed. I can't seem to determine Roman's antidote no matter how hard I try." He gazes at me with a face full of defeat. "And until I can come up with some other option, something I haven't yet tried, well, I'm afraid this is as good as it gets for us. But if it's becoming a source of frustration, then maybe we should stop coming here—or at least for a while anyway?"

"No!" I look at him, shaking my head, that's not at all what I meant, not in the least. "No, no, that's . . ." I'm quick to wave it away. "It's not like I wasn't caught up in the moment too, because I was. I was enjoying her flirtatious game just as much as you were. And, trust me, I'm as surprised as you that this happened. I mean, while I've definitely had the occasional thought that seemed out of character, this is the first time one of those thoughts has knocked me right out of character. I didn't even know this was possible—*did you*?"

He looks at me and shrugs, always too caught up in the moment to have even bothered with thinking about it.

"But still, now that we're here . . ." I pause, wondering if I should really go through with this, then deciding I have nothing to lose. "Well, there is a point I wanted to make, something that recently came to me."

He waits, waits for me to stop with the prefacing and get to it already.

I press my lips together and gaze all around, trying to organize my thoughts, gather just the right words. I hadn't actually planned on broaching it, had no intention of going there, and yet, that's not enough to stop me from turning to him, the words rushing forth when I say, "I've been thinking—okay, I'm not sure how to say this, but, you know how every time we come here we choose between my lives?"

Damen nods patiently, though his gaze betrays just the opposite.

"Well, there's a part of me that can't help thinking: Why do we always choose between my lives? What if being Damen Augustus Notte Esposito wasn't your first life?"

He doesn't gape, doesn't gawk, doesn't flinch, shuffle, fumble, or mumble or any of the nervous little time-stalling maneuvers I would've gladly bet my money on.

Nope, he just continues to stand there, his face a complete blank, devoid of expression, as though he has no thoughts on the idea I just raised. Looking as though I'd just spoken in one of the few languages he's not quite proficient in.

"Right before you got here, I used the remote to punch in the numbers—you know, eight, eight, thirteen, oh, eight? I though it might be an important date or something—a time when we both lived before. And even though nothing happened, still, I can't help thinking it's a very real possibility. I mean, we both know I lived as a Parisian servant named Evaline, right? And a Puritan's daughter named Abigail; a spoiled London socialite, Chloe; the artist's muse," I point directly at her, "Fleur; and the young slave girl, Emala—but what if you weren't always Damen? What if you were once, a long time ago, a very long time ago, someone else entirely?"

What if you reincarnated too?

Leaving that last bit unspoken but knowing he heard it just the same. The words swirling all around us in a way that can't be ignored, even though it becomes immediately clear that Damen has every intention of doing just that.

His stiff shoulders and shadowed gaze are pretty much polar opposites of my glowing face and thrumming body. And try as I might to temper it, it's no use. I'm so overcome with the excitement of this new idea—this perhaps undiscovered possibility—that I can practically feel the energy shimmering around me. And if I had an aura, no immortals do, but if I did have one, I'm pretty sure it would be shining the most beautiful, brilliant purple flecked with lots and lots of sparkly gold bits, because that's exactly how I feel.

It's how I *know* that I'm right.

But, apparently I'm the only one feeling it. Which means I watch in jaw-dropping dismay as Damen turns and leaves me in a field of blazing red tulips without a single parting word.

I pop out of Summerland and appear back at the house, finding Damen looking visibly deflated as he slumps on the couch.

I glance down at myself, noticing how the flimsy slip of silk is instantly replaced with the jeans and blue sweater from before, just as Damen's flowy white shirt and black pants are traded for the clothes he chose this morning.

But even though his clothes are transformed, his mood, unfortunately, is not. And as I survey his face, searching for a hint of kindness, an opening of some kind, I get nothing more than a stony gaze in return. So I head for a nearby wall and park myself there, vowing to lean against it for however long it takes for him to make the next move. Unsure what angers him more—my breaking free of the scene, or the idea that he might've lived before. But whichever it is, it's obviously unleashed some kind of inner demon of his.

"I thought we'd moved past this," he finally says, his gaze landing on mine but only briefly before he's pacing again. "I thought you were ready to move on and have a little fun. I thought you realized you weren't getting anywhere, that you were wrong about Summerland, the dark dreary part of it, the old lady—*all of it*. I thought you just wanted to make a stop in the pavilion so we could have a little past-life fun before we headed off on vacation. Then the minute we finally start to have a good time, you change your mind. What can I say? I'm a little disappointed, Ever. Truly."

I wrap my arms around myself, as though they'll ward off his words. It's not like I was trying to disappoint him; that wasn't at all what I intended. Still, I just can't shake the idea that unraveling the old woman's riddle will lead to a happier, brighter future for us. Which is all I really want, and I know that's all he really wants too—despite the downer mood that he's in.

But I don't say any of that. Mostly because Damen—my soul mate—the love of my lives—is always the one I can count on to diffuse my emotional land mines well before they have a chance to explode in our faces. So the least I can do is return the favor.

He looks at me, still clearly unhappy. So I keep my voice purposely soft and mellow, relaxing my body and holding my hands out before me, fingers splayed, palms open in a gesture of peace when I say, "Are you upset because I stopped the scene and popped out of character? Or are you upset because I insinuated you might've lived before, as somebody else? Or—or both? And if it's both, which is upsetting you more?"

I wait for him to respond. Braced for the worst, braced to hear just about anything at this point, and yet still taken by surprise when he says, "This whole thing is ridiculous. I mean, a *previous life*? Ever, *please*. I've been around for over six hundred years already, doesn't that seem long enough to you?"

"O—*kay* . . ." I drag out the word, intent on making my point, but knowing I need to tread carefully, this whole subject has clearly hit a nerve. "And I've popped in and out of existence for four hundred years . . . *that we know of.*" I nod, knowing it's sure to upset him but it has to be said.

"That you *know of*?" He looks at me, choosing to take that personally. "You think there's more that I'm hiding from you? Another slave life perhaps?"

"No." I shake my head, quick to refute it, wanting desperately to diffuse it. "No, not at all. I was actually thinking more along the lines of there being other lives that—that we're *not* aware of. I mean, Damen, seriously, you've got to at least admit the possibility. I mean, what? You think the world just sprang up all around you the day you came into the world as Damen Augustus Notte? You think you were some newly hatched soul with no past? No karma to pay off?"

His brows draw together as his eyes grow dark, but his voice remains calm, even, when he says, "I'm sorry, Ever. Sorry to trump your idea with the truth. But the fact is, a soul has to start somewhere, to be 'newly hatched' as you call it. So why not then and there? Besides, if there'd been another life, an earlier life, I would've known about it by now. I would've seen it in the Shadowland."

"So, you're telling me you didn't?" I'm unwilling to let it go, despite the undeniable point he's just made, despite the steam running out of me.

"I did not." He nods, face solemn, resolute, determined not to gloat with the victory of winning this one.

I sigh, close my eyes, and shove my hands deep into my pockets. Recalling my own trip to Shadowland, the blur of images that played out before me—all around me—never once seeing anything that wasn't expected—no prior lives I wasn't already aware of.

No other version of me that went by the name Adelina.

Nothing that took place in the year 1308.

My lids lifting only to find Damen standing before me, his gaze soft and gentle, pressing a bundle of tulips into my hand. The words *I'm sorry*, written in an elaborate bold purple script that hovers between us.

Me too, I write just underneath. *I didn't mean to disappoint you.*

"I know," he whispers, his arms moving around me as I close my eyes and lean into the hug, savoring the feel of his body against mine. "And I know I'm going to live to regret this, but you can have your week back. Really. Investigate your heart out and I'll do what I can to help you search. But when the week is over, Ever, you're all mine. I'm making some serious vacation plans."

SEVEN

"**When I agreed to help you search,** I thought we'd be in the Great Halls of Learning. What are we going to do here? Set up camp for the next six days?" He looks at me, face aghast by the very thought of it. Having assumed his days of roughing it, of going without the things he's grown accustomed to, like magick, and manifesting, not to mention indoor plumbing, were solidly behind him, he's more than a little dismayed to find himself here. "What if she doesn't return? What then?" He settles in beside me, his body heaving a little more forcefully than necessary, or at least it seems that way to me. His movements causing the plastic tarp to sink and shake, resulting in a disgusting slurping-type sound as the ground burps and settles beneath us.

A sound that sets me off in a fit of giggles, I can't help it. But he just shakes his head and rolls his eyes, totally and completely over it.

Having been smart enough to manifest two big plastic tarps—one to sit on, and one to shield us from the constant on-slaught of rain—along with a few other essentials just before reaching this point—the part of Summerland where magick goes unrecognized, and manifesting does not exist—I can't help but think we should've made something more—like a fully loaded RV perhaps that we could've parked off to the side. Still, I'm determined to make the best of it, to wait it out until the old lady shows up again.

And she better show up or I'll never live this one down.

The ground continues to sink and slosh every time one of us makes even the slightest adjustment, forcing me to swallow a whole new set of giggles and return my focus to Damen when I say, "Instead of worrying about what you'll do if she *doesn't* come, maybe you should start thinking about what you'll do when she *does* come. I mean, after all, isn't that why we're here?"

He looks at me, swipes a hand through his hair, pushing it away from his forehead when he says, "Honestly, Ever? The only reason I'm here is because I've sworn my eternal allegiance to you. You know that part about 'for better or worse'? I figure this must be the *worse* part, which means it can only get better from here."

I glance at him, tempted to make some crack about us not being married, but decide it's better not to push my luck, so I let it drop.

"So what are you going to do? If she comes, I mean?" Damen leans back and gazes up at the tarp hanging over us, no magick, no manifesting, nothing better to do.

"I'm going to confront her head-on. I'm going to ask her to stop speaking in riddles and get to the point. I'm going to—"

He looks at me, waiting to hear more. But there is no more. That's as far as I've gotten with the plan. So I fold my hands in my lap and end it with that.

"Okay, and between now and then?" He lifts his brow.

I look at him, my face a blank until I remember the duffle bag I'd manifested earlier. I run off to retrieve it, dropping it before him and watching as he sits up, perks up, and peers inside. Riffling through a supply of magazines, a couple of paperbacks, a deck of playing cards, some board games, and several chilled bottles of elixir.

"I don't get it," he says, seeming a little confused by the stash. "What's all this?"

"It's a little something I like to call, 'making the best of a not so great situation.'" I nod, holding my breath when he hesitates, stills, then decides to go with it. Lifting the top off a board game and going about the motions of setting it up, I settle in beside him.

Stretching my legs out before me until they're nearly even with his, glancing all around, on the lookout for *her*, but seeing only the usual landscape of gray skies, drenched earth, and a rain that refuses to stop or slow down, I plead a silent wish for her to show, sooner rather than later, then return my focus to Damen, motioning for him to take the first roll.

EIGHT

Three games, one nap (Damen, not me), and two and a half bottles of elixir later, she appears.

And I mean, she just—*appears*. Like, one minute it's just us, no sign of anyone else, and the next she's standing before us, those ancient eyes focused on me as though they'd never left.

"Damen!" I spare a moment to glance at him, seeing the way he stirs in his sleep and starts to roll over. I grab hold of his leg, giving it one, two good shakes as I repeat, "Damen— wake up! She's *here!*"

Saying it as though the mere sight of her holds the promise of something great—like I'd just spotted Santa with a sleigh full of presents and a fleet of flying reindeer.

Damen bolts upright, allowing his hand a quick swipe of his eyes, clearing the sleep before reaching for me. A delay that causes him to miss contact, the chance to pull me back to him, as I haul myself to my feet and make my way toward her. Having no idea what I'll say, but I've waited too long in the rain to miss the opportunity.

"You . . ." she begins, her arm slowly lifting, though I'm quick to stop her right there. No need to go into full-on chant mode, not when we've all heard it before and really don't need to hear it again.

"About that . . ." I stand before her, careful to keep a cushion of a few feet between us, even though at her advanced age I'm pretty sure she's ill equipped to harm me in any real way. "I've heard the song, memorized the lyrics, and trust me, I mean no disrespect, but do you think we could just communicate in English? Or, at least the kind of English I'm used to, the kind that actually makes sense?"

My eyes travel over her, taking in the silver wisps of hair, the startling eyes, the skin that appears so fragile and thin it looks as though it might snag. Searching for a reaction, some sign that she took offense at my words, but unable to find any response other than a rheumy old gaze that switches to Damen as he claims the space by my side. His shoulders squared, legs steady, feet placed just so, readying himself to spring into action, do whatever it takes to defend me from this strange centenarian should it come to that.

A thought that seems so silly on the surface, I could easily burst into yet another fit of laughter if this wasn't so serious.

I rise up on my toes, well, as much as one can when knee-deep in muck, remembering how one of the last times I saw her, Misa and Marco surprised me by stepping out from behind her, but from what I can see, today they're not here.

So far it's just Damen, the crazy old lady, and me. And, from what I can tell, she doesn't seem the slightest bit surprised to find us both waiting.

I'm about to speak again, determined to move this thing forward and get what I came for—determined to clear my conscience of the overwhelmingly nagging doubt that Damen might be right after all—that this is all some sort of cruel cosmic joke—that I'm being played in the very worst way—that there's no way either of us lived before—when she looks at me and says, *"Adelina."*

That's it. She just says, *"Adelina."* Then lowers her lids and bows ever so slightly, her palms held fast to the center of her chest, the movement directed at me as though she is the worshipper and I'm some kind of hallowed deity.

"Um, see, the thing is," I start, unsure how to respond to such an awkward gesture and eager to move past it, pretend it didn't happen. "I have no idea what you're talking about. My name is *Ever* and this is *Damen*—" Damen shoots me a look of absolute horror, unhappy at being pulled into it. So I shoot him a frown, taking a moment to tack on an eye roll to go along with it, returning my focus to her when I add, "As you *already* know," shooting Damen another quick look, reminding him that his identity is hardly a secret where she's concerned. In fact, she seems to know all about him, or at least his full name anyway. "And, I have no idea who this Adelina is, or what she could possibly have to do with me, so maybe you can fill me in, what do you think?"

"I am Lotus," she says, voice like a whisper as her gaze lights on mine.

O-*kay,* not exactly what I asked, but still progress. I guess.

"Damen is the reason." Her head turns toward him. "Your love is the symptom." She glances back and forth between us. "But you, Adelina, are the cure. The key." She settles on me.

Oh boy.

Just because I keep myself from sighing, doesn't mean I keep myself from thinking: *Here we go again—more cryptic ramblings that make absolutely no sense.*

"Listen, here's the thing, like I just said, my name is Ever, *not* Adelina. In fact, I've *never* been Adelina. I've been Evaline, Abigail, Fleur, Chloe, and Emala but never Adelina. You got the *wrong* girl."

I sigh and turn away, annoyed by the game. Catching a glimpse of relief in Damen's gaze—a glimpse that soon turns to rage—when the old woman steps forward and grabs ahold of my sleeve.

"Hey—" Damen's voice is sharp, but Lotus ignores him, her grip tightening on my arm as she peers at me intently.

"*Please*. We've waited so long. Waited for you, Adelina. You must return. You must make the journey. You must find the truth. It's the only way to release them. Release me."

"Where are Misa and Marco?" I ask, though I have no idea why. Maybe it's because they're the only things that feel tangible and real in this otherwise surreal scene.

"There are many who await you. The journey is yours. Yours and only yours."

"*What* journey?" I ask, voice trembling like a sob. "I'm sorry but none of this makes any sense. If it's so important for me to do this, even though I'm *not* Adelina, then maybe you can quit with the puzzles and explain it in a way that'll mean something to me."

"The journey back." She bows her head again, leaving me with a view of silvery hair with no discernable part.

"Back to *where*?" I plead, face flushing with the makings of hysteria—and knowing I need to dial it down a notch, or maybe two.

"Back to the beginning. To the scene you've yet to see. Back to its very origin. You must see it. Learn it. Know it. All of it. Though, you must be warned it is only the start. The journey is long, arduous, but the reward very great. The truth begets true happiness—but only the pure of heart may seize it." Her gaze switching to Damen as she adds, "The journey is yours and yours alone, Adelina. Damen is not welcome there."

Damen cuts in, having heard more than enough. "Listen," he says, "I don't know what you're trying to do here but—"

His anger halted by the surprising sight of her palm rising, followed by the shock of it pressing to his cheek. It's like, one minute he's yelling, a good two feet yawning between them, and the next, she's practically pressed up against him, her rheumy old gaze boring into his, transmitting something, some kind of message or memory meant only for him.

I watch, fascinated, wondering just what it is that transpires between them. Knowing only one thing for sure, that whatever it is, it's causing her to glow in a way that prompts a stream of light to radiate all around. The color spectrum so intense, it's as though it originates from somewhere so deep, it can't help but seep outward until the glimmer surrounds her.

But while she glows, Damen does the opposite. His normally tall, lean form appears to darken and shrink until he's barely a shell of himself.

"Damen Augustus Notte Esposito," she says. "Why do you deny me?"

I watch, startled to see him so flustered he's unable to respond, unable to find his own voice, much less fight his way out of whatever it is that she shows him. Just about to intervene when he shakes his head, straightens his spine, and yanks himself right out of her spell, pulling himself together enough to say, "You're crazy. You're wrong *and* you're crazy. And while I have no idea what your deal is or what you're trying to do here, I do know you better stay away from Ever. Far, far away, do you hear? Otherwise, I can't be held responsible for what happens to you, regardless of how old you claim to be."

But if he expected her to back off or run away scared, well, he must've been just as surprised as I was to see her smile instead. The two of us watching her face brighten, her cheeks widen, her lips spreading and lifting enough to display a startling array of teeth—startling in that a good deal of them are either graying, yellowing, or entirely missing.

Her attention shifting as she moves from him to me, taking my hand in her soft papery dry one, her words confident and sure when she says, "His love is the key."

I look at her, release myself from her grip. "I thought you said Adelina was the key?"

"It is one and the same." She nods, as if that made any sense. "Please. Please consider the journey. It is the only way to release me. To release you as well."

"The journey back—back to the beginning?" I say, sarcasm blooming. "And just where does this journey start? Where does it end?" I look at her, noticing how she still appears lit from within.

"The journey begins here."

She points down at our feet, or maybe the mud, I can't be too sure. I'm more confused now than I was when this started. But when our eyes meet again, I know the instruction is literal—the journey begins in the very muck where we stand.

"And it ends in the truth."

And before I can say another word, before I can beg for a little more clarification, Damen swings his arm around my waist and pulls me away.

Hurling the words over his shoulder, not bothering to look back when he says, "No one's going anywhere. Don't bother us again."

NINE

"**So what do you make of it?**" Ava swings her wavy auburn locks over her shoulder and levels her brown eyes on me, lowering herself onto one of the old plastic fold-up chairs Jude dragged into his office in an attempt to accommodate us all in this impromptu meeting. "What do you think it all means?"

I venture a glance toward Damen, who, having refused a chair, chooses to lean against the wall, arms crossed before him, face bearing a look that reads loud and clear: *I thought we were through with this? I thought I warned her to stay away? I thought you said you were merely planning to swing by, pick up a book or two, and be on your way?*

Meeting it with one of my own that says: *You promised me a week and I'm holding you to it—unless, of course, you want to tell me what the old woman showed you?*

He frowns, looks away, just as I figured he would, so I turn away from him in favor of Ava.

"I have no idea what it means," I admit, doing my best to

pretend I didn't just hear Damen sigh even though that was clearly his intent.

Jude glances between us, his gaze cautious, correctly sensing there's trouble in paradise and wanting nothing more than to steer clear of it. Still, since he also promised to help, he takes his place behind his desk, tilts his chair way back, and pretends to be lost in deep thought as he stares into space, when really, he's just dreaming of being some other place. Summerland would be my best guess.

"So, she thinks you're Adelina, or that you were Adelina, or . . . whatever . . ." Miles frowns, tapping his pen against the pages of the leather-bound journal I gave him before he left for Florence, busying himself with intense note taking, trying to make sense of it, while I busy myself with taking him in. Noting how his freshly cut hair makes him appear a lot more like the old Miles again, the one who so willingly befriended me on my first day of school, though the baby fat he shed when he went to acting camp in Italy is clearly gone for good, transforming him from comfortably cute to, well, really, really cute.

"Yeah." I nod, still not used to talking about this so openly, or at least not with him.

Even though he's all caught up to speed, pretty much informed of all the more sordid details of our lives thanks to both Roman's interference and the fact that he was there the night I killed Haven. Caught in her snare, eyes about to pop right out of his head, as she went about the business of trying to choke him to death.

By killing her, I saved him. And by doing so, I lost all hope of ever getting my hands on that antidote.

Still, I'd do it again if I had to. He's one of my very best friends, and he did absolutely nothing to deserve that from her.

"I have no idea who she is." I frown. "All I know is that the old lady calls herself Lotus, and is convinced I'm Adelina." The words mumbled in a way that makes it sound as though I was talking to myself.

Yanked from my mire of confusion when Romy and Rayne pipe up and say, "We need to start at the beginning."

I look at them, so perplexed by it all that I don't even know where that is. But before I can respond, they spring forth from their chairs, rush down the hall, and into the store. Returning just a few moments later, they reclaim their seats and peer at the book they've propped open on Romy's lap.

Rayne's voice piercing the silence when she leans over her twin sister, her huge brown eyes widening under her dark fringe of razor-slashed bangs as she says, "Okay, you said her name was Lotus, right?"

I nod.

"So, according to this, the lotus flower grows out of the mud, struggling through the muck to make its way toward the light. And, once it reaches that light, it blossoms and grows into something extraordinary, something very, very beautiful."

I suck in my breath, realizing we may have just made a little progress at last. *Mud, muck, crazy old lady named Lotus—it all fits, but what does it mean?*

"It's a symbol for awakening," Ava says, interrupting Rayne, who was about to speak again. "Awakening to the spiritual side of life."

"But it also represents life in general," Jude says, bringing his chair forward, settling his elbows onto his desk, and pushing his dreadlocks off his face as he gazes at us. "You know, overcoming the hardships and struggles life brings in order to blossom into your true self—the beautiful being you were destined to be."

He looks at me when he says it, and there's nothing I can do to stop the flush from rising to my cheeks. I know all too well about Jude's hardships and struggles, having seen them firsthand the day I pretended to read his palm so I could prove my psychic prowess and secure a job in his store. I saw it unfold as clearly as though I was standing right there alongside him. Gifted with psychic abilities his parents worked hard to deny, he lost his mother at a young age, only to have his grieving father shove a gun in his mouth and soon follow. Abandoning Jude to a series of intolerable foster families until the cycle of abuse became so unbearable the street seemed like a much better option. His life saved the day Lina found him, saw the promise in him, and managed to convince him that he wasn't a freak, but rather a unique and gifted soul. That the limited views of others should have no bearing on the person he already was, the man he'd become.

And now Lina's gone too.

I press my lips together and look at him, wondering how he's handling that, if it's why he's spending so much time in Summerland, or if that's more due to me—his attempt to get over the choice that I made.

His gaze meets mine, holding for only a moment, but still long enough for me to wish I could love him. He deserves to be loved. But my heart belongs to Damen. Despite our current conflict, I've no doubt he and I are meant for each other. This is just a minor rough patch we'll get through in no time.

"They also make for a pretty popular tattoo," Jude continues. "People who've overcome hard times, struggled their way out of the muck so to speak, like to use them as a sort of marker of having survived the journey and come out the other side."

"Do you have a tattoo?" Rayne asks, eyes widening as she

leans toward him, practically falling out of her seat with excitement.

"One or two." He nods, face bearing the slightest hint of a smile.

She gapes, hardly able to believe he plans to leave it at that, causing her to ask, "So, what are they?"

"One's an Ouroboros. It's on the small of my back."

And even though I can feel his gaze flit my way, I deflect the look entirely. I've seen the Ouroboros. Oh, yeah, that one did not go unnoticed.

"An Ouroboros?" She squints, glancing at her identical sister, who mirrors her in every way except for the clothing. Romy favors pink, Rayne prefers black, and sometimes, when they're not around, I refer to them as Good & Plenty because it makes Damen laugh. "I thought that was evil," she adds.

"It's *not* evil," Damen says, deciding to contribute since he has virtually no choice but to be here 'til it's over. "It's an ancient alchemical symbol of life, death, rebirth—immortality." He lifts his shoulders, gazing around the room but settling on no one in particular. "A whole slew of theologies have adopted it again and again throughout history, all of them attributing their own meanings to it, but it's *not* evil. Although Roman and his rogues adopted it and made it seem that way, on its own, it bears no ill will." He nods, meets the wall again, his speech halted, or at least for now anyway.

"O-*kay* . . ." Rayne smirks. "If I ever have to write a term paper on it, I'll go straight to you, but for now, back to the tattoos." She shakes her head, falling just shy of rolling her eyes. Her complete and total adoration of Damen is the only thing that spares him from that. "What's the other one?" she asks, turning back to Jude.

"The other is the Japanese symbol for the lotus blossom. I thought an actual flower seemed . . . well . . . a little girly."

She peers at him, brow arched high.

"I was younger, less evolved, what can I say?" He lifts his shoulders and swipes a hand over his hair.

"And—so—where's that one?" she ventures, but Jude just flashes his palm and shakes his head, terminating that particular topic right then and there.

Rayne turns to Ava, shooting her a dark, angry glare, her eyes narrowing even further when Ava just laughs in reply. And from what I can hear of the thoughts swirling between them, Rayne's been begging for a tattoo for the past several weeks, and can't understand why she's forced to wait another five years until she's eighteen. Having been around for three centuries already, the majority of which was spent in Summerland living as a refugee from the Salem Witch Trials, she doesn't see why her time served there can't be recognized here.

But it's hardly my argument, so I tune out just as quickly as I tuned in, more than a little eager to get back on track.

"So anyway, what about the song?" Miles asks. "How did it go again? Something about rising from the mud toward the sky, or the dreamy sky, or . . . or something?"

"From the mud it shall rise, lifting upward toward vast dreamy skies, just as you—you—you shall rise too," I sing, my voice echoing the same tune Lotus used.

"So obviously she thinks you're like the lotus flower," Romy adds, while her twin, still miffed about the tattoo, and never having been a fan of mine despite the recent bear hug she gave me in Summerland after seeing I'd survived Haven's attack, slumps down in her seat and levels her steely gaze right on me. Clearly doubting the truth of such a thing, and choosing then and there to side with Damen, thinking for sure the old lady has got to be crazy to see that kind of promise in me.

"And the rest, how did it go?" Miles prompts.

"From the deep and dark depths it struggles toward the light . . ."

"Again, lotus flower." Romy nods, tapping the page of the book with her pink painted nail, seemingly pleased with herself.

"Desiring only one thing—the truth! The truth of its being."

"Your destiny." Ava nods. Dashing any hope that she just might know what that is when she adds, "Whatever that may turn out to be."

"Okay, and . . ." Miles's head bobs as his pen races across the page, writing it all down.

"Um, okay . . ." I stall, trying to remember where I left off, where it goes from there. "Oh yeah, then it goes: *But will you let it? Will you let it rise and blossom and grow? Or will you damn it to the depths? Will you banish its worn and weary soul?*"

"So basically you're the lotus blossom, or, at least the keeper of the lotus blossoms, and you're either gonna let them fulfill their destiny and bloom, or, more likely, you're gonna screw it all up and damn them to the depths."

"Rayne!" Ava scolds.

But Rayne just shrugs, claiming, "What? It's not like *I* said 'damn', *the song* did. I was merely repeating."

"That is not what I meant and you know it. Your intent far outweighs your words." Ava's face darkens.

"Sorry," Rayne mumbles, and though she looks at me when she says it, it was clearly for Ava's benefit.

"You know what this reminds me of?" Damen says, prompting us all to turn, surprised to hear him speak up again. "It reminds me of 1968 when the Beatles released the *White Album* after their stay in India. Everyone was trying to interpret the lyrics, searching for some kind of deeper meaning, and, as it turned out, most of them were wrong—some of which ended in tragic results."

"Charles Manson." Jude nods, leaning back in his seat again, his fingers picking at the ancient Mayan symbol on the front of his T-shirt. "He thought the entire album contained an apocalyptic message, calling for a race war, and he used it to justify killing the wealthy, which he and his family of followers did."

I shudder. I can't help it. The whole idea is too creepy. Still, that's hardly what we're doing here, and I've a pretty good idea Damen knows it.

"While that may be all well and true," I say, carefully avoiding his gaze, "there's definitely a message *here*. And, according to Lotus anyway, there's also a journey that only I can make." Then, surprising just about everyone, including myself, I look right at Jude when I say, "All that time you've spent in Summerland, all that time you've studied your past lives—*our* past lives—have you ever seen one I don't know about? One that surprised you? One where I was named Adelina?"

I hold my breath, allowing myself to exhale only when he shakes his head and says, "Sorry, no."

"Okay then." Damen nods, divorcing himself of the wall, signaling that this meeting is now officially adjourned. "I think we've covered about all that we can here, no?"

And even though I want to protest that the answer is, indeed, *no,* I just nod and go with it.

Partly because I know he's only doing what he thinks is right. Trying to protect me from Lotus, the dark part of Summerland, and heck, maybe even myself.

And partly because, well, he's probably right. There probably is no more to do here. Even though I'm reluctant to admit it, it appears we've uncovered all that we can.

Or at least for now anyway.

As for the rest—well, I'm hoping it'll reveal itself somewhere along the journey.

TEN

"Are you going in?"

Damen stands beside me, right beside me. His body so close to mine I can feel his swarm of tingle and heat, his warm breath brushing softly along the curve of my cheek.

"No," I whisper. "I—I can't do it." I swallow hard, wrapping my arms around myself as I continue to peer inside. Feeling like the worst kind of creepy stalker for standing out here in the dark, spying on Sabine and Munoz instead of just going around to the front, opening the door, and going in to join them like a normal person would.

But I'm not normal.

Not even close.

And that's pretty much what keeps me crouching out here in the dark, on the wrong side of her window.

If you're not going in, can you at least tell me what we're doing out here? The words thought instead of spoken, he doesn't want to risk being heard.

I'm saying good-bye. I sigh. *I'm preparing for a future without her.*

Though I'm facing the wrong way to see his expression, I can feel the way his energy shifts, the way it broadens and expands until it swallows us both. Providing a wonderful, warm, hug-like embrace that lingers well past the point when his arm catches up and follows suit.

"Ever . . ." he whispers, hands clasped at my waist, lips pushing through my curtain of hair to land on my cheek. And even though it seemed like something might follow, he chooses to end it right there. Allowing the kiss to do what words fail to.

We huddle together, watching as the happy couple picks at the remaining scraps of dinner. Each of them urging the other to claim the last slice of pizza before Sabine waves her hand and reaches for her wineglass and Monoz laughs and digs in.

But despite their playful attitude, it's not hard to locate the glint of remorse in Sabine's gaze, the flicker of defeat at having taken a chance, issued an ultimatum, only to fail at the one thing that truly meant something to her.

A look that's *almost* enough to rouse me from my position at the window so I can hurl myself in there and show her that all is okay, all is forgiven.

Almost, but not quite.

Instead, I remain right in place, observing their date. She still in her suit, which, coupled with the pizza, signals a late night at work; while Munoz is dressed far more informally, wearing a pair of broken-in jeans and a long-sleeved white shirt with the cuffs rolled halfway to his elbows, enjoying a little time off from school, using his winter break to work on his book.

The one he was about to give up on.

The one I told him would be published someday.

Well, at least some good came of my abilities. They may have alien-
ated Sabine, but at least I managed to convince Munoz to not give up
on his dream.

And I'm so lost in the thought, and Damen's so lost in the act
of comforting me, that neither one of us is prepared for Munoz
to burst through the side door with an overstuffed trash bag in
hand.

"Ever?" He stands before us, Hefty bag dangling by his side,
squinting as though he stopped trusting his eyes the moment
they landed on me.

I flash my palm, my gaze pleading with his to keep quiet,
keep the news to himself, keep on heading for the trash as
though he didn't see us stooped beneath the windowsill.

But it's a lot to ask of someone who's been searching for you.
And while he makes for the trash can and drops the bag in, he's
quick to circle right back to where Damen and I stand.

"Where the hell have you been?" His words take me by surprise, mostly because they didn't come out nearly as angry as
they could have. They sounded more like a huge sigh of relief.

"I'm staying at Damen's," I say, as though that somehow
covers the full extent of my absence. "And Sabine's fully aware
of that since Damen called to tell her as much." I glance at Damen, glimpsing the wave of shock that plays over his face. He
didn't realize I knew that.

"Sabine's been worried sick. You've got to go in there—
you've got to let her know you're okay." He glances between us,
his brain still trying to catch up with what he sees before him.

"You know I can't do that." My voice is flat, matter of fact.
"And you know why. In fact, you know way more than you
should—way more than I ever intended." I sigh and shake my

head, remembering the day, just a few weeks before, when, in a frantic rush toward a disaster I didn't foresee, I manifested a bouquet of daffodils and a black BMW right before his eyes. Basically showing him right then and there that the full extent of my weirdness—my powers—goes far deeper than the psychic telepath he knew me to be. He saw me run like the wind, make things appear where there was once only air—and I'm pretty sure that after getting over the shock of that, he probably started wondering just what else I might be capable of. Or at least that's what I would've done if our positions were switched.

"Are you part of this too?" Munoz asks, shifting his focus to Damen as though looking for a nice convenient place to dump all the blame.

"I am the reason, yes," Damen says, without hesitation, no pause of any kind.

And I can't help but gape, so startled by the words, the way they echoed what Lotus said earlier. Wondering if that's what he meant, or if it's just a coincidence that his words mirrored hers.

Munoz ponders, tries to make sense of it. He was headed in one direction when Damen went in another, and now he's forced to catch up, or at least meet somewhere in the middle.

"I always thought there was something very strange about you," Munoz finally says, his voice low, almost dreamy.

Damen nods, and I've no idea how he took that, his voice, like his face, gives nothing away.

"It's almost as though you're not from this time," Munoz adds, as though musing to himself.

"I am not from this time." Damen looks right at him, the reply so simple, so direct, so unexpected, it takes my breath away.

Munoz nods, taking the answer in stride, acting as though he just might believe him when he says, "And so, which time are you from, then?"

"One of your favorites." Damen's lip curls, allowing for a ghost of a smile. "The Italian Renaissance."

Munoz gulps, nods, and glances all around as though he expects to find further explanation planted in the garden, floating in the pool, or maybe even taped to the lid of the barbeque. Processing the statement with more calm than I ever would've expected, acting as though he's not at all surprised to find himself having such a serious conversation about such a peculiar subject.

"So, alchemy is real then?" he ventures, hitting the bull's-eye in a way most people fail to.

I mean, when it was me trying to pin down Damen's strangeness, I went straight for vampire. Miles did too. But apparently Munoz is not nearly as influenced by the current pop culture phenomenon, and so he shot straight for the truth.

"Alchemy has always been real," Damen admits, his face controlled, voice steady, giving absolutely no hint as to how much this is costing him—though I have a pretty good idea.

For six centuries he's fought to keep the truth of his existence a secret, only to meet up with me in this lifetime and watch the whole thing unravel like a moth-eaten sweater. "Real, yes—but not always successful." Munoz's eyes light on Damen, considering him in a whole new way, as Damen nods in agreement. "And you, Ever?" Munoz looks at me, trying to see me in a whole new way too. But despite all of my unmitigated weirdness, I'm clearly a product of the modern world, there's no getting around it.

I shake my head, lift my shoulders, and leave it at that.

"Wow. There's just so much to talk about—so much I want to ask you—"

I peer anxiously at Damen, hoping Munoz won't launch into a whole string of inquiries that Damen, for whatever reason, will feel compelled to answer.

But, as luck would have it (something I haven't had much of lately, but I'll happily take in any form that it comes) Sabine saves me by calling, "Paul? Everything okay out there?"

He sucks in his breath and glances back and forth between us. And since I can't risk speaking, can't risk having her hear my voice coming from just outside her window, I settle for shaking my head, and shooting him a deep, pleading, meaningful look.

Overcome with relief when he says, "Yeah, I'm . . . fine. Just enjoying the night, doing a little stargazing, searching for Cassiopeia, you know how I like to do that. I'll be inside in a second."

"Should I join you?" she asks, her voice lowered, seductive, leading straight into something I *so* don't want to witness.

"Nah, it's pretty cold out here. Hold the thought and I'll meet you inside," he answers, much to my relief.

He gives us a thorough once-over. His lips parting as if to say something more, but I just shake my head, close my eyes, and quickly manifest a bouquet of daffodils I urge him to give her.

"What am I supposed to tell her? What should I say?" he whispers, casting a cautious glance toward the window.

"I'd prefer you not say anything, not mention it at all," I tell him. "But, if you feel you have to, then just tell her I love her. Tell her I'm sorry for all the trouble I've caused, and to not spend another moment feeling guilty about anything she might've said out of frustration and anger. I know it sounds cold, and probably pretty awful from your point of view, but please just try to trust me when I say that it's better this way. We can't see each other again. It's impossible, she won't accept it, and there's just no way to explain."

Then before Munoz can react, before he can take a stance, make a promise one way or another, Damen squeezes my hand, pulls me along the stone path, and out the side gate.

The two of us fading into the night until Munoz can no longer see us.

The two of us refusing to look back, knowing it's better to look forward, toward the future, than to long for a past that's gone forever.

ELEVEN

Since it's our last night together—or at least our last night for an indeterminate amount of time anyway—I'm hoping to do something special.

Something memorable.

Something that Damen can look back on with a smile.

And yet, it probably shouldn't be *too* memorable since I can't afford for him to catch onto the fact that I'm withholding something I'm not quite willing to mention just yet.

While I made up my mind to set off on Lotus's journey not long after having left Summerland, Damen's not exactly clued in to that fact. And since getting him clued in will no doubt lead to an argument of mammoth proportions, I'm hoping to keep the news to myself until I have no choice but to share it with him.

So while he busies himself with the business of brushing his teeth and getting ready for sleep, I slip between the sheets and try to come up with something with which to surprise him. But a moment later, when he pauses in the doorway looking like a glorious vision wrapped in blue silk, the best I can do is gulp, stare, and manifest a single red tulip that floats from my hand to his.

He grins, closes the distance between us in less than a handful of steps, and slides in beside me. His fingers softly tracing the line of my brow as he pushes my hair from my face, gathers me into the crook of his arm, and settles me snugly against him. My cheek pressed hard against his chest as I close my eyes and lose myself in the hum of his heartbeat, the *almost* feel of his lips, the way his hands play across my skin. Tossing my leg over his, I anchor him to me, concentrating on his essence—his energy—his being—determined to brand every last detail of this moment onto my brain so it never slips away.

And even though I want to speak, to say something meaningful and significant, something to make up for anything bad that might've passed between us earlier, with the way his hands smooth and soothe—with the way his voice is reduced to a faint murmur that plays at my ear—it's not long before I'm lulled away from my waking state and into a deep dreamless sleep.

I wait until midmorning to tell him.

Wait until the showers are taken, the clothes donned, and we find ourselves downstairs in his kitchen, sitting at the breakfast table, enjoying some chilled bottles of elixir while Damen scans the morning papers.

I wait until I have no more excuses to delay what I know must be said.

It's cowardly, I know, but I do it anyway.

"So, what is this? Day two or three of your week of research?" He looks up, folds his paper in half, and flashes me an irresistible smile as he tilts the bottle to his lips. "Because I think I lost track." He wipes his mouth with his hand, then his hand on his knee.

I frown, tipping my bottle from side to side, watching the elixir spark and flare as it races up to the rim then back down again. Gnawing my lip, trying to figure out just where to start, then deciding it's better to dive in, that there's no reason to delay the inevitable when all paths ultimately lead to the same destination. I discard the usual preemptive pleas of: *Please don't be mad,* or, just as ineffective: *Please hear me out,* in favor of the cleanly stated truth, saying, "I've decided to go on that journey."

He looks at me, face lifting, eyes brightening, the sight of it filling me with instant relief—a relief that's short lived, vanishing the moment I realize he mistook my use of the word "journey" for the vacation he's planning.

"Oh, no, not . . . not *that,*" I mumble, feeling about *this* big when I see his face drop. "I meant the journey that Lotus referred to. Though if things go as I well as I hope, then we should have plenty of time for that too." My hands flop in my lap as I try to force a smile onto my face, but it doesn't get very far. It's a false move on my part, and he knows it too.

He turns away, seemingly speechless at what I just said. But by the way his fingers grip his elixir, by the way his jaw tightens and clenches, I know he's at no loss for words, he's merely attempting to gather and sort them. He won't stay silent for long.

"You're serious." He finally faces me. The words sounding more like a statement than the accusation I expected.

I nod, quick to chase it with an apology. "And I'm sorry. I know you're probably not very happy to hear that."

He looks me over, arranging his face in a way I can't read. His words careful, measured, when he says, "No, I can't say that I am." The tone exhibiting an enormous amount of self-control his energy can't seem to mimic. Even though he has no visible aura, I can feel his vibration. I can feel his pulse quickening.

He starts to speak again, but before he can get to the words I flash my palm and stop him right there, saying, "Listen, I know what you're going to say, trust me I do. You're going to tell me she's crazy, that it's dangerous, that I need to ignore her and move on, to give you some more time to find a way for us to be able to touch each other again . . ." I pause for a beat, not allowing enough time for him to respond before I'm at it again. "But here's the thing, it's not just about us being together in the way that we want. It's about my destiny. My fate. My reason for being—the reason I keep coming back, being born over and over again. I have to go, there's really no choice. And while I know you don't like it, and while I know you won't like it no matter how good an argument I wage, I'm willing to settle for mere grudging acceptance. Basically, I'll settle for whatever I can get. Because Damen, while there's definitely a good chance that she's stark-raving crazy, there's also just as good a chance that she's onto something real. And I just know in my heart that this is what I need to—no, scratch that, I know in my *soul* that this is what I'm *meant* to do. It's like she said, it's a destiny only I can fulfill. And while I wish you could join me, while I wish that more than anything, she made it very clear that you can't. And . . ." I gulp, the lump in my throat like a hot, angry fireball, but still I push past it and add, "And I just hope you can find a way to accept that, even if you can't get around to supporting it."

Damen nods, taking his time to formulate a reply. Thrusting his legs out before him, crossing them at the ankle as his fingers trace the rim of the bottle. "So, what you're telling me is that nothing I can say or do will stop you from going through with this? From setting out on your own?"

I lower my gaze, thankful that our conversation has steered far from the screaming match I envisioned, and yet in some ways I'm surprised to realize it's worse. Impassioned arguing is pretty easy to hurdle once enough time has passed, but this, this sort of grudging acceptance I thought I'd be happy to get, well, it leaves me feeling sad, lonely, and depressingly bleak.

"And when do you plan to head off on this journey?"

"Soon." I nod, forcing myself to look at him when I add, "Pretty much now. No reason to delay, right?"

He buries his face in his hands, spending a few silent moments rubbing his eyes, doing his best to avoid me. And when he does look up again, he stares off in the distance, past the meticulously landscaped yard, past the pool, past the ocean beyond, to some troubling mental landscape viewable only to him, carefully shielding his thoughts.

"I wish you wouldn't do this," he says, the words simple but heartfelt.

I nod.

"But if you insist, then I insist on going with you." He looks at me. "It's too dangerous—too . . ." He frowns, pushes his hair off his face. "Too vague, too uncertain—I can't just let you trot off into the muck on your own. Ever, don't you see? You're my whole world! I can't just allow you to head off on some crazy old lady's journey!"

His eyes meet mine, showing me the full extent of his determination. But I'm determined too, and Lotus's instructions were crystal clear: *It's my journey—my destiny—Damen is not welcome there.* And I can't help but think that there's a reason for that—I can't help but think that maybe this time, it's up to me to protect him by insisting I go it alone.

And I'm just about to say as much when he reaches across the table, reaches for my hand, and says, "Ever . . ." His voice cracking in a way that forces him to swallow, clear his throat, and start again. "Ever, what if you don't return?"

"Of course I'll return!" I practically jettison out of my chair, sliding all the way to the edge, hardly believing he'd even think such a thing. "Damen, I would never leave you! Sheesh, is that what's got you so upset?"

"No," he says, voice steadier now. "I was thinking more along the lines of: What if you *can't* come back? What if you get trapped? Lost in the muck? What if you can't find your way out?" His stricken gaze meets mine, and it's clear that he's already experiencing some imagined, future loss despite the fact that I'm still here, still sitting before him.

But it's not like I don't get it. In fact, I completely understand.

Having lost me so many previous times, he's terrified at losing me again just when he was sure he had me for eternity. The sheer depth of his emotion robbing me of breath, leaving me speechless, humbled, with no easy reply, no easy way to comfort him.

"It won't happen," I finally say, hoping to convince. "You and I are meant to be. It's the only thing I'm absolutely sure of. And while I have no idea what to expect, I promise I'll do whatever it takes to find my way back. Seriously, Damen, nothing can keep us apart—or at least not for long. But for now, I have to go. And I have to go it alone, Lotus was clear about that. So please, please just let me do this, please just let me see where this leads. I can't rest until I try. And while I know it's a lot to ask, I really wish you would try to understand. And if you can't do that, then I wish you'd at least try to support me. Can you do that?"

But even though my voice practically pleads with him to look at me, to respond in some way, he continues to sit in silence, lost in his own mental scenery.

Choosing to take a wild leap of faith and hoping he'll come along for the ride, I add, "Damen, I know how you feel, believe me I do. But I can't help thinking there's more to our story. An entire lifetime we're both completely unaware of. I think it's the clue, or maybe *the key,* as Lotus put it. The key that'll lead us to the reason behind all of the obstacles we've been plagued with for all of these centuries, including the one we face now."

But, like I said, it was a leap.

A leap that lands flat on its face when Damen rises from his seat, moves away from the table, and looks at me briefly. His gaze bleak, his voice cold, clipped, telling me he's a million miles away when he says, "So I guess that's it then. Your mind is made up. In which case I wish you all the best, and I look forward to your return."

TWELVE

"You sure you don't want to come in?"

I shake my head, meeting Jude's gaze for a moment before shifting my focus to the barren winter stems that once bore the beautiful pink and purple peonies that lined the path from the drive to his door.

"So, you're really going through with this?"

I nod. Realizing I should probably try to answer at least one of his questions verbally, but at the moment, I'm feeling far too choked up to speak. Unable to keep my mind from replaying that last scene with Damen—his final words, what he said about the possibility of my not returning, getting lost in the muck, unable to find my way back. The way he pulled me into his arms just after, stopping just short of storming out of the room to circle back to me, his body moving toward mine almost against his will. His embrace so warm, so all-encompassing, so loving, so . . . *brief*, it served as a complete and total contrast for his words, which were nothing shy of cold and perfunctory.

And even though I could sense his inner struggle, even though

I recognized the signs of someone striving to detach from an outcome they're convinced can only end in heartbreak, I couldn't help but expect something more.

Even though I knew I had to go it alone, even though I insisted the journey was mine and mine alone, I still thought for sure he'd at least escort me to Summerland.

Pushing the thought from my mind, I resolve to focus on the present—on the space where Jude stands before me, the two of us flanking either side of his doorway.

"So where's Damen, then?" He peers at the empty space to my right then eyeballs me carefully. "He's going with you, right?"

I lower my gaze. All too aware of the horrible way my throat tightens as my eyes start to sting—the usual warnings that a flood of tears is in the making, but I stop it right there. I won't let myself cry.

Not here.

Not in front of Jude.

Not for something I've elected to do.

Finally pulling myself together, I say, "It's just me. This is something I've got to do alone. Lotus made that abundantly clear." Lifting my shoulders as though it's no big deal, and hoping he'll buy it too.

He leans against the door, hands shoved deep into his front pockets. And from the look of his quirked mouth, and from the slant of his spliced brow, it's clear he's doing just the opposite, trying to determine what could be going on between Damen and me.

But that's not why I'm here, so I'm quick to wave it away, my eyes meeting his as I say, "Listen, I just wanted to stop by and say thanks. Thanks for being such a good friend to me throughout all of these . . . lifetimes."

He frowns and looks past me, focusing on the street just beyond, emitting some kind of sarcastic sound, a cross between a
grunt and a groan, before he says, "Ever, you might want to
save your gratitude for someone who deserves it. None of my
actions have proved to be the least bit helpful. In fact, it's pretty
much the opposite—I've made everything worse. Seems I've
got a really bad habit of messing things up in a pretty big way."

Since there's no point denying it, I'm quick to agree, though
I'm also quick to add, "Still, I'm not convinced that's your fault.
If anything, I'm pretty sure it's your destiny."

He tilts his head, scratches his stubble-lined chin. "My destiny is to mess up your life?" He shoots me a skeptical look.
"I'm not really sure how I should feel about that."

"Well, no, not *just* that. I'm sure there are much better things
in store for you—things that have nothing to do with me. What
I mean is, maybe that's our combined destiny, you know? Like
maybe you and I keep meeting throughout all of these centuries
for a reason neither of us has ever thought of before . . ." I peer
at him, trying to get a read on how that went over, but his head
is leaning in a way that causes a tangle of dreadlocks to fall
sideways, obscuring his face. "So, anyway . . ." I pause, starting
to feel more than a little foolish for having come here. "I'm
hoping the journey will reveal that and more."

"So, this is it then?" He pushes his hair away, allowing his
tropical gaze to light on mine.

"Looks like." I try to smile, but just barely make it.

He nods, body jerking ever so slightly, like he's holding
something back—caught in a struggle between saying what he
wants and what his better sense will allow. Finally settling on
the latter when he says, "Then I wish you Godspeed."

He moves away from the door, moves as though he just

might embrace me but changes his mind at the very last second and drops his hands to his sides.

And before the moment can get any more awkward than it already is, I breach the space between us and hug him tightly to me. Holding the embrace for a moment, a moment that feels somehow suspended, then I pull away and end it. Aware of the wave of Jude's energy, his usual calling card of cool, calm serenity that continues to flood through me.

Holding, lingering, strangely enduring, as I make my way toward my car, and head for my next set of good-byes.

After stopping by Miles's only to learn he wasn't home, I swing by Ava and the twins' only to find they're gone as well. Then I stop by Haven's old house, the one she shared with her little brother Austin and their parents. Parking on the street, seeing a FOR SALE sign stuck in the lawn and an open house in progress as a long line of looky-loos stream in and out.

And I wonder if her parents even realize she's gone, that she'll never return. Or, if they're still looking past her, all around her, everywhere but at her, just like they did when she was still here. And since I'm already mired in a deeply blue mood, I decide to drive by Sabine's, but that's all that I do. I don't stop. I don't go inside. I already said a silent good-bye last night.

And with no further reason to delay, I cruise down the next street, abandon my car at the curb, close my eyes, and manifest the portal that leads me to Summerland. Landing in the vast fragrant field with its pulsating flowers and shivering trees, and stealing a moment to enjoy the pure, unadulterated splendor of it all—the unmitigated mass of beauty, love, and everything good—before I find my way out and venture toward its opposite side. The place where the trees are all barren, flowers don't grow, and magick and manifesting do not exist.

My suspicions confirmed the moment I notice the thin trail of muck leading from Haven's memorial all the way to the dark side I first stumbled upon.

It's growing.

Encroaching.

But even though I'm not at all surprised to see it like that, I have no idea how to stop it. No idea what I'll do once I arrive. And though I tried to mentally prepare myself for just about every possibility of what I might find, I failed to prepare myself for the one I stumble upon.

I stop, my eyes wide in wonder, jaw practically dropped to my knees when I see Jude, Ava, Romy, Rayne, and . . . *Miles?*— standing there waiting for me.

The only person who could make this reunion complete is Damen, but sadly, he's absent.

"How did . . ." My voice trails off as I gape at Miles, the biggest surprise of them all.

"Well, it took some doing, more than a few tries for sure, but between the four of us pooling our energy and Miles's own fervent desire to see you off on your journey, in the end, we managed to pull through."

"I hope you at least showed him around the nicer parts first." I cringe, thinking how he must've felt to go through all that only to step through the beautiful, shimmering veil and into such a dark, dreary, bleak place.

"Later," Ava says. "We were in too big of a hurry to catch you before you leave."

"But—why?" I glance at Jude, correctly assuming he called

them, convinced them all to meet me here, just after I left him standing in his doorway.

"Because you deserve a proper send-off," Romy says, nudging her sister hard in the gut until she nods in reluctant agreement.

"I—I don't know what to say." I swallow hard, warning myself not to cry in front of them.

"You don't have to say anything." Miles grins. "You know I'm more than able to handle the talking for all of us."

"True." I laugh, still getting used to seeing him here.

"Oh, and we brought gifts." Ava nods excitedly.

I try to look pleased, though the truth is I have no idea what I'll do with them, or if I'll even be able to bring them where I'm going—wherever that is. The thought extinguished the moment Rayne steps forward, motions for me to lower my head, and drapes a small silver talisman dangling from a tan leather cord around my neck.

I grasp the pendant between my forefinger and thumb, lifting it to where I can better see it, unsure how I'm supposed to interpret the message behind it, especially considering it came straight from her.

"An Ouroboros?" I gape, my voice sharp, my brow raised in question.

"It's from Romy and me," she says, eyes wide and serious. "It's for protection. Damen was right. It's not at all evil and we're just hoping it'll remind you of where you started, where you'll end up, and where we hope you'll find yourself again."

"And where's that?" I ask, my eyes never once straying from hers.

"Back here. With all of us," she says, her voice full of sincerity. Her dual nature, her ability to run so hot and cold, especially where I'm concerned, is so confusing I can't seem to get a grip on her. Reminding me of the old man I ran across that time in Summerland, the one who insisted the twins bore opposite personalities to the ones I've grown used to. Claiming Rayne was the quiet one and Romy the stubborn one, and I can't help but wonder just how often they play this game.

Before I can formulate some kind of reply, Ava comes forward and hands me a small shiny crystalline stone made of a blue-green so brilliant it reminds me a bit of Jude's eyes.

"It's cavansite," she says, studying me closely. "It enhances intuition and psychic healing. It also prompts deep reflection, inspires new ideas, helps rid oneself of faulty beliefs, and aids in inducing the memories of one's prior lives."

Our eyes meet and hold as she shoots me a meaningful look, and I can't help but wish Damen were around to hear that.

I nod, slip the stone into my pocket, and turn toward Jude. Not because I'm expecting something from him, but because I can tell by the way his aura flares, the way his energy radiates, that he has something to tell me.

"I'm coming with," he says.

I squint, unsure I heard him correctly.

"Seriously. That's my gift. I'm making the journey with you. You shouldn't have to go it alone. I don't want you to go it alone."

"But—you can't," I say, the words slipping out before I've even had a chance to stop and consider them. But for some reason, it seems like the right thing to say. If Damen can't go, then Jude can't either. Besides, there's no need to involve him in this any more than I already have. "Trust me, I appreciate the sentiment. Really, I do. But Lotus's instructions were clear—I need to do this alone. Without you, without Damen, with no one to rely on but myself. It's my destiny, only I can make the journey."

"But I thought our destinies were entwined? You said so yourself."

I pause, unsure how to reply. Glancing from the twins, to Miles, and then over to Ava and back to Jude, about to reiterate what I just said, when I sense her.

Lotus.

She's here.

I turn, my gaze instinctively finding hers, noticing how she looks even older than the last time I saw her, more delicate, frail, somewhat feeble even. Her movements slow but determined, her slim frame stooped slightly forward, her hair freed from the braid she normally wears, left to hang loose around her shoulders in long silvery wisps. The waves floaty, springy, providing the usual halo effect—its color blending into skin so pale it makes the blue of her eyes pop out like two startling chunks of aquamarine dropped into a snowy-white landscape. And unlike the other times I saw her, this time she leans heavily onto an old carved wooden walking stick. Her fingers wrapped around the curved handle, arthritic knuckles blanching and bulging. Yet her face still lifts as she makes her approach, her rheumy old eyes taking me in as her lips curl in delight.

"Adelina." She bows, stopping just a few feet shy of me, her gaze fixed on mine as though she's yet to notice I have company. "You are ready? Ready to make the journey? Ready to release me?"

"Is that what I'm doing?" I study her closely, her words planting a seed of doubt that has me second-guessing my purpose all over again.

"We've been waiting for so long now. Only you can make the journey, only you can reveal the truth."

"But why only me?" I ask. "Why can't Damen come—or Jude?"

"Please," she whispers, voice low and throaty, pressing her left palm to her heart as she bows toward me, a thin gold band she wears on her ring finger glinting in a way I can't miss, and I wonder if she's always worn it, and if so, why I failed to notice it until now. "You must choose to believe."

For the first time since she arrived, I glance back toward my friends, seeing them looking upon her with such awe and reverence I can't help but wonder if they see something I miss.

But when I turn to Lotus again, I see it as clearly as they do—the beautiful golden glow that emanates deep from within, growing and expanding until it glimmers all around her.

"You are ready then?" She looks at me, her face so luminous I just nod, unable to resist.

Lifting one gnarled old finger, she beckons for me to follow—to take the first step toward a destiny I can't yet imagine.

I turn back to my friends, turn to wave good-bye, only to find Miles, Ava, and the twins waving back, and Jude standing right there behind me.

And just as I'm about to explain yet again why I need to go it alone, Lotus stops, glances over her shoulder, and takes him in as though seeing him for the very first time. Her eyes moving over him as though she somehow recognizes him, taking me by surprise when she waves him forward, inviting him to join us.

"This is your destiny too. The answers you seek are now within your reach," she says, her voice both sage and true.

I glance between her and Jude, wondering what the heck that might've meant, but she's already turned back, and from the look in his eyes, he's just as confused as I am.

She leads us through the muck, through a forest of burnt-out trees with cruel barren branches bearing no trace of foliage despite the constant supply of rain. Her feet moving with surprising surety as I struggle to keep up. Keeping my eyes glued to the back of her head, not wanting to lose sight of her, aware of the *slip-slop* of Jude's feet as he trudges behind me.

And even though I'm grateful for the company, I can't help but think it should be Damen instead.

Damen should be making the journey alongside me. Damen, who wanted to come, wanted to keep me safe—despite the fact that he disagreed with my coming here in the first place.

Having Jude here feels wrong in every way.

We push on, following Lotus for what feels like miles, and I'm about to ask how much farther it is, when we reach it.

I know it the moment I see it.

The landscape is basically unchanged, the ground is still muddy, the rain still falls, and the surrounding area is as dreary and barren as ever—but still, there's just no denying it. The air is different. Cooler. The temperature dropped so low I wish I'd worn something a little heavier than an old pair of jeans and a long-sleeved T-shirt. But even more noticeable is the way the area just before us seems to glisten and glow—to glimmer and gleam. Looking less like the shimmering veil that marks the portal to Summerland, and more like a change in atmosphere. The space turned suddenly hazy, swirly, allowing for only a blur of shapes, a mere hint of what might lie beyond.

Lotus stops, lifts her hand to her brow, and surveys the scene, as I stand right beside her, and Jude beside me, wondering if he'll insist on continuing now that we're here.

I turn to Lotus, hoping for some sort of instruction, advice, a heads-up, words of wisdom—willing to settle for just about anything she's willing to give, but she just points straight ahead, motions for me to keep moving, to make that big leap between the space where I stand and the great unknown just beyond.

"But what will I do when I get there?" I ask, practically reduced to begging.

But instead of addressing me she turns to Jude and says, "Go forward. Learn. You will know when it is time to return."

"But . . . I'm going with Ever . . . *aren't I?*" He glances at us, his face a mask of confusion that matches my own.

Lotus gestures impatiently, gestures ahead, and as I follow the direction of her crooked old fingers, I'm forced to blink a few times to take it all in, to see what she sees.

Still, despite my efforts, all I get is a blurry hologram. Like a shadowy mirage that could represent a village and its people, but could just as easily be something else entirely.

"Your journeys begin here. Where it ends is for you to discover."

Jude grasps my hand, determined to support me, to go with me, but I'm not ready just yet.

Much as I care for Jude, Damen rules my heart. He's the one I want beside me on this journey—on any journey.

Lotus touches my arm, presses a small silk pouch into my palm. Curling my fingers around it, she says, "Everything you think you need is in here. You decide what that means."

"But *how? How* will I know? *How* will I—" I start, a million unanswered questions storming my brain.

Not getting very far before she looks at me and says, "Trust. Believe. It is the only way to proceed."

She nudges me forward, nudges me with a surprising amount of strength. And I can't help it—I glance back again. My eyes scanning the area, desperately seeking Damen, as if the sheer force of my longing will magically transport him here.

But not finding him anywhere, I square my shoulders, tilt my chin, and take that first step, Jude right beside me, my hand grasped in his.

The two of us moving tentatively toward something we can't quite make out, though it's not long before we're pulled along by the irresistible force of it—like a whirling mass of energy, a vortex that's sucking us in. And I'm just about to merge into it, when I feel it.

That familiar swarm of tingle and heat.

Soon followed by the plaintive cry of my name on his lips.

I turn, catching the flash of pain in his eyes when he sees me with Jude, assumes I've replaced him.

I drop Jude's hand, watching helplessly as Jude's swallowed into the whirl, while I strive to hold on, to straddle two worlds.

My fingers grasping, yearning, reaching for Damen, and though he moves fast, it's not fast enough to keep our fingers from just barely grazing, the tips lightly brushing as our gaze briefly meets. And the next thing I know, I can't stop it.

I'm yanked out of his reach.

Lost in the swirl.

Hurtling into an unknown place—into an unknown time.

Aware that Damen is here—somewhere—but unable to find him.

Already making the trip back.

Way back.

Back to the very beginning.

THIRTEEN

"Adelina!"

The voice that calls to me is hushed, whispered, taking great care to be heard only by me.

"Adelina, my sweet, please tell me you have come for me!"

I move away from the corner, out of the darkness and into the fading stream of light just beyond. Fighting to keep my tone calm, stoic, I say, "I have come for you, Alrik." Bowing low before him, my hands buried in the folds of my skirt so he can't see them shake, desperate to hide my excitement, to appear respectable, ladylike, sedate.

But the moment I lift my head, the moment I see the way his dark brown eyes light on mine, his gaze partially obscured by the tumble of dark waves that fall past his heavy fringe of lashes, past his straight nose, along the curving angle of his beautifully sculpted cheekbone—when I see the way his long, lean form fills the doorway—my face betrays me.

My gaze sparks, my cheeks flush, and my lips begin to quiver and curl, unable to contain the surge of extreme pleasure and joy the mere sight of him brings.

And if his expression is anything to judge by, then he clearly feels the same way. I can tell by the way he pauses in the threshold, the way he lifts his torch high, allowing the light to spill over me.

Allowing his eyes to devour me.

I can tell by the way his breath grows labored, the way his jaw tightens, the way his gaze clouds with desire—we bear the same effect on each other.

And when he closes the space between us in a handful of steps and hugs me tightly to him, when he covers my face with his kiss, his lips capturing mine, fusing, melding, exploring—all of my doubts slip away. I focus only on *this*.

Here.

Now.

My entire world shrinking until nothing else exists.

Nothing other than the crush of his lips, the warmth of his skin, and the swell of tingle and heat that always manages to find me whenever he's near.

Refusing to think about a future that can never be ours.

Refusing to think about such cruel things as class and position and obligation and the strange game of chance that birth order brings.

Refusing to think about the fact that despite the depth of our love, we can never belong to each other in the way that we want. A truth that was decided long before we had a chance to meet, our futures determined by others, not us.

Despite the fact that he loves me and I him—we will never marry.

Can't marry.

He's been betrothed to another since he was a boy.

One whose family boasts far more wealth than mine.

One who happens to be my cousin, Esme.

"Adelina," he whispers, my name like a prayer on his lips. "Oh, Adelina, tell me you have missed me as much as I have missed you."

"Yes, m'lord." I pull away quickly, the bliss of a few moments before rudely smothered by the reality we find ourselves in. Reminding me of who I am—a poor relation to the distant cousin he'll marry; who he is—the future king of our tiny city state; and where we both stand—in an empty, darkened stall in his stable, the air thick with the smell of horse flesh and hay, a pile of freshly laid straw at our feet.

"*M'lord?*" He quirks his brow, allowing his dark eyes to graze over me until meeting my blue ones, leaving me to wonder if he sees the same things in mine as I see in his: disappointment, doubt, and a fervent but futile desire to change the status quo. "What is this? Is that how you see me now, as *lord*?"

"Well, aren't you? In principle anyway?"

It's cheeky, I know, but it's also the truth. I happen to know he likes that about me, the fact that I don't play the usual games, especially where courtship is concerned. I'm neither silly, nor flirty, and sometimes, I tend to veer far more toward tomboy than girly. But I'm forthright, direct, and I try my best to tell it like it is.

I try my best to live without regrets.

He cups my face in his hands, traces his finger from my temple to my chin, where he presses his finger and lifts, forcing my eyes to meet his. "What is the reason for all this formality? You act as though we've just met. And even then, if memory serves, you were hardly formal that day—you pushed me right into the mud, face-first no less. Your manners were certainly lacking, though you managed to make quite an impression. I'm certain I have loved you from that very moment. Covered head to toe in muck—I knew right then my life would never be the same."

A smile sneaks onto my face, remembering the moment as clearly as he. Me at ten, he thirteen, I'd been staying with much wealthier relatives and paid him a visit with my spoiled cousin Esme, who so enjoyed lording her wealth over me, always comparing her fancy dresses to my more drab ones; she was becoming a chore to tolerate. And so, annoyed with her constant preening and prancing and bragging with no end in sight about how handsome her future husband was, how wealthy, and how wonderful it would be when she was made queen and I'd be forced to bow down and kiss her feet, well, I just couldn't take it anymore, so I marched right up to him, caught him off guard, and pushed him straight into the pond, then I turned to her and said, "Still think he's handsome?" and watched her cry and scream and run off to tell someone what I'd done.

"It was a pond," I say, looking right at him.

"A *very muddy* pond." He nods. "It never quite came out of my clothing. I still have the shirt that bears the stain."

"And, if I remember correctly, I paid a grand price for that. I was sent home immediately, and Esme never invited me to visit again. Which, come to think of it, really wasn't much of a punishment at all, was it?"

"And yet, you found your way back. Or at least back to me anyway." His arms circle my waist, as his fingers traipse up and down my spine. The feel of it so calm and soothing, it's all I can do to stay focused, on point, to not succumb to his spell.

"Yes," I say, my voice barely a murmur. "Are you glad of that?" Knowing that he is, but it's always nice to hear the words spoken aloud.

"Am I glad?" He throws his head back and laughs in a way that exposes a glorious column of neck it takes all of my will not to kiss. "Shall I show you the level of my gratitude?"

He kisses me again, at first playful, a series of light pecks and nips, but then it grows deeper, much deeper. But even though I try to respond with the usual fervor, something is off. And he senses it too.

"What has happened since we last met? You are different. Has something occurred to change your feelings for me?"

I force my gaze away. Force myself to breathe, to speak. But the speech I rehearsed as I made my way over suddenly escapes me.

"Adelina, please tell me—do you no longer love me?"

"No! Of course not! It's nothing of the sort! How can you even say such a thing?"

"Then what? What terrible event has you refusing me?"

I gather the words, struggle to move them from my head to my lips, but I can't do it. Can't say what needs to be said. So, like a coward—a word that has never been used to describe me—I gaze down instead.

"Is it Rhys? Is my brother bothering you again?" His jaw tightens as his eyes begin to blaze.

But before it can go any further, I'm quick to shake my head.

His brother Rhys is fair of hair and even fairer of face—his obvious outer attractions going a long way to belie a much darker inside—the fact that he's ruled by a long string of jealousies he can never overcome.

Second in line not just for the crown—the chance to rule his father's small Iberian kingdom—but also for his father's attentions, only to learn that the girl whom he loves, my spoiled cousin Esme, is destined for his brother—the one who, in Rhys's opinion was born into everything, yet deserves nothing.

And while I've tried to gaze upon Rhys with compassion, if for no other reason than the fact that we share something in common—we're both being kept from a chance at true happiness—being kept from the one we love due to politics, finance, and traditions we just barely understand—my sympathies were soon thwarted by his undeniable mean streak, and his abject cruelty toward me.

As though it's my doing. As though it's my fault that Alrik is betrothed to the one Rhys loves.

As though I wouldn't change that if I could.

As though I wouldn't reverse it, switch up the birth order so that I could live happily with Alrik, and he could live happily with Esme, and we could all live happily ever after—preferably far apart from each other.

But alas, that is not to be.

For one thing, Esme has no interest in Rhys. She loves Alrik. She can't wait to be married.

For another, sometimes, when I'm trying very hard to be logical and reasonable, I remind myself that while I've no doubt Alrik loves me, loves me in the way that I love him, I'm not sure I fully believe him when he claims he has no interest in the crown.

It's his birthright. As the firstborn son, as his father's heir, it's what he's been destined for ever since he came into the world. To turn his back on all that, well, it seems like a sacrilege.

"Adelina, please don't look so sad." Alrik's lips sweep my face, desperate to brighten my darkening mood. "Not when I happen to have the most wonderful surprise for you."

I lower my gaze, assuring myself I can do this. That I'm really, truly ready to go through with it, then I meet his eyes and say, "And I have one for you."

I take a deep breath and gather my strength. Virtue isn't something one gives away easily, not without marriage, or at least the promise thereof. And if word got out, well, there's no doubt it would ruin me. And yet, I don't care. I don't care about rules and conventions that have everything to do with the head while steadfastly ignoring the heart.

I can't care about a future I can't even see, much less imagine.

All I know for sure is that Alrik will marry Esme, and, eventually, someone will marry me. There've been offers. Serious offers. But for now anyway, I refuse to entertain them, no matter how much my parents may beg and plead. Even though I fully expect to one day lie with my husband in our marriage bed, even though I expect he will be a good and kind man with much to recommend him, I know in my heart that I will never love him in the way I love Alrik.

The kind of love we share only comes once in a lifetime— and for some, not even then.

And it's for this reason alone that I'm prepared to risk it all.

If I do nothing else with this life I find myself in, I want to experience love in its absolute, deepest, truest form. Otherwise, I just can't see the point in going on.

"You first," he says, eyes glinting with anticipation, as he grasps my hands in his.

I lift my chin, lift my arms to circle around him, my hands clasped at his neck, looking straight into his dark eyes when I say, "I've decided that I am ready and quite willing . . . to make myself yours."

His brows merge, at first not quite understanding the meaning behind my words. But he soon catches on, reacting in a way I didn't expect. As many times as I rehearsed this scenario in my head, not once did I imagine he'd reply in a burst of uncontrolled laughter. Deep and hearty laughter. So deep and hearty I'm afraid someone will overhear, find us sequestered in here.

Then, just as quickly, he pulls me back to him, covers my face with his kiss once again, lips pressing softly against my flesh as he says, "My dearest Adelina, there is no need for you to sacrifice your virtue when you are soon to be mine."

I pull away, stare into his eyes—my gaze incredulous—his resolute.

"I—I don't understand," I stammer.

"We are to be married." He smiles. "You and I. Just like we've dreamed. It's all been arranged. Just you and me and a member of the clergy. I'm sorry it won't be grand, the kind of wedding befitting my future queen, and I'm sorry your family can't be there to witness our union, though I'm sure you understand the need for great secrecy. But soon, very soon, once word is out and my father has no choice but to accept what I've done and allow both his sons to forge a future with the ones they love, well, then we'll have the grandest party you've ever seen. Adelina, I promise you that."

My eyes search his face, wishing I could match his level of elation, but I'm left with far too many questions to even attempt that. "But how will we do this? *Where* will we do this? And, more importantly, Alrik, your father will *kill* you!"

But Alrik just laughs, erasing the notion with an impatient wave of his hand. "Kill his firstborn son? Never! My father will adapt. And when he meets you, gets to know you as well as I do, well, he won't be able to resist loving you too—you'll see!"

But even though I'd love to believe that, I can't. I'm less idealistic than Alrik. Having made do with far less fortune and privilege, I've experienced firsthand some of the more searing disappointments life brings.

But before we can discuss any further there's a shuffle of footsteps, the unmistakable sound of boots trudging along the long dirt path that runs between the stalls. Stopping just outside of ours, it's soon followed by a swift knock on the door and a deep male voice that calls, "Alrik? You in there?"

"I am," he says, lips still kissing me, covering every square inch of my face, before exploring the deep square neckline of my dress. "And you may come in. Though I warn you, I am not alone, I am enjoying some time with my bride."

I start to pull away, feeling embarrassed by this public display and longing for the shadowed corner again. But Alrik won't have it, and he pulls me back to him. Crooking his arm tightly around my waist as Heath comes into the room, bows deeply, and barely taking a moment to venture a glance at us, says, "M'lord and Esme." His back straightening again only to reveal a look of pure horror that plays across his face. "Oh, *Adelina*, forgive me. I misspoke. I assumed . . ." His face heating to a thousand degrees, allowing the words to trail off from there. Having nowhere to go with that, no elegant way to take the words back.

Even worse is the fact that Heath has only very recently asked for my hand—something known only to Heath, my parents (who scolded me to an unbelievable degree for denying him), and I. Luckily, Alrik hasn't a clue. If he did, he certainly wouldn't be welcoming his oldest and dearest childhood friend, his father's most favored knight, in the way he is now.

My eyes graze over Heath, taking in his coarse, golden-brown hair, his startling blue-green gaze, his lean, muscled form—feeling terribly guilty at his finding us like this, knowing my life would be so much simpler if I could just force myself to return his affections. But that's like saying if it weren't for the existence of the sun you'd be satisfied with an onslaught of rain everyday.

The heart knows no logic, and rarely corresponds with the brain.

When Alrik is present, everyone dims.

And as handsome and kind and well intentioned as Heath is, he becomes nearly invisible when he's next to Alrik. It may sound cruel on the surface, but it's the stone cold truth.

"Nonsense, my friend!" Alrik cries, not at all bothered by Heath's glaring faux pas. "Come join us! I sent for you for a reason, I wanted you to be the first to hear our happy news—Adelina and I are to be married!"

"Sir." He bows, mostly out of respect, but partly to hide an expression that is clearly conflicted. And by the time he straightens again, he's back in control, though he still makes an effort to avoid looking at me.

"I trust you will keep this under wraps until it is time to reveal?"

"And when will that be, sir?"

"Tomorrow we will marry. And the day after that, I will share my joy with the kingdom. But for now, I must go. I have some last-minute details to attend to. So, may I trust you to escort Adelina, my future bride, safely home?"

"Of course, m'lord." He bows once more. But this time, when I remove myself from Alrik's kiss, I catch Heath peering at me in a way I can't read.

His face bearing a look I continue to ponder long after he's exchanged it for another, more malleable one.

A look I continue to guess at as we make our way out of the stables and into what's left of the daylight.

A look that while I still can't define it, manages to linger—the sheer insistence of it leaving me profoundly uneasy.

FOURTEEN

We ride in silence. Or rather I ride, Heath walks alongside me with the reins held loosely in hand, the two of us lost in our own mental landscapes. And though he's had plenty of opportunity to address me, it's not until we've nearly arrived when he chooses to speak.

"Do you love him?" he asks, the words simple, direct, as though we'd been engaged in the sort of conversation that naturally brought us to this point. And though he strives to mask the pain behind the statement, he fails miserably. I can feel his despair from up here.

I press my lips together and look away, wishing I could refuse to answer. Most females would. Claiming great offense to have their heart questioned, their privacy trespassed upon, that it could hardly be considered his business, and so on.

But I'm not like most females. I detest that sort of falsity, that sort of game.

Besides, Heath is kind and decent. I owe him something

better, an honest answer at the very least. No matter how much it hurts.

After all, we've shared a kiss.

Or rather, several kisses—a series of kisses, if you will.

Kisses that, from what I can tell, came to mean much more to him than to me.

I was merely experimenting. Trying to see if my head could influence my heart. Wanting to see if all kisses were like Alrik's. His being the first left me with none other to judge by. And though it was nice kissing Heath, while it left me feeling soft, and calm, and serene—like floating on a luxurious raft in a beautiful, tranquil blue sea—it still couldn't compete with Alrik's rush of warmth. His swarm of tingle and heat.

Though unfortunately, it wasn't until my experiment failed that I realized Heath's intentions were entirely different. He wasn't testing the waters. He was expressing his interest in me.

And though my life would surely be easier if I could return his affections, I just can't, and it would be cruel to pretend otherwise.

I take a deep breath. Allow him to lift me out of the saddle and onto the ground, where he places me gently before him. His face mere inches from mine, hands still grasping either side of my waist, the feel of them resulting in the usual stream of calm, cool energy I've come to associate with him.

"Yes," I say, trying to soften the word, but no matter how it's spoken, I imagine it feels like a dagger to him. "Yes, I do love him." I sigh, feeling the need to further explain when I add, "I can't help it. It's just . . . unexplainable. It's just one of those things."

"You don't have to say any more. Really. You owe me no explanation." His eyes bore into mine, his gaze betraying his words. He's desperate to understand, desperate to make sense of it, desperate to know why I chose Alrik over him.

I try to smile, but only make it halfway. My voice sounding thin, unstable, when I say, "Oh, I'm not so sure about that. It feels like I do owe you an explanation, or . . . something."

His hands grow warmer, his gaze deepens, and before it can go any further, he moves away, the move so abrupt it's a moment before I adjust.

"Adelina," he says, voice low and sweet, loaded with a reverence he's reserved just for me. "You are aware of my feelings for you, so I won't bore you there. But please, allow me to speak as your friend when I say I have great cause to worry about your and Alrik's plan."

Not my plan, Alrik's plan. I really had no part in it. Still, it's not like I denied him. It's not like I said *no*. Then again, I don't remember saying *yes* either. I'd barely gotten a chance to ask a few questions before Heath barged in and put an end to our discussion. Though I choose not to share that with him.

"For one thing, the most obvious thing, the king will be furious. Alrik's match to Esme was planned long ago. No one's ever fooled themselves into thinking it was a matter of the heart—except maybe Esme . . ." He muses, getting back to the point when he adds, "But there is much to consider, much money at stake. As it happens, Alrik's family desperately needs Esme's money if they are to continue their rule. And, as if that wasn't enough, well, then there is Esme and her family to consider. They will gladly hand over a very large dowry if it means their daughter may someday wear the crown. And though I don't claim to be well versed in Esme herself, having only met her a handful of times, I do think it's safe to assume that she'll be quite furious when she discovers what you two have done. And I've a feeling her anger could prove to be even more frightening than the king's. There's something about that girl—something untamed, something that knows no limits, no boundaries of any kind." He shakes his head, hands fumbling by his sides. "And then, of course there is Rhys, who, well, I'm sure he will be the only one, other than you and Alrik that is, who will be over-joyed by the news—a thought which is frightening in its own way, is it not?" His voice lifts in question, though his face remains the same, solid, fixed, with no hint of amusement. "While it may free him to pursue Esme, his doing so will only anger her sister. As I'm sure you know, Fiona has been interested in Rhys for some time now."

I blink at Heath, struggling to take it all in. Even though I was well aware of the triangle of jealousies and attractions I'm immersed in, it's still quite startling to have it so plainly laid out.

"What a tangle love is," I whisper, almost as though speaking to myself. Then meeting Heath's gaze, I ask, "So what do you propose I do then? How would you suggest I choose?"

"I would suggest you choose me." He sighs, the sound as bereft as the look in his eyes. "I will know going in that you will never love me like you do Alrik, and I will accept that. I will also do all that I can to make you happy. I promise you, Adelina, I will dedicate my entire life to seeing that you are well cared for, content."

"Heath . . ." I shake my head, wishing he hadn't just said that.

"I'm sorry if I've made you uncomfortable, but I'd never forgive myself if I didn't at least express my concerns and try to offer you a way out of what I fear will only end in trouble, if not heartbreak, for nearly all involved."

I nod, his words lingering, swirling with the current in my

head, and the worst part is, there's not a single thing to refute. His worries mimic my own.

Still, I look at him and say, "And now that you've expressed your concerns—what now?"

"Now, I bid you good-bye and wish you much happiness." He bows low before me.

And before he can rise, I leave him. Pressing my lips briefly to the crown of his head, pushing against the coarse golden-brown strands, before making my way toward my door. Musing to myself that no matter what happens, come tomorrow, I will never look at my house, my life, or Heath, in the same way again. I will be changed in a most profound way.

Aware of the weight of Heath's gaze still hovering, his cool, calm energy streaming, lingering, as I make my way over the stoop and inside the house.

FIFTEEN

It's a pebble at my window that wakes me. One sharp tap, followed by another, and then another, until I'm fully roused from my sleep.

I reach for my dressing gown and pull it tightly around me, stealing a moment to brush a quick hand over my hair, before I move forward, eager to see who is there.

Expecting just about anyone, except the one whom I find.

"Rhys?" I squint, taking in his deep blue eyes and golden-blond hair. "What is it?" My heart beats in triple time as a swarm of possibilities overcome me—each one worse than the one that came before. *Alrik's had an accident—Alrik's taken ill—Alrik's changed his mind about me . . .* until I finally gather my wits enough to ask, "Is it Alrik? Is he all right?"

Rhys laughs, laughs in a way that lights up his face—laughs in a way that makes him irresistible to females of all ages, all stations—everyone from matrons, to princesses, to the lowliest chambermaids—everyone except me, that is.

"Trust me, your precious Alrik is fine. Just fine. Like a bitch in heat he can't wait to see you, which is why he sent me to fetch you and bring you to him."

"I don't believe you," I say, the words coming before I've had a chance to properly vet them, but once spoken, I find I don't regret them. "Alrik would never send you—or at least not to fetch me. He's well aware of your cruelty, Rhys. The demeaning way in which you enjoy treating me."

Rhys smiles, runs a hand through his glossy golden waves, blue eyes sparkling in the dark as he says, "I will neither deny, nor apologize for that. In fact, I fully admit to believing that my brother is an idiot for choosing you when he could have the lovely, bewitching Esme instead. But then, as it turns out, my brother's idiocy is now working in my favor. Because of his bizarre attraction to you, Esme, my beautiful flame-haired goddess, is free for me to pursue. And so, it seems, under the circumstances, my brother and I have called for a truce. And as he busies himself with his duties, he has sent me for you. So come now, your marriage awaits. Don't make me wake your whole house."

"Now?" I blink into the darkness, sure he misspoke.

"Yes, *now*. It's all very cloak and dagger—top-secret business. So come, grab what you need, get yourself dressed, and come around back to where my horse waits."

But despite his instructions, I remain rooted in place, refusing to budge from the window, knowing better than to take Rhys at his highly unreliable word. Sure that if Alrik were to send anyone for me, it would be Heath, not Rhys, the brother he doesn't trust, the brother he detests.

Rhys sighs. Sighs and shakes his head. Reaching into the pocket of his overcoat when he says, "Fine. Here. Read it and weep. But whatever you do, make it fast. I'd like to get back to my own bed at some point. I've a plump little dairymaid warming my sheets at this very moment."

Suppressing an irresistible urge to roll my eyes, I pretend to ignore that last part and watch as he deftly climbs the trellis just outside my window, body moving swiftly, catlike, thrusting the folded paper into my hand as he perches himself on the ledge.

I step away, pull my gown tighter around me, then push my long golden hair over my shoulder so it hangs down before me. Trying to deflect the way his eyes hungrily roam me, pausing everywhere they shouldn't and not being gentlemanly enough to make any attempt to hide it.

Recognizing the red wax seal Alrik always uses to mark his correspondence on his numerous letters to me, I unfold it quickly, smooth out the creases, and read:

My dearest Adelina:

   If you are reading this now, it's because you refused to take Rhys at his word.

   Good for you!

   Once again, you've done me proud. Though, just this once, I ask that you trust him. It seems my brother and I have finally forged some common ground and now find ourselves working together—working for our own greater good, so to speak. So it is with an easy heart and a clear conscience that I beseech you to go with him.

   Unable to locate Heath, I found myself in need of an ally and turned to Rhys, correctly assuming he'd be delighted by the news of our secretly marrying, or, as he's more prone to put it: "Alrik's ridiculously romantic, foolhardy blunder." But laugh as he may, I'm afraid the joke is on him, for he will never experience the kind of love you and I have found in each other.

Still, despite his making fun, he is sharp enough to understand that my marrying you frees him to pursue Esme and ultimately to pursue the crown, and probably the position as "Father's favorite son and heir" that I once occupied as well. But none of that matters in light of what I now stand to gain—the ability to fulfill my long-held dream of a life lived with you.

So now, I await you, my darling—my bride—my wife! Please hurry to me!

Yours always and forever—

Alrik

"So, what do you think? Does it pass the test?" Rhys lounges on the ledge, one leg dangling into my room, the other bent, propped on the shelf, serving as a rest for his hands.

I glance between the note and him, having to admit that it was certainly written by Alrik's hand, and clearly not under duress, so I take a deep breath and nod my consent.

"Good," Rhys snaps, reaching toward me and snatching it back. Shoving it deep into his pocket without first taking the time to properly fold it, he looks at me, tells me to hurry, then hurtles right out my window, right out of sight.

SIXTEEN

"Climb on up."

I look at him. Frowning as I say, "Up there? With *you*?"

"Unless you prefer to walk." His shoulders rise and fall as though he's prepared to let me do just that.

"Why don't *you* walk and I'll ride?" I place my hands on my hips, vowing to tell Alrik about this later.

"Nope, not a chance." He shakes his head. "For one thing it's dark out. For another it's cold. And, for another . . ." He prolongs the pause, making me wait for it, as though I actually care. "I'm not all that big on acting nobly or gentlemanly. Especially when I don't expect to get anything out of it. Though, if I *were* to get something out of it, then I may reconsider."

I gaze up into those glinting blue eyes, the haughty arc of his golden-blond brow, the flash of white teeth in the blackened night sky. A sight that leaves most girls feeling faint, weak in the knees, ready to succumb to his every whim and need—but for me, it just makes my stomach turn, makes me feel as though I might heave.

"Is this how you flirt with Esme?" I ask, knowing I shouldn't engage him, but it's not like that stops me. "If so, I can't imagine why she'd reject you in favor of your brother. Tell me, Rhys, has she seen this oh-so-charming side of you?"

I wait for his reply, expecting him to get mad, to say something cruel about my looks, my family's low status and lack of finances, but instead he just laughs, his smile growing wider when he says, "Nah, with Esme, it's all pomp and show, and nothing but the deepest courtesy and respect. You have to know how to play a girl like her. She's greedy, superficial, and vain. The only thing she sees in my brother is what's soon to be mine—the power of his position, and, more importantly, the crown. We're a lot alike, Esme and I. We were made for each other. We *belong* together. She and I are twin souls, and someday she'll realize it too."

I continue to gaze at him, fishing around for some kind of sarcastic reply, but the ones I come up with die right on my lips. What he said is remarkably true. They are shallow, and vain, and extremely narcissistic—and his ability to realize that truth reveals an amazing amount of self-awareness and insight I never would've expected.

"So how long are you planning to stand there like that?" he asks, voice bored, thumbs tapping against the horn of the saddle.

"Why didn't you bring a carriage?" I ask, still not willing to ride tandem with him, though clearly my options are limited.

Watching as he heaves a deep sigh and springs from his mount until he's standing before me, a smattering of inches the only thing that separates us.

"Because a carriage attracts far too much notice at this hour," he says. "Remember, this is supposed to be a secret. Which means I didn't think you'd want to let your parents in on the fact that you're eloping—even if it is with the local royalty. But I'm afraid if you insist on continuing to dicker like this, well, there will be no need for secrecy as the whole damn village will soon be in on your tryst. So come on, Adelina, what do you say? You still planning to push against me, or are you ready to submit to the path of least resistance? Be a good girl and hop up—Alrik is waiting."

I swallow hard, swallow my pride, and nod my consent. Bracing against the feel of his hands at my waist as he lifts me up high and gets me all settled, before he hops up himself and warns me to hold on tight or risk tumbling off. Something which he seems to enjoy a little too much—something I do my best not to think about.

We ride for miles. Ride for so long that at one point I allow sleep to claim me. Awakened by the sound of Rhys's voice at my ear, soft and surprisingly tender when he says, "Hey, Adelina. You can wake up now. We're here."

I rouse myself from his shoulder, brush my hand over my eyes, my hair, and take in my surroundings, try to get a feel for our location, but it's not one I recognize.

"It's a hunting lodge," he says, lips tickling at the very edge of my ear. "It's our hunting lodge, Alrik's and mine. And while it's nowhere near as grand as the palace, I will say it's not bad either. I think you'll find it surprisingly comfortable. I know that many, many, many of my conquests have greatly enjoyed themselves here."

Yep, he's back to being Rhys again.

"Where is Alrik?" I ask, yanking free of him.

But I've barely gotten the words out before a whispered voice says, "I am here."

He reaches toward me, carefully catching me as I slide from the horse and into his outstretched arms. His body so warm, so comforting, that for a moment his awful brother is all but forgotten, until Alrik breaks away and says, "Brother, thank you. I owe you for this one."

But Rhys just laughs, turns his horse around, and glances over his shoulder. "Forget it. Your bride for the kingdom—" He shakes his head. "Hate to say it, brother, but I'm afraid it is *I* who will owe *you* once your little honeymoon is over and you realize your folly. I just hope you're not foolish enough to try to collect once you've sullied your bed. And while I wish you much happiness and joy and all that, I'm afraid I must return. My sweet little Sophie surely has *my* bed nicely heated by now."

"Still bedding the chambermaids?" Alrik calls.

Only to have Rhys reply, "Dairymaid, brother, dairymaid. Try to keep up!"

His horse gallops off, taking Rhys along with him, as Alrik pulls me toward the lodge, lips brushing my cheek as he says, "I apologize for him. I was hoping he'd spare you from that brand of crudeness, but perhaps that was just foolish on my part. Still, all that really matters is that he brought you to me. He did as I asked, and you've arrived safely." He gazes down at me with a face filled with so much love and devotion, I swallow everything I was about to tell him about just how crude his brother really is, not wanting my words to mar his expression.

"Actually, I slept through most of the journey, if for no other reason than to tune him out," I say, finding a compromise that succeeds in making him laugh.

"Then you are not tired? You are not longing for bed?" His eyes glint on mine.

I gaze from him to the still-darkened night sky, to the door he's propped open that leads to a rustic yet sumptuous room just beyond.

"Oh, I'm feeling quite rested." I smile. "But I have no objection to bed."

SEVENTEEN

After an hour or two of giggling, cuddling, and whispering to each other—making grand plans for our new life together, a life that begins tomorrow afternoon, Alrik and I fall to sleep. He still fully clothed (minus his boots of course), me stripped of the dress I arrived in, stripped down to the same dressing gown his brother found me in.

Alrik's arm is tossed around my waist, anchoring me tightly to him. Our bodies conforming, pressed so snugly together I can feel the beat of his heart at my back, the rustle of his breath at my ear. And I'm determined to sink into the feel of it, to push aside any stray worries, any lingering fears, in favor of this moment together. Eager for tomorrow, when our exchange of vows will allow us to love each other freely, openly—no longer relegated to vacant horse stalls, or secluded spots in the forest that surrounds my parents' house. No longer forced to pull ourselves back just when the moment becomes truly heated.

It's a change I look forward to.

But while those are the kinds of thoughts my conscious mind is all too happy to dwell on, the moment I fall unconscious my guard slips and a long list of worries seeps in. Manifesting themselves in the strange language that only dreams speak, immersing me in a bleak and foreign landscape where Alrik is nowhere near and a dark hooded being chases me.

I race through brambles and bushes. I race for my life. Wincing against the sting of sharp thorns that snare at my skin and tear at my clothing—leaving me tattered, battered, bruised, but still I race on.

Yet, no matter how fast I run, it's not fast enough.

I can't seem to escape it.

Can't escape the dark hooded being that's coming for me.

Bearing down on me.

Claiming me.

Ending me . . .

I bolt upright, a horrifying scream piercing my sleep. Not realizing until Alrik bolts upright beside me and pulls me tightly to his chest that the sound came from me.

"Adelina! My darling, my sweet, are you okay? What has happened? Was someone here? Speak to me, please!" His hands cup my cheeks, making me face him as he stares into my wide, frightened eyes.

"I—" I blink rapidly, taking a moment to pull away, to gaze around the room, as I fight to get my bearings, to remind myself of where I am, who I am, but still haunted by the horrible visions I saw, as though the dream has continued.

Alrik leaps from our bed, reaches for the torch and shines it on every corner of the room. Finally assured that no one else has joined us, he returns to my side and says, "My sweet Adelina, relax. It was only a dream."

He murmurs a stream of sweet words in my ear—promises, declarations of love, a steadfast assurance that it doesn't mean anything—that I'm perfectly safe—that I will not be harmed in any way.

But I know better.

Know there is no such thing as *just a dream.*

My dreams are not the kind other people have.

My dreams have an uncanny way of coming true.

Prophetic my mother calls them. Warning me from a young age, when I first started having them, to never speak of them again—to do my best to block them out, lest anyone find out. *It will wreck your life,* she'd said. *That sort of thing is deeply frowned upon.*

But tonight, I've no choice but to tell Alrik, to warn him of the terrible thing yet to come. I've had this dream before, many times since I was a girl. Though this is the first time I've come to realize what it means.

That the time has now come.

From the warm, safe shelter of his arms, I allow my eyes to sadly roam his face, my voice low, nearly a whisper, as I say, "We will never be married." I look at him, making sure he understands that my softened tone should not belie the intensity of my words. "I won't make it to the ceremony."

Alrik balks, shakes his head, searches for a way to comfort me. "That's preposterous!" he says. "It was merely a nightmare, nothing more. It means *nothing,* absolutely *nothing*—or at least nothing more than a perfectly normal display of pre-marriage jitters. Our lives are about to change in a very big way—we are about to embark on the life of our dreams. And while I know you're excited, I suspect you're also a tiny bit frightened as well, and this is how that sort of fear often chooses to manifest itself.

But my darling, my sweet Adelina, please know that you have nothing to worry about. I won't let anything bad happen to you. Not now, not ever. Do you hear? You will always be safe with me."

I nod. Swallow hard. Wanting more than anything to believe him, for his words to be true.

But deep down inside I know different.

He's wrong.

Dead wrong.

He didn't see what I saw.

Doesn't know what I know.

Didn't feel the cold hand of death as it grabbed hold of my flesh and refused to let go.

"Kiss me," I say, seeing the way his face softens, falsely believing it's over.

"Kiss me and make me forget. Make it go away," I urge, knowing this is it, my one and only chance to experience our love in its absolute, truest, deepest form. If I can't convince him now, well, then it's a love I'll never know.

"Kiss me as though we have already taken our vows. Kiss me as though I am already your bride."

I loosen the ties of my gown, allowing it to fall away from my body as my gaze holds on his. Aware of his quick intake of breath, his tightening jaw, his widening eyes. Gazing upon me in wonder. Gazing upon me as though he's never seen anything like it before.

But I know differently. Having heard most of the stories, I'm well aware that I'm hardly his first. Though not quite a rake like his brother, he's known to have enjoyed his share of willing partners.

But the thought doesn't bother me. If anything, I find it reassuring. Out of all the girls that he's been with, out of all the girls he could still be with, he chooses to be with me, and only me, for as long as our hearts shall continue to beat.

No matter what happens to me, no matter what the future may bring, I've no doubt that in Alrik's own heart I will always remain his true intended queen.

"Adelina, are you sure?" he asks, his breath coming faster as my fingers creep toward his shirt with the sole intention of ridding him of it.

He's trying to provide a way out, to spare me from doing something he fears I'll regret. An attempt to do the right thing, to be noble, gallant, but the words bear no meaning, he's as eager as I am.

I press my finger to his mouth, only to remove it a second later and replace it with my lips. "You were married to me the day I pushed you into the pond, and I was married to you the day you sent me flowers in response. Red tulips. Who would've thought?" I smile, pausing long enough for my lips to explore his earlobes, his neck, as my hands roam the glorious expanse of his newly bared chest.

His handsome face hovers before me, as he pushes me back onto the pillows, back onto our bed, his lips moving over me, kissing every inch of bared skin, kissing me in places I never would've imagined. Fingers moving quickly, deftly, removing the sparse layer of clothing standing between us, the task finally completed, he says, "Adelina?"

I nod, having never felt more certain.

Then a kiss.

A sigh.

And there is no going back.

I have done this.

We are doing this.

Our bodies moving together—melded, fused, connected as one.

And it's every bit as glorious as I dreamed it would be, if not more.

EIGHTEEN

"My darling," Alrik whispers, turning onto his side and peering at me, his sight aided by the stream of light sneaking in through the windows and creeping up from under the door. "Did you sleep?"

I murmur something inconsequential, not wanting him to know that I didn't. That I couldn't risk ruining my perfect night, the love that we made, with yet another dream that heralds the grim reality of what I'll now face.

"How do you feel? Any regrets?" He shoots me a worried look.

"Regrets?" I shake my head and grin, pressing my lips to his forehead, the place between his brows. Capturing a stray lock of hair in my fingers and smoothing it away from his face to better see him. "What could there possibly be to regret? Are you referring to the second time? Or maybe the third?"

He smiles, maneuvers his body until it's covering mine once again. "I was thinking more like the fourth?"

"Fourth?" I squint, as though trying to recall. "I don't seem to remember a fourth? Is it possible I was sleeping?" I bat my eyes flirtatiously, aware of his hands already at work, already warming me, as I lift my arms to his neck and bring him back to me, voice softly teasing when I say, "Perhaps you should refresh my memory . . ."

When it's over, he shows me where to wash and dress, shows me the wardrobe stuffed with new gowns he brought just for me. Telling me to choose whichever one I want for today's secret ceremony—that they're all beautiful, all elaborate, all appropriate enough for the woman who will one day be his queen, then he leaves, mounts his horse, and gallops away. Promising to send a maid to help me dress, something he'd failed to think of before—promising to return just as soon as all the other last-minute arrangements are taken care of.

I take my time washing, marveling at how everything can look the same on the outside, while inside everything's changed in an irreversible way. No matter what happens from here, at least I now know what it's like to be loved so fully, so thoroughly, so utterly and completely, it's as though the strength of our love has also strengthened me. And that, along with the warm assurance of a freshly drawn bath and a bright and sunny new day, leave me feeling a bit silly for giving so much credence to last night's dream.

Alrik was right. I put far too much importance on what was probably nothing more than a few deeply harbored worries coming to life in my dreams.

Still, I don't regret my decision to lie with Alrik, not for a minute. If anything, I look forward to reliving the experience as his wife, wondering if it will feel any different.

I prolong my bath, wait for the maid to arrive, but when I've washed all I can, when my fingers and toes grow all wrinkled and prune-like, I decide to dry myself and make liberal use of the variety of creams and powders Alrik's left for my use. Then I slip back into my dressing gown and attempt to pick out something to wear for the ceremony, hoping the maid will show soon to help me dress. What with all the layers and ties and things that are meant to cinch impossibly tight, it's impossible to clothe oneself without some assistance.

And I'm just working on my hair, ridding it of snarls and tangles while wondering how I should wear it—knowing Alrik likes to see it left long and loose, flowing in soft golden waves that fall around my shoulders and tumble to my waist, but knowing that as far as the marriage is concerned, it would probably be far more appropriate to wear it braided or pinned in some complicated manner—when I hear a knock at the door and quickly move to answer it, hoping it's the maid and that she's good with hair too.

Barely having a chance to move past the dressing table when I see she's let herself in. And, far from the lady's maid I was expecting, I find my cousin Esme instead.

"Well, well . . ." Her brilliant green eyes burn upon mine. Taking me in with a gaze so searing, so hate filled and angry, it takes a moment for me to gather myself, get my bearings. "It seems the rumor is true. Just look at you standing there, barely clothed." She clucks her tongue in disgust. "You really are planning to elope with him, aren't you?"

"Who told you?" I demand, seeing no reason to deny it. She knows what she knows. Sees what she sees. The story is clear.

"Does it matter?" She arches her brow and roams around the room, surveying the place and everything in it as though she has some sort of personal claim to it. Taking a moment to appraise a picture, straighten its frame, before fixing herself at the edge of the rumpled, unmade bed where her eyes continue to blaze as her small pink mouth pulls into a tight angry frown.

"It matters," I say. "In fact, I expect it will matter very much to Alrik. I'm sure he'd like nothing more than to know the name of the one who betrayed him."

She continues to glare at the bed before casting her gaze my way, saying, "Well, in that case, it was Fiona." She lifts her shoulders, easily giving her sister, my cousin, away. "You know she's had her eye on Master Rhys for some time now, and so she made sure to befriend his latest domestic conquest. Some daft little dairymaid from what I hear. It was quite crafty of Fiona, I must say, and she did manage to learn all she could." She quirks her mouth to the side, as though she finds it all terribly amusing, but not something she prefers to dwell on for long. "Anyway, as it turns out, our dear Rhys likes to talk in his . . . *sleep* . . . so to speak, or at least according to his latest bedmate. And so, Fiona, being the good sister she is, couldn't wait to fill me in on your very happy news. Of course I didn't believe her at first. You'll have to forgive me, Adelina, but the thought of you and Alrik together is simply ludicrous, now, isn't it?"

She looks at me, her eyes flashing as though she fully expects me to nod my agreement, and when I don't, when I just continue to stand before her with my mouth grim, eyes narrowed, and arms folded before me, she sighs and says, "But the way she insisted, well, I decided to come see for myself. But all I see here is one very mussed bed and one very sad, very pathetic, incredibly naive girl who seems to have fallen for the oldest trick in the book." She shakes her head and *tsks*, her tongue repeatedly tapping the roof of her mouth. "Really, Adelina, just how pathetic are you? Gladly forfeiting your virtue with the false promise of a ring on your finger. A ring that, I've no doubt, Alrik never intended to give you." She slants her eyes and looks me over. "Not a very smart move, cousin. Not smart at all. You do realize you have willingly, stupidly, ruined yourself for good. You're spoiled. Used up. No one will ever want to marry you once the word gets out. Hell, you'll be lucky if that lovesick Heath will have anything to do with you. Nobody enjoys dipping into seconds, cousin, if you know what I mean?"

"You need to leave." I straighten my back, square my shoulders, having heard enough of her insults, and not wanting Alrik to return and find us like this. There's no telling what he might do.

But Esme will have none of it. She's not going anywhere. She remains rooted in place, lips curling into a sardonic smile that perfectly matches the look in her eyes.

"You need to leave now, before the maid gets here and before Alrik returns," I say, hoping that'll be enough to convince her.

But she just scoffs. "Oh, no need to worry about that." She checks her nails, runs a hand over her coif of red hair. "The maid won't be getting here anytime soon, if ever. From what I hear it seems she's had a little detour. And as for Alrik . . ."

I swallow. Hold my breath. Wait. A horrible feeling creeping over me, knowing before she can say it, that she's done something bad, found a way to thwart all our plans.

Her words confirming my worst suspicions when she says, "I expect the king is giving him a stern talking-to now. Sorry to break it to you, Adelina, but it seems that your little secret is out, and as for your *marriage,* it seems that it's over before it could start."

I turn away. Struggle to breathe. Having no idea how to respond to anything she just said. I should've known. Should've known it was too good to be true. Should've known Esme would find a way to barge in, interfere; it's what she's best known for.

"The only question that remains now is what will become of you?" She moves until her eyes find mine, her gaze betraying her words. There's no calculating, no pondering, she knows exactly why she's come, what she plans to do, and has no intention of leaving until she sees it all the way through.

Her eyes narrowing, glistening as she raises her arms, reaches behind her, and secures her hood up over her head.

Her black velvet cloak an exact replica of the one in my dreams.

The one I mistook as a mere symbol of death.

Never once thinking that I should take it literally.

Never once thinking it would be the last thing I'd see before my whole world dropped out from under me.

NINETEEN

I am cold.

Hurting.

My only source of warmth coming from a trail of something slippery that streams down my face, causing my eyes to burn and sting and a coppery taste to loll over my tongue.

Blood.

My blood.

It must be. Esme never had a chance to shed any.

She was too quick. Too focused. Too sure of her intent. And I was woefully unprepared to handle her.

Despite being warned by the dream, I never stood a chance.

Never imagined she'd be the one to bring me my death.

And now, after arranging it to look like an accident, she's gone.

Leaving me to fall deeper and deeper into a never-ending pool of blackness.

* * *

I can hear his voice drifting from miles away.

The sound garbled, distorted, as though traveling from the depths of a very deep sea, as though grappling for the surface, grappling for me.

And though I want more than anything to nod vigorously, to wave my arms, to shout out loud and clear that I've heard him, received his message, that I'm aware that he's near—I can't seem to manage those things.

I can't see. Can't move. Can't speak.

It's like I'm already locked in my coffin, buried alive, aware of what goes on all around me, but unable to participate.

Struggling with all of my might to hang onto his words, his presence, to find a way to reach him before I'm gone for good.

He is frantic, mournful, despondent, and stricken when he cries, "Who has done this to her? I will kill them!" Followed by a long stream of threats that spew forth from his lips, pausing every now and then to alternate between begging favors of God and demanding to know why that same God has betrayed him—robbed him of his one and only chance at true love.

"It appears to be an accident," says a voice I instantly recognize as belonging to Rhys. And I can't help but recoil, can't help but hope against hope that it wasn't his hand I just felt at my brow.

"Get away from her! Don't touch her!" Alrik cries. "This is your fault—you and your big mouth. Damn you, brother! Look what you've done!"

"Me?" Rhys laughs, a deeply sarcastic sound. "How could I possibly have caused this when I've only just arrived?"

I strain to hear, wondering if Alrik suspects the truth, that it's Esme, his betrothed, who left me like this.

My hopes crashing when he says, "If you hadn't told Father, I wouldn't have been delayed. I would have been here to save her from . . . from this . . . *fall.*" He shudders, his hand quivering, breath like a sob. "This never would've happened, if it wasn't for you."

"Brother, please. Get ahold of yourself. Why would I do this when I have as much to lose as you do?" Rhys's voice remains steady, firm, a cruel contrast to his brother's never-ending sorrow, his deep-seated grief.

"You haven't lost anything," Alrik says, his words just barely audible. "You can have the crown—I don't want it. You are free to marry Esme, as well—I couldn't stand to look at her now. It is I who have lost. I've lost everything—the only thing that's ever meant anything to me . . . Adelina," he whispers, fingers smoothing my brow, my cheek, trailing down to my neck, where they pause, linger, his voice pleading when he adds, "Adelina, *why?* Why has this happened? Why are you leaving me?"

Because of the dream, I try to say, but no words will come, so I concentrate on thinking it instead. *I tried to warn you, tried to prepare you, but you brushed it away . . .*

"Oh, Adelina, you saw this, didn't you? You tried to warn me last night when you woke from your nightmare, but I only wanted to soothe you, I refused to listen . . ."

For a moment, I felt myself drifting, losing my grip, but when he just spoke, his words echoing my own, something deep inside of me jerked to attention.

Did he . . . is it possible that he somehow heard me? Sensed the thoughts I was sending to him?

Alrik! Alrik, can you hear me? Please know that I love you. I concentrate on the words, concentrate with all of my might, all that is left. Wondering, hoping that he'll sense those words too. *I have always loved you. I always will love you. Nothing can keep us apart, not even my death.*

"I love *you*, Adelina," he whispers, one hand at my brow, the other entwined with mine, frantically pushing some cool, round piece of metal, what could only be my wedding band, onto my finger. "I have always loved you, I always will love you. You will always live in my heart . . . you will always be my bride . . ." His voice breaks, as a flood of fresh tears rain onto my face.

Well, how about that? I think, willing a smile but not quite succeeding. I'm immobile, locked in, and yet, we have *this*— the thoughts that stream between us.

I'm just about to attempt it again, eager to let him know that all is not lost, that I'm not gone yet, that a glimmer of me still exists, when I hear a rush of heavy footsteps followed by Heath's voice saying, "The doctor is here."

The next few moments are spent poking, prodding, and feeling for a pulse so faint the doctor nearly misses it. His voice grave, his prognosis grim, his final pronouncement the last thing Alrik wants to hear.

I am not long for this world.

But Alrik won't accept it. "There are other ways," he insists. "I have money. Lots and lots of money. You can have my entire fortune, whatever you want—just bring her back to me. I've heard the rumors, I know about the elixirs, the secret potions and tonics—the special brew that cures all ills, extending life for an indefinite amount of time . . ."

"I know nothing about that," the doctor insists, his tone sharp, resolute. "And, I assure you that even if I did, that is nothing you want to play with. I am sorry for your loss, truly I am. But this is the natural order of things and you must find a way to make peace with it."

"I will not!" Alrik shouts. And if I could see him, well I'm sure I'd find his face as stony and cold as his voice just resonated.

"Where there is life, there is hope, and you know it! What kind of doctor are you if you do not believe that to be true? I will never make my peace with futility when there are other options still left to explore. I have money, no expense will be spared—do you hear me? You cannot say no to me! Don't you know who I am?"

It goes on like that, Alrik eliciting a long stream of threats I'm sure he has no plans to make good on. It's the ramblings of a man driven mad with grief, and fortunately the doctor recognizes that.

His words compassionate, forgiving yet firm when he says, "Alrik, m'lord, while I am truly sorry for your loss, I have done all that I can. Now I beg of you to keep her comfortable, to say your good-byes, and to let her pass easily, painlessly, with no further outbursts from you. Please, Alrik. If you love her as much as you claim, then let her go in peace."

"Out! *OUT!*" is Alrik's only reply. Followed by the press of his lips on my cheek, a rush of words whispered into my flesh. Our palms pressed together as he utters a string of prayers, pleas, questions, recriminations, and threats, then returning to prayers and beginning all over again.

The litany broken only by Heath's quiet voice saying, "Sir, m'lord, I know someone who may offer the sort of assistance you seek."

Alrik stops, stills, and asks, "Who?"

"A woman who lives just outside the village. I've heard rumors. Can't say for sure if they're true. Though it might be worth a try . . ."

"Bring her," Alrik says, burying his face into the hollow where my neck meets my shoulder. "Go. Fetch her. Bring her to me."

TWENTY

I must've fallen into an even deeper state of unconsciousness because the next thing I know more people have joined me. And from the sound of their voices I'm guessing them to be Alrik, Heath, an older female whom I assume is the one Heath was sent to fetch, and two younger female voices that probably belong to her daughters, or apprentices, or both.

"You must know right up front that there is no guarantee. This is only to be tried as an absolute last resort," the older female voice says.

"Does it look like I have other options?" Alrik cries, teetering on the edge of hysteria.

"It worked on a cat. Brought him right back. He went on to live for another full year," one of the younger female voices cuts in. "But the last human who drank, well, it didn't go over so well."

"What does that mean? What does she mean?" Alrik is frantic.

"It means he died in spite of it," the older woman says. "He could not be saved. Not everyone can."

"Adelina's not just anyone. She's young, beautiful, in good health. It will work for her—you will make sure that it does!" Alrik demands.

"I will try. That is all I can promise. I've recently used it on myself—just six months ago when I fell ill the drink cured me, brought me back from the brink so quickly it was as if it never happened. Still, like I said, there are no guarantees."

"So what are you waiting for? Give it to her already! Hurry, before it's too late!"

She moves toward me. I feel the warmth of her body sidling up beside me. Her fingers sliding under my neck, cupping the back of my head, bringing me to her as she presses something hard and cold to my mouth. Urging a cool bitter liquid to slip past my lips and over my tongue, until it sinks down my throat and I do what I can to struggle against it. But it's no use, I can't fight it. I'm immobile, paralyzed, my thoughts locked inside, and I've no way to tell them to stop—it's a waste of their effort.

It's too late.

It won't work.

My energy is gathering, compressing, shrinking down into a small vibrating sphere of color and light. Preparing to rise and lift—to drift right out of the center-most part of my scalp, what's called the crown, and merge into whatever it is that lies just beyond.

They continue to fuss all around me, voices clamoring, hands prodding—making it clear that I'm the only one aware of the fact that I'm close to being gone.

This life is ending.

I won't be returning—or at least not in this form.

My formerly sightless eyes suddenly filled with a vision of a beautiful golden veil I can't wait to merge into. Still, I strain to hold on for just a few seconds more—I need to reach Alrik, need to convince him that it will all be all right.

My tongue bitter with the useless concoction they insist on feeding me. Wasting precious time, choosing to focus on absurdities when there are far more important things.

Alrik! I concentrate on his name with every last ounce of my being. *Alrik, please, can you hear me?*

But my plea falls on deaf ears. He misses it entirely.

His attention is claimed by his grief.

And now it's too late.

I can't ignore the pull. Can no longer fight it. Don't want to fight it. And so I heave my last breath and allow myself to soar. Hovering up near the ceiling as I gaze down upon the scene, seeing Heath drowning in anguish with his head bowed low, the older female still feeding me the elixir, while her two young apprentices, who bear such a striking resemblance I'm sure they're her daughters, hover over me, whispering a long string of words I cannot decipher. And finally, Alrik, my dear Alrik—frantically grasping the hand that bears my wedding band, futilely searching for signs of a life that no longer exists.

Letting out a bloodcurdling howl when he realizes the truth.

My body's been reduced to an unoccupied shell.

My soul has been freed.

He empties the room, wanting to be alone with his grief. Then numbed, broken, completely defeated, he throws his body over me. His lips seeking my mouth, desperate to bring me back, unable to accept what he knows deep down inside to be true.

So lost in his sorrow he has no idea that I kneel right beside him, longing to reach him. Desperate to assure him of a truth he couldn't even begin to imagine—that I haven't gone anywhere—that I'll never truly leave him—that the body may wither, but my soul, just like the love that we share, never dies.

But it's no use. He's shut down. Unable to hear me. Unable to sense me.

Convinced that he now walks alone in the world.

And it's not long before I feel the pull again. This time so strong there is no way to escape it.

Yanking me away from Alrik, out of the lodge, and into the sky. Sending me spinning, soaring, racing through the clouds, flying over mountain peaks, peering down upon an earth so different from the way I used to see it, becoming a place where everything shimmers, where everything vibrates and glows.

The truth of our existence so clearly revealed, I can't imagine why I failed to see it before.

Every living thing, from plants, to animals, to the very people who populate the planet—are all connected to each other.

We are all one.

And though we may pass in and out of existence, our souls, our energy, our essence, never fade.

We are infinite beings—every last one.

The realization dawning like a lightning bolt crashing over-head, and I instinctively know this is *it*.

This is what I'm supposed to learn.

This is what I must never allow myself to forget, no matter what happens from this moment on.

And then, before the next thought can form, I pierce through the beautiful shimmering golden veil of light and find myself right back in a place I instantly recognize.

TWENTY-ONE

I land on the riverbank. Land with a thud.

Toes caught in the water, butt caught in the sand—the events of a lifetime, my first lifetime, still swirling through my head.

Aware of a soft rustling sound coming from somewhere behind, I turn to see her smiling as she makes her approach, offers an old gnarled hand, and helps me to my feet.

My lips parting as a slew of questions rush forth, all of that halted when Lotus shakes her head, places her hand on my arm, and says, "You have discovered the truth."

I nod, clinging to what I now know, what I must always remember, never forget, but at this exact moment, I'm burdened with more pressing concerns. "And Damen?" I ask, my voice betraying my anxiety. "Where is he?"

She lowers her lids for a moment as though watching a scene that plays deep within, lifting them again when she says, "He still has much to see. Much to learn. For him, it's not over. Not yet anyway."

She motions toward the river, and I follow the tilt of her

finger. Watching the current swirl and change until it smooths out again and the remnants of the scene I just left are reflected upon it. Showing Alrik's life still in progress, showing him consumed by a never-ending grief.

He is broken, defeated, wrecked to the core, so greatly misguided all he can manage is to seek revenge for my death. Having no idea Esme caused it, he's eager to place the blame on someone, anyone, ultimately seeing that the woman from the village, along with her two young apprentices, are charged with dealing in witchcraft and magick and put to their deaths. Soon falling into an even deeper despair when the act of his vengeance brings no sense of peace, no sense of redemption. Fails to compensate for his loss. Fails to bring me back to him.

The rest of his life lived in a fog of lost passions and thwarted dreams, his fervor and fight buried right along with my body. He goes through the motions, does what's expected, settling into the path of least resistance, settling into the life his father had planned.

Marries Esme.

Claims the crown.

Each passing day causing his heart to harden and shrink into a small bitter stone.

Not daring to believe he'll ever see me again.

Not daring to believe in anything, ever again.

And it breaks my heart to watch it, to watch him eventually brought down in a revolt secretly staged by a brother turned against him. Rhys ultimately marrying Fiona, Esme's sister, only to find he can't seem to stop longing for Esme, the one woman who will never be his.

The four of them trapped in their own private hell, unable to find a way out.

Having no way to know what I've learned: When we harm one another, we also harm ourselves.

"Alrik is Damen." I switch my gaze from the water to Lotus, surprised to hear myself say it, but knowing it's true. "And Rhys is Roman, Heath is Jude, the village woman is Ava, her apprentices are the twins Romy and Rayne, Fiona is Haven, Esme is Drina . . ." *Of course.* I frown and roll my eyes. "And the doctor? Do I know him?" But before I can finish the sentence, I *know*. "The doctor is Miles." I shake my head, allow a small laugh, then I add, "The only reasonable one in the group. The only one who wanted nothing to do with mystical cures."

Sighing when I realize we've already done this, centuries earlier—only to fall into a similar trap, repeat a modern-day version of a nearly identical existence.

Glancing at the river, watching it clear, the images quickly fading when I say, "How did we not know this? Why do we keep making the same stupid mistakes over and over again?"

Facing Lotus, her gaze narrowing in a way that sets off a riot of wrinkles that fan either side of her eyes. Her voice low and grave, she says, "It is the plight of man. And while the blame lies partly on the river," she gestures toward the swiftly moving dark waters before us, "most of the blame lies on man's inclination to tune into the noise that blares all around him, instead of the beautiful silence that lies deep within."

I gaze out at the river, turning her words around in my head, realizing how they mirror everything I just learned. We spend our lives getting caught up in all the wrong things—led astray by our minds, our egos, seeing ourselves as separate from each other, rather than listening to the truth that lies within our own hearts, the truth that we are all connected, we are all in it together.

"The universe is patient," she says. "Providing multiple opportunities for us to learn, to get it right, which is why we reincarnate."

"So, it's true then. Damen and I lived before as Adelina and Alrik." I glance at her, seeing her nod in confirmation. "And I'm assuming he died in that life—a mortal death?" My eyes graze over her silver hair, down to the long white tunic stitched with gold, all the way down to her surprisingly bare feet, though it's a moment before I notice that the cane she used the last time I saw her is gone. She is able to stand on her own.

"Oh yes," she says. "He is caught in it now. Reliving the moment. Though it should be over soon."

I press my lips together and fiddle with the hem of my T-shirt, thinking it over. Having no reason not to believe her, but still, there's something that doesn't make any sense, something she needs to explain.

"But if that's all true, then why is it that neither of us saw that life when we died and went to the Shadowland? And why didn't Jude see it on any of his trips to the Great Halls of Learning? I'm sorry, Lotus, but despite how real it all seemed, it just doesn't make any sense."

But despite my voice rising at the end, despite my getting more than a little caught up in my own argument, Lotus remains calm, serene, completely unruffled when she says, "You are familiar with the saying, 'When the student is ready the teacher appears'?"

I nod, remembering how Jude once said it to me.

"It is the same with knowledge. The truth is revealed when you are ready to receive it, when you need it in order to move forward, to take the next step in your journey, to move on toward your destiny. You were not in need of that knowledge before, nor were you ready for it. And thus you saw only that which you needed to know and not a single thing more. But now that you are ready the knowledge was revealed. Each step leads us to the next. It is as simple as that. And the same goes for Damen and Jude."

"And what about Jude? Is he still stuck in that lifetime too?"

Lotus nods. Her gaze faraway when she says, "Jude has his own journey. You may not see him for a while. Though you will see him again. Not to worry."

My gaze lands on the river, noticing it's grown darker, murkier, and glad to be standing safely on its banks rather than closer to its shore. "So is this it then?" I turn to face her. "Is this the journey? Is it over—have I completed what you've asked me to do?"

Lotus shakes her head, those rheumy old eyes meeting mine. "That was merely the beginning, the first test of many. Much lies ahead. You have more to discover."

And before I can ask what that means, before I can ask her to clarify for me, the ground begins to shake, the river begins to slosh and bulge, as the earth beneath my feet begins to shift and separate in a way that reminds me of my first California earthquake.

I fight to locate my voice, fight to free the scream that sticks at the back of my throat, when Lotus disappears—just simply evaporates—as a swell of red tulips sprout up all around me, taking her place.

A sign that can only mean one thing—Damen has joined me.

Hundreds of tulips sent fluttering, their soft petals whispering against him, as he rushes over them, rushes toward me—grasping me into his arms, he picks me up off my feet, twirls me all around, and presses his lips to my face, my hair, my lips, my cheeks, then starts the procession all over again. Desperately reassuring himself that I'm here, that it really is me—Adelina/ Evaline/Abigail/Chloe/Fleur/Emala/Ever—his love of so many lifetimes, bearing so many names, but being of only one soul all the same. Finally made aware of the truth, that I never really left him despite what he may have convinced himself of.

"Adelina!" He pauses, smoothing my hair from my face, his eyes hungrily roaming over me, drinking me in, as he laughs, shakes his head, realizes he's still caught up in the past, and says, "Ever!" He kisses me again, holds me tightly to him. "You were right. You were right all along. There was a life before—an entire lifetime I never could've imagined." His eyes pore over me, still a bit overcome by what just transpired. "But now that we know, what do you suppose it all means?" he asks, almost as though musing to himself.

I thread my fingers through his hair, aware that his question was meant to be serious, but eager to erase any trace of his lingering grief in favor of a much sweeter memory.

"Well, for one thing, it means I wasn't *always* a virgin." I smile, remembering the beautiful night we spent together as Alrik and Adelina, and the wonderful part of the morning that followed.

Watching as he throws his head back and laughs, his hands clasping tighter around my waist as he says, "Now that's a moment I wouldn't mind reliving in the pavilion."

He finds my lips again, warm, deep, then he pulls away and says, "And Jude?"

"Jude or Heath?" I lift a brow. "You do know they are one and the same?"

He nods, having figured that out.

And not sure exactly which part he wants me to explain, I say, "He insisted on joining me, and for some reason, Lotus allowed it. Said the answers he sought would be found there."

"He loved you then too, didn't he?" Damen's mouth pulls down into a frown as his eyes stare into mine.

I nod.

"And the rest—did you see it? All of it?"

I take a deep breath and nod again.

Damen sighs, tries to turn, to pull away, but I won't let him. I keep him clutched tightly to me.

His eyes pulling down at the sides when he says, "No wonder Jude keeps reappearing in my life. He's trying to keep us apart, but not for the reason I thought. He must recognize me, sense who I am, knows innately *what* I am. That I later succeeded where I first failed, ensuring my own immortality before going after yours." He shakes his head. "All of this time, for all of those lifetimes, without even realizing it, he was trying to stop me, trying to save you from me." He rubs his chin, looks at me wearily. "I thought I would die from the pain of losing you. I wanted to die. And trust me when I say my death did not come soon enough. I was left hollow, a shell of a man without you." He swallows hard, swipes a hand across his eyes. "Heath begged me not to prosecute against Ava and the twins, or rather the people they were then. And when he couldn't change my mind, he begged me to take him instead. He never forgave himself for bringing them to me. Never got over the guilt. Having summoned them as much for himself as he did for me. He couldn't bear to lose you. Would do anything to keep you around, even if it meant having to watch you marry me. But, when you died in spite of our attempts, he was quick to accept what I stubbornly resisted. What we did was wrong, unnatural, something best not attempted. He understood that; I did not. Neither in that life, nor the one that followed, where I eventually found a way to finish what I'd started." He shutters his eyes, musing at the folly of the last several hundred years. "Did you see the rest of his life? Did you see what became of him?"

I shake my head.

Damen sighs, his hands warming my arms, gaze distant when he says, "He retreated somewhere far away, died alone, still a fairly young man. I'm afraid my karma is more of a mess than I ever could've guessed."

Not knowing what to say, I don't say anything, but that's okay, since Damen speaks in my place.

"So what now? Do we wait here—see if Jude or Lotus reappear? Make our way back and try to make amends for the deeds of prior lives we can't really change? It's your call, Ever. Your destiny. Your journey. I won't doubt you again."

I look at him, more than a little shocked by his words, knowing how much he likes being right, being in charge; most people do.

But he just lifts his shoulders and says, "Isn't that the whole point? Isn't that why you keep showing up in my lives? To teach me about grief, to teach me to feel it, to accept it, but to not try to outwit it. To lead me out of the dark and into the light—to show me the real truth of our existence—that I've had it wrong all along—that the soul is the only immortal part of us. Isn't that why all this has happened, why you and I can't find true happiness, why we keep facing obstacles that are impossible to surmount? Isn't this why we find ourselves here now, because I got it all wrong and managed to mess up on such a colossal scale?"

The silence gathers around us. Damen absorbed by his past, while I'm left speechless by his words. Eager to move past it, not wanting to dwell here for long, I'm just about to tell him that I have no idea what could be next, that his guess is as good as mine, when I see a small boat anchored by the shore, anchored right alongside us. A boat that appeared out of nowhere, wasn't there less than a second ago.

And knowing there are no accidents here, no coincidences of any kind, I grasp his hand in mine, and start leading him toward it, saying, "I think we're meant to go for a sail."

TWENTY-TWO

I settle onto the seat, busying myself with rearranging the velvet pillows at our backs as Damen slides in beside me. The boat is long, painted a dark glossy red with gold ornate swirls marking its sides, narrowing into a curving crest at both the front and the back in a way that reminds me of the gondola Jude and I once manifested in the Summerland version of Venice. But with no oar, no motor, no way to steer or guide ourselves, we're at the mercy of the river. Left with no choice but to sit back and hope for the best.

The boat pulls away from the shore, drifting deeper into the water just seconds after we board, following the current, giving no hint as to what might be in store. Damen slides a protective arm around me as we peer at the passing scenery; the way the river widens so swiftly it's not long before we're surrounded by nothing but deep dark water, the banks we once stood upon reduced to a slim speck of gold on a distant horizon.

I lean into Damen, wishing I could do something, say something to erase the hint of worry that plays at his brow, to ease the regret that burdens his heart. Seeing the way his eyes widen, the way he sits up higher, on full-scale alert, as he looks all around and says, "It's the River of Forgetfulness."

I squint, vaguely remembering him mentioning such a place once before. Saying something about the soul taking a trip down the River of Forgetfulness before it's reborn into the next life. That the purpose of that particular journey is so we don't remember what came before—that we're not meant to remember the lives we've just lived—that each incarnation offers a new journey of self-discovery, a chance to right our previous wrongs, to balance our accumulated karma, to find new solutions to old problems.

That life is not meant to be an open-book test.

Remembering how Lotus recently said something similar— that man's folly, his penchant for making the same mistakes over and over again, can be blamed partly on the river—and taking that as proof that Damen is right. It's exactly what he thinks. Though it's anyone's guess where it will end.

"Are we going to relive them *all?*" Damen asks, voice betraying a deep-seated reluctance, bearing no desire to ever revisit those painful early days he lived back in Florence, Italy.

But before he can get too bogged down in the thought, I look at him and say, "No. It's a test. We have to do whatever we can to not let ourselves forget all that we've learned. Lotus came to me just before you arrived, she said knowledge is revealed when we need it, which means we need to hang on to all we just saw. We can't forget a single moment. I'm pretty sure we're gonna need it for later."

"It's a lot to hang on to." He frowns. "The river is tricky. And other than the fact that I've made a mess of the last several hundred years—that I owe Ava and the twins big time for taking their lives—what would you suggest I choose to concentrate on? There's a good chance that when we get off this ship and go back to our normal lives we won't remember any of the things we've just experienced."

I steal a moment to gather my reply, partly because he may not like what I say, and partly because I'm still amazed that he's looking to me for the answers. Taking a deep breath, venturing a quick look around, before I return to him and say, "You need to remember that the soul is eternal. That love never dies. And that your failure to realize that, your attachment to the physical world is what brought us both here—brought us both to this point."

There, I said it. It's his fault. Still, my voice bears no blame. He's not the first to make that mistake. As Lotus said, it's the folly of man. Damen's just one of the few to actually succeed at his attempt to thwart physical death—or at least for a while anyway.

"Then later, when we get through this, and wind up . . . well, wherever we'll wind up, we'll need to use that knowledge to find a way to reverse what we've done—the mistakes that we've made," I add, the words coming so quickly and easily it's as though they emanate from some other place, but I know deep down inside, know in my gut, that they're true. "That's my journey." I nod, suddenly knowing it for sure. "That's the truth I'm supposed to reveal. How?" I peer at him, attempting to answer the question that marks his brow. "I'm not sure, but there's no doubt in my mind that it's what I'm destined to do."

Damen looks at me, features hardened, conflicted, though sticking to his vow to follow my lead.

And though I search for a better argument, a better way to persuade him that'll erase any lingering doubts, there's no time to dwell. No time to assure him of what I know deep down inside to be true.

Not with the current growing swifter.

Not with the sky darkening in a way that instantly erases the horizon.

The line between heaven and earth, water and air, up and down, suddenly blurred. Catching us in a swirling, whirling surge of rogue waves, each one bigger than the one that came before, causing the river to expand and surge, to ripple and roar, until all we can do is hang on to each other, to keep from going overboard, capsizing into the water.

The sky cracking open with a rumble of thunder so loud, we seek shelter in the only place left to us—each other. The two of us trembling under a cloudburst of rain—an unrelenting monsoon—as great bolts of lightning strike down all around.

"Concentrate!" I cry, eyes squeezed shut against the downpour, my lips at his ear. "This is part of the test, hang on to the past, refuse to forget, no matter how scary it gets!"

Not quite sure where that came from, but again, sensing it to be true. Knowing firsthand the mighty power of fear, having been ruled by it before.

It's the opposite of faith.

The opposite of trusting in the universe.

The opposite of believing in one's higher self.

Fear leaves you sweaty and shaky and insecure enough to question everything you know to be true.

Fear makes you turn your back on what matters most.

Resulting in rash decisions, false moves, and later, the unrelenting burden of regret. And if Damen and I are to get through this, move forward on our path, we'll have to beat this river and overcome this storm by doing whatever it takes to block it all out.

The waters continue to churn and dip as the boat creaks and tilts in a terrifying way. Damen and I huddle together, clinging to our memories, clinging to each other, as a bolt of lightning burns up the bow, cracks it in half, and allows a torrent of water to gush in. Causing the bottom to fall out from the weight of it, as the river rises to swallow us whole.

The two of us reaching, grasping, fighting for our lives, fighting to hang on to each other—but it's no use.

Our skin is too wet, too slippery, too slick to grab hold of.

And though I try to keep my eye on Damen, try to determine the direction from which he calls out my name, it's too dark, too confusing, I've no sense of time or place, no sense of up or down—and the next thing I know, I'm sinking.

It's over.

Too late.

The river has claimed me.

TWENTY-THREE

I'm gagging.

Gagging on mud, and muck, and totally icky bottom-of-the-river sludge. Something hard and metallic clanging against my upper molars and floating on my tongue—something I'm determined to rid myself of.

I push up onto my elbows, and then onto my knees. Balanced on all fours, I spit onto the ground, scoop a finger around the inside of my mouth, and rid it of rocks and debris along with a strange medallion that pops out and dangles before me—hanging from a brown leather cord I wear at my neck.

I lean back on my heels, pinching the piece between my forefinger and thumb as I peer at a small silver circle of a snake swallowing its own tail. Thinking it curious, more than a little interesting, but having no idea where it came from.

No idea why I find myself wearing it.

No idea what it could possibly mean.

I fall back in exhaustion, close my eyes against the sun. At first enjoying the feel of it, the way it dries my clothes and warms my skin, but it's not long before the pleasure's diminished by rays so intense they leave me sweaty and breathless and suddenly overcome with a deep parching thirst that has me scrambling back toward the river, hoping to drink, only to find the river is gone. Replaced by a landscape of sand, a multitude of cacti, and two blazing suns overhead emitting dual sets of harsh, unforgiving, searing hot rays.

My skin begins to blister and burn as my lips crack and bleed, and with no shelter to be found, and too weakened by my thirst to go searching for one, I'm left with no choice but to curl my body into a ball. Bowing my head until my chin is tucked tightly to my knees, my hair hanging down before me, hoping it will shield me, only to end up sacrificing the back of my neck in order to spare my face.

Think. I squinch my eyes tightly, try to center myself, try to concentrate.

Think, I scold. *Remember.*

But the heat's so intense it's impossible to focus on anything but my scalding skin and unquenched raging thirst.

I yank my sleeves down, down past my wrists and over my hands, all the way down to my fingertips. Trying not to cry out when the cotton rubs against the blisters, splitting them open and allowing the juice from the wounds to sizzle right there on my flesh. Working past the pain, I shove them deep into my pockets, attempting to make myself smaller, less of a target, trying to hide from the heat, but it's no use. With dueling suns, one at my front, one at my back, there is no escaping their wrath.

My fingers squirm deep, and then deeper still. Ultimately coming across something slick and hard with rough edges—a stone of some kind.

A stone I cannot remember.

I work my way along the sides, along the cool smooth surface, knowing I need to think, to concentrate, to remember . . . *something* . . . but having no idea what that something might be.

I turn the stone over. Explore each side, again and again, until a flicker of light plays on the underside of my crusted, shuttered lids. A flash of color, a myriad of varying hues, creeping into my vision—my inner vision—accompanied by a string of words meant to prod me, nudge me, insistently swirling through me, demanding my notice—though I've no idea what they mean.

Words that continue to loop and repeat, playing over and over, each and every syllable stressed with greatest urgency, until it sounds something like:

Dark—like his eyes.

Red—like the blood that flowed from me.

Blue—like the river, like the stone in my pocket.

A stone I must *see*.

I work it up past my hip, slide it across my belly and over to where I can see it. Marveling at how it's managed to stay cool despite the raging inferno around me, daring to slit one eye open, despite my lashes singeing, my skin scalding, and my retina searing, I peer upon it, twirling that brilliant blue-green crystal around in my fingers, awed by the sight of it, until I notice something even more wondrous—the energy that radiates from my skin like a halo of the brightest, most radiant, golden-flecked purple.

The color reminding me of the one I *felt* earlier. The one that thrummed right through my body, back when I was in Summerland, just after I'd inadvertently traded Fleur's experience for mine. That colorful feeling convincing me there was more to Damen's and my story. That we'd both lived a life we'd yet to acknowledge.

And suddenly I know what it means—know what it is.

That brilliantly shimmering shade that I see is the color of my soul.

My *immortal* soul.

It's what my aura would look like if I had one.

The truth descending upon me so hard and fast it leaves no room for doubt in my mind.

I can't die here.

Can't die anywhere.

While it's true that my body may not outlast this heat, no matter what, my soul will live on.

Like the snake that hangs from the cord at my neck—each life feeds into the next.

And the moment I acknowledge that, accept it for a fact, a soft spring rain begins to fall and I jump to my feet, smiling, laughing, as I tilt my head back. Opening my mouth as wide as it will go, encouraging a small pool of water to collect on my tongue. Aware of the sand fading beneath me as my toes curl into a lovely expanse of flowers and grass that springs up to replace it. Aware of my skin healing, regenerating, as one sun sparks and fades and burns itself out, while the other one dims into a warm, forgiving, life-sustaining glow.

I spread my arms wide and twirl in the field, skipping, and leaping, and dancing in a rain that, having healed me, is now reduced to a light, shimmering drizzle.

I did it! I can't help but smile triumphantly. *I won! I outsmarted the river—remembered the one thing that matters most—with a little help from my friends, of course!*

Friends.

I stop, my breath coming ragged, too quick, as I gaze all around, my joy vanishing the moment I realize two truths I've forgotten 'til now:

—I'm not like my friends. My body's immortal, my soul is not.

—Damen's not here. Which means he forgot. Couldn't hold on to the memories. Allowed the river to get the best of him.

And, having traded the soul's immortality for physical immortality there's only one place left to find him.

Trapped inside the Shadowland.

TWENTY-FOUR

Though I've been there before, three times at last count, I have no idea how to find it. No idea where it actually exists, or how to locate it on a map.

My first visit was via the experience Damen shared with me in his head. The second was when I telepathically showed Roman the place where Drina's soul went. And the third was when Haven killed me, sent me to that horrible abyss for what felt like forever but was probably only a matter of minutes.

That's how the Shadowland works.

But it's not like I ever made the trip by foot. It's not like I ever set out to find the physical manifestation of it.

So, hoping for answers, I fall back on all that I've learned, the things Ava taught me. And instead of allowing my mind to run amok with questions and thoughts that only result in creating panic and uncertainty while never actually arriving anywhere helpful or good, I choose to focus on the silence within. Trusting it to guide me, to lead me, to see that I arrive in the place I'm most meant to be.

Determined to follow my gut, my heart, my intuition, the hidden truth resting inside—I blaze my own trail, led solely by my own instincts, but when it feels like the trek is taking too long, I decide to speed it up a bit and manifest a partner.

Riding my mount for as far as she'll go, I slide off her back the second she halts just shy of the perimeter, the place where the grass turns to mud, where the trees are all burned out and barren despite the constant deluge of rain that never ceases to fall. It's exactly like I first thought, this horrible place really is Summerland's yin—its shadow self—its opposite side—providing a clear demarcation between the two worlds—one light, one dark—leaving me with no doubt in my mind that it marks the entrance to the Shadowland.

I tap my horse on her rear, urging her to head for greener pastures, as I glance all around, hoping to find Lotus, or maybe even a guide of some kind, but realizing I'm all on my own I trudge deep into the muck. Trudge past what feels like mind-numbing miles of bleak, dreary, desolate, drenched, and soggy landscape, wondering if there will ever come a point where it turns into something else, stops looking the same. That point coming much sooner than imagined when I stumble upon a scene so drastically different, I stop, swipe a hand over my eyes, and blink a few times to make sure I'm not hallucinating, that I really am seeing what I think I'm seeing. And even then, I still have my doubts.

I creep forward, my head swiveling as my eyes strive to take it all in. It's surreal, surely a crazy mirage of my own mental making. And yet, no matter how many times I blink, no matter how long I hold my breath and stare, it refuses to yield in any way until I've no choice but to accept the fact that the scene that lies before me is not only real, but an exact replica of the one in my dream.

The dream I was sure Riley had sent me.

The dream I had again very recently.

The dream I was sure had been merely symbolic, something I was meant to take my time pondering, analyzing, dissecting, until I could finally break it down into manageable bits that actually meant something.

Never once thinking I was supposed to take it literally.

Never once thinking that an entire landscape of rectangular blocks—a maze of glass prisons—could really exist.

I take a deep breath, take a few cautious steps, and squinch up my gaze. Peering at a crowd of tormented souls, knowing exactly how they feel, having been there myself.

Alone.

Isolated.

Devoid of all hope.

Surrounded by silence, an infinite darkness, forced to relive their very worst choices, their most tragic mistakes and wrong turns, the bad decisions and selfish acts that caused others pain—forced to relive their own personal hell over and over again. Experiencing the pain they've caused others as though it's their own—just like I did when it was me in their place. Having no way of knowing that there are others just like them—that while they may feel alone, the irony is they're actually trapped among their own kind. All of them ruled by an assault of images, age-old regrets, with no way to turn off the pictures, no way to silence their heads.

And just as I wonder what I'm expected to do from here, the memory of Lotus's voice plays in my ear.

There are many who await you. Await you to release them, to release me.

And I know this is what she meant. I have to start here.

I approach the first block, observing a frenzy of energy that belongs to a tormented, agonized soul I don't recognize. Though there's no doubt it's one of Roman's, since other than me, the only ones Damen turned were the orphans. And I can't help but wonder just how many immortals Roman might've made, remembering how he once answered Haven when she posed the question: *That's for me to know, and the rest of the world to find out.* Not to mention how many might've inadvertently, accidently, ended up here.

I close my eyes, press my palms to the glass, and wait for some kind of sign, further instructions, an order that will soon be revealed, only to be met by a blast of despair so dark, a torment so bleak, I can barely contain it. Soon followed by a surge of bitter cold so intense I can't help but jerk back. Gaping at my freezing, frostbitten palms, knowing that as long as I'm here, there's no chance they'll heal.

Desperate to end it, for myself as well as them, I kick at the glass, kick as hard as I can, and when that doesn't work, I pound with both hands. And after hurling my body against it to no avail whatsoever, I dig deep into my pocket, locate the bit of crystal Ava gave me, the small piece of cavansite that enhances intuition, and psychic healing, prompts deep reflection, inspires new ideas, helps rid oneself of faulty beliefs, and aids in inducing the memories of one's prior lives, hoping it can help me here as well. And when my hand lights up, when my palm heals, when my skin emits that brilliant golden-flecked purple hue I glimpsed earlier, I know exactly what to do.

I take the sharp edge, the jagged tip that narrows to a point, and drag it vertically up one side of the glass, then horizontally across the top, and then vertically down the other, cringing at the high-pitched, squeaky, nails-on-a-chalkboard, wince-inducing kind of sound that results, but knowing I've succeeded when the prison collapses, shatters onto itself, and a cool blast of air whizzes by as the trapped soul rushes out.

My heart hammers hard in my chest as the entity hovers before me, growing, stretching into a varying collection of personas—a full array of prior-life guises, none of which I recognize. Emitting a bright flash of color as it shrinks down into itself once again and takes flight, soaring high into the sky, quickly disappearing from sight.

I pause to catch my breath, amazed by what I just witnessed, what I've just succeeded in doing, then I head to the next cube and repeat the sequence again, and then again. Releasing one trapped soul after another, having no idea where they go, but figuring anywhere's got to be better than here.

And then, just as I move for the next, I find him.

Damen.

Though it's not at all like I thought, not at all like I expected.

Rather than being trapped like I feared, he also wanders from block to block.

His hair wildly mussed, his eyes haunted and red-rimmed, his voice thick with remorse as he begs forgiveness for all that he's done.

Begs forgiveness for their being here.

"This isn't your fault," I say, quietly approaching him. "You had nothing to do with this, Roman's the one who turned them. You know how proud he was of his elixir, how he liked to share it freely, or at least with whomever he deemed worthy, whereas you only gave it to the orphans and me. Unless . . ." I swallow hard, look at him, a whole new thought occurring to me, one I pray is just pure paranoia and not at all true. "Unless there were others you haven't told me about?" I suck in my breath.

Relaxing only when his bereft gaze meets mine and he says, "Six orphans. Plus you. That's the grand total of my personal legacy." He lifts his shoulders, *breathes* deeply, looks all around, before returning to me. "Still, in the end, it doesn't really matter who fed them the elixir, doesn't matter who decided to turn them, because all of this—" he sweeps his arm wide, hand arcing before him, all around him, "everything you see here—it all stems from me. I was the first. I planted the seed. Roman never would've gotten there if it hadn't been for me. So, you see, Ever, this *is* my fault. It's like Lotus said, *I'm the cause and our love is the symptom.* I couldn't let you go. Couldn't handle the pain of a life lived without you. And while you, my sweet Ever, my dearest Adelina, may very well be the cure, I have to do all that I can to correct my karma, to right all my wrongs. And what better place to start than right here?"

I pause, taking a few moments to consider his words, while carefully sifting through a few of my own. "Well," I say, my voice low, quiet, my eyes never once straying far from the elegant planes of his face. "From what I've experienced so far, the best way to make up for all that is to release them. That's pretty much all we can do at this point."

I show him the crystal, show him how I've been using it to break through the glass and set the souls free. Motioning for him to join me, and watching as he places his palms to the surface and sends a silent plea for forgiveness. His flesh throbbing, blistering, blackening, before becoming almost mummified looking—refusing my offer of the crystal that will allow him to heal, he prefers to suffer, convinced he deserves it, as he follows me from one to the next. The two of us repeating the sequence—Damen expressing his regrets as I send the glass shattering so another soul can rush out.

When we get to the next one, we halt—immediately sensing something different. Instantly alerted to something unusual that sets it apart from those that came before. And even though the energy within is just as frantic as all the others, thrashing furiously, crashing from top to bottom and side to side, moving so fast it's hard to get a handle on, to see it for anything more than a confusing blur—it's still an energy we both recognize.

So I bow out. Step to the side.

This particular soul is Damen's to release, not mine.

While we all share a past, a long and convoluted history of jealousy that always ends in murder, my murder, the two of them have memories that don't involve me, have nothing to do with me—and not all of them bad.

I hand him the crystal, listening as he calls to her silently, telepathically, but still I can hear. And when he places his hands on either side of her cube, everything stills.

Damen? she calls, sensing his presence, his energy, or maybe it's just wishful thinking. Maybe she's been calling for him since the day I killed her and sent her soul here.

I am here. He closes his eyes, presses his forehead to the glass, holding on to the sides with each hand. *I have failed you. Failed you in so many ways. Failed to love you in the way that you wanted, in the way that you needed. And though I may have saved your life, may have spared you from the black plague, I'm afraid that in the end, I stepped in where I didn't belong, and, because of it, I've reduced you to this.*

His breath fogs up the glass, prompting him to swipe a finger across it, then clear it with the scorched palm of his smoldering hand.

Drina Magdalena, you are Poverina no more. So please go. Be free. You have other places to be. I was never meant to be your destiny.

He taps the crystal to the glass, drags it down each side, a bit

across the top. Encouraging it to shatter into long, thin strips
that fall to the ground before breaking into much smaller
pieces that crumble at his feet.

I brace myself. Brace for just about anything. Expecting
an angry whirl of energy that, if history is any indication, will
most likely hurl itself straight at me.

Which is why I'm surprised when she chooses to seep out
slowly.

Her energy hovering before us, expanding, stretching, at
first forming into a brief image of herself as my cousin Esme
that lasts only a few seconds before she settles into her last incarnation as the gloriously beautiful, red-haired, green-eyed
Drina—a beauty so startling even death cannot mar it.

She floats closer to Damen, her gaze moving over him,
drinking him in as a quiet communication passes between
them. And even though I can hear it, even though neither one
of them tries to hide it from me, I still turn away, try to grant
them their privacy. Catching only about every third word,
leaving their dialogue sounding something like:

*Sorry—forgive you—forgive me—wrong—wasted—misguided—
regretful*—then back to *sorry* again.

She reaches toward him, cups his face between her fingers,
her mouth tugging down at the corners when he involuntarily
flinches at the feel of her—her gaze saddening at the bottomless pool of regret she finds in his eyes.

And when she turns to me, it's not at all what I expected.
The usual score of hate, taunts, and threats has been replaced
with a soft lilting reverence.

I should've known the first time I killed you, she thinks. *I should've
realized back then that even without your presence beside him, your
love never died. I may have succeeded in borrowing him for a time, but*

he was never really mine, and it was never very long before he went searching for you again. Throughout all of these years, from the very first moment he met you as Adelina, his heart was claimed for good. He belongs only to you. You and Damen are meant to be. And I've been a fool for interfering. She sighs, shakes her head, reaches forward as though to touch me, but then, remembering Damen's reaction, she thinks better, returns her arm to her side.

And I'm not sure who's more surprised, her, Damen, or me, when I choose to step forward—when I choose to reach for her hand and grasp it in mine. Suddenly knowing why Damen flinched the way he did, it's not so much the cold, it's more the buzz of her energy—the sheer, vibrating intensity is hard to get used to.

The words streaming into my head when she thinks: *If you can forgive me, then soon, I'll be leaving.*

I gaze into the eyes of the person who killed me time and time again. Trying to rid herself of me, rid the world of me, only to find that she couldn't. No matter how hard she tried, I kept coming back. And I'm amazed to find I can no longer think of her as the enemy. Now that I know the truth, know that we're connected, that I'm as much a part of her as she is of me, I can no longer hate her. And even though this seems like the end, this good-bye is probably only temporary. I've no doubt we'll someday meet again. I just hope she can manage to hold on to some of the wisdom she's gained.

She smiles, her face lighting up in a way that leaves her looking positively radiant, and at first I think it's a response to what I just thought, only to see her eyes moving over me, motioning for Damen to look too.

Look—you're glowing! Her expression changing to confusion when she adds: *But . . . how can that be? Immortals don't glow.*

You never glowed. But now you do. It's so odd—what do you suppose that it means?

Damen squints, unable to see what I see—what she sees—the faint trace of purple that emanates from me, all around me.

She pauses, waiting for me to explain, but since I don't even know where to begin, I just lift my shoulders and quirk my mouth to the side.

And Roman—have you sent him here too? She looks straight at me.

I pause, wanting to stress that it wasn't *me* who killed Roman—that, contrary to some people's opinions I'm *not* some crazy immortal killer. But soon realize that two out of three is hardly a record worth bragging about, much less defending, I gulp down the words and nod toward the last two remaining cubes.

And just like when Damen approached hers, when she approaches Roman's, all activity halts as he senses her presence and cries out for her. And the second Damen cracks it open, Roman whirls out in a furious storm of energy that expands and forms, spending a few seconds as the handsome, rakish Rhys before he settles on the way he looked as the even more handsome, even more rakish Roman. Complete with golden tousled hair, piercing blue eyes, suntanned skin, faded jeans that hang dangerously low, and an unbuttoned white linen shirt that showcases his finely sculpted abs.

But even though Damen and I stand right there before him, ready to explain, defend our actions, do whatever it takes to ease what could very easily become a precarious situation— just like in life, his sole focus is Drina.

She's all he can see.

Though unlike the past six centuries, Drina can finally see him.

The two of them drawn to each other, gazing at each other for so long, Damen clasps my hand in his and starts to move away, nearing the last remaining block when Roman calls: *Brother.*

Soon followed by: *Friend.*

And then: *Enemy.*

Though that last part is chased with a dazzling, white-toothed smile.

We meet Roman's gaze. Noting the way the grin lights up his face, lights up his energy, making it spark and glow as he shuts his eyes tightly and concentrates on a long stream of words he wants us to hear.

A long stream of words I can't seem to put into any sort of context, can't make any kind of sense of.

A long convoluted list of herbs, potions, crystals, and . . . *moon phases* . . .

I gasp, eyes wide with disbelief, gaping at Damen, wondering if he hears what I hear, understands what, for me, just became clear.

It's the antidote!

Roman is willingly, without being asked, bullied, manipulated, or tortured, holding up his end of the deal.

The one we struck just minutes before he was killed and sent here.

The one where I agreed to give him what he wanted most, in exchange for what I wanted most.

Drina for the antidote that'll allow Damen and me to be together in the way that we were as Alrik and Adelina—with no need for energy shields, no fear of our DNA clashing, no threat of Damen dying.

Roman's making good on his word.

Taking a moment to repeat it once more, make sure that we got it, took note of it, committed it to memory, because he'll soon be moving on, with Drina by his side, and he doesn't expect to see us again, or at least not for a very long time. This is our last chance. The opportunity won't come again.

I gulp, nod, brimming with so much gratitude, so overcome with happiness, my eyes sting, my throat swells, and I've no idea where to start, what to say.

But I don't have to say anything. He and Drina have already joined hands, already turned away. Already headed to the next cube, where, having no further need of us, they pool their energy in a way that splits it wide open, allowing Haven to burst out of her own personal hell.

She shoots straight for me. An angry ball of raging red energy that, from all appearances, is still furious with me.

Still blames me.

Still intends to make good on her last spoken words—her threat to undo me.

Damen shouts, jumps between us, his arms spread wide, doing his best to cover me, to defend me from whatever she's planned.

But just as she reaches us, hovering a mere razor's width away, she stops, slows, and I watch, eyes wide with wonder, as the furious red glow of her simmers into a much softer rose-toned pink. Shifting between all of the personas of her previous lives, beginning with my cousin, Esme's sister, Fiona, before transitioning into several more I vaguely recognize from scenes I've viewed of my past incarnations. Amazed to learn she's been with me all this time, usually from a distance, never as a close friend or even a sister, but still, wow, I had no idea.

I start to apologize, want her to know how deeply sorry I am, but she's far too impatient, and quickly waves it away. There's still more to show me, she's not quite through yet, and I watch as she transitions into all of the guises she wore in her most recent life. Everything from her prima ballerina phase, to her J. Crew preppy phase, to the goth phase she was in back when we first met, to the short-lived Drina-wannabe phase that followed, to the emo phase that came shortly after, to the black leather and lace rock 'n' roll gypsy look that didn't last long before transitioning into her super-scary immortal witch phase, as Miles once called it—the one her life ended with—until finally settling upon a version of herself I've never seen before. One where her hair is long and shiny and well cared for, her eyes clear and bright, her clothing slightly edgy, Haven-like, but not crying out for attention or in-your-face angry. But the biggest change of all is the radiant smile that lights up her face, telling me she's finally found herself—finally at peace.

Finally likes who she is.

Jabbing her thumb between Damen, Roman, and Drina, a love triangle that spanned way too many centuries, she shakes her head, rolls her eyes, and lets out a long wistful sigh that soon turns into a contagious laugh I can't fight. The two of us giggling in a way that reminds me of better days spent with Miles at the lunch table, lazy afternoons holed up in her room with a stash of magazines piled high between us, Friday nights hanging in my Jacuzzi after having devoured an entire pizza.

Her focus shifted back to me when she thinks: *I don't hate you. Though I'm not gonna lie, I used to. And not just in that last life, but in most of the others as well. But that's only because I was so unhappy with myself, I was sure that everyone else had it better, had what I needed. I was sure that if I could only claim what they had, then I could be happy too.* She shakes her head, rolls her eyes at the absolute folly of it. *Anyway, you'll be glad to know that's all over now. I'm free in more ways than one. Now I'm just looking forward to whatever comes next.*

I swallow hard and nod, her words pretty much the opposite of what I'd prepared for, which makes them even more welcome. Ones I won't soon forget.

And then, the next thing I know, Drina points, Haven squeals, Roman grins, and they all join hands, the three of them rushing toward something viewable only to them, disappearing into a brilliant flash of white light without once looking back.

TWENTY-FIVE

Damen pulls me into his arms, grasps me tightly to him, then lifts me into the air and swings me around. My hair swirling behind me like a shiny gold cape as we twirl and spin and dance and laugh, gazing in wonder as this once-barren field begins to transform itself.

The jagged shards of prison glass sinking deep into the ground—recycling first into sand, then into a rich dark soil that provides instant nourishment for the formerly burned-out trees. Allowing them to straighten and stretch, to sprout a thick blanket of leaves, as a swath of purple and yellow wildflowers bloom at their roots.

The two of us overcome with excitement, brimming with the glee of our triumph, Damen's voice like a song in my ear when he says, "We did it! We freed them—made amends—we even secured the recipe for the antidote, and it's all because of *you!*" His lips find my forehead, my cheek, my nose, and my ear, then pulling away, he adds, "Ever, do you realize what this all means?"

I look at him, my grin so wide my cheeks are stretched to their limits, but still wanting to hear him say it, wanting to hear the words spoken out loud for both of us to hear.

"It means we can finally be together." He stops, presses his forehead to mine, his breath coming fast and quick. "It means all of our problems are solved. It means that we'll never have to visit the pavilion again—not even as Alrik and Adelina—unless, of course, we want to." He wiggles his brow, emits a low, deep laugh. "All we have to do is head back to the earth plane, get working on the brew, and . . ." He pauses, smooths his thumb over my cheek, then leans in to kiss me again.

I return it with an intensity and fervor matching his. Aware of the slim veil of energy hovering between us, keeping him safe from what, thanks to Roman, has become my lethal DNA, which, also thanks to Roman, won't be a threat for much longer. Hardly able to believe that the days of what we've come to refer to as our *almost kiss* are so close to being over.

Soon, very soon, we'll be able to live just like everyone else. Able to touch each other openly, freely, without any worries. Like we do in the pavilion—only better, because it'll be real.

Soon we'll embrace as ourselves—our present-tense selves—instead of in our various past-life guises.

I pull away ever so slightly, close my eyes and turn my face to the sky, stealing a moment to send a silent thanks to Roman, wherever he is, for giving us this wonderful gift.

Then just when I'm about to kiss Damen again, his face falls and he moves out of my reach, answering the question in my inquiring gaze with a curt nod toward Lotus, who kneels at a distance.

She sits at the edge of a pond just a few feet away, her wispy silver strands flowing freely about her, murmuring softly with her hands clasped tightly to her chest. Gazing upon an abundance of lotus blossoms that rise through the murky dark waters to bloom above the surface. Their soft white and pink petals lifting upward, surrounded by shiny green scallop-edged leaves, one popping up right after the other until you can barely see the water for the flowers.

She remains like that for some time. Content to meditate on the wondrous view before her, until she turns to face us, wearing an expression that, while not exactly what I'd call *troubled*, hardly matches the flood of triumph Damen and I are currently in the midst of.

Damen's eyes narrow, his jaw clenches, bracing for whatever bad news he's sure that she brings.

The two of us cautiously moving toward her, meeting halfway, both of us equally startled when she rises from the muddy banks, looks at us, and says, "Congratulations."

We wait. Wait for something to follow. But, for a while anyway, that seems to be all.

"You may return to the earth plane if you wish." She glances back and forth between us.

Damen squeezes my hand, in need of no further prodding. He's more than ready to leave right now, doesn't see the point in wasting another second hanging around. But I stand firm. Dig my heels in. Sensing it's not over yet, there's something more Lotus is waiting to share.

"You have done well. All is in bloom." She gestures toward the flowers that are still blossoming, and to the landscape beyond. "You have even freed the lost ones." She presses her palms together, forming a steeple she holds close to her heart, her simple gold band glinting at us. "And so you are free to leave. Free to return to your immortal lives. Yet, I wonder . . ."

We look at her, me curious, Damen on guard, fingers curling at his sides.

"I wonder if you will want to return to your lives after all you have learned. I wonder if you will choose a life of physical immortality after having learned the truth of the soul."

Damen rolls his eyes, grunts, and again, tries to haul me away. But I stay right where I am, looking at Lotus when I say, "Are you implying we actually have a choice?"

She lifts one gnarled old hand, brushes a stray wisp of hair away from her face. "Oh yes," she says, her gaze moving over me. "There is a choice. A way out."

I press my lips into a frown, trying to determine just what that might mean. Deciding I don't like the conclusion I come to, don't like it at all, when I say, "If you're referring to *death* as a way out . . ." I shake my head, blink a few times, hardly believing she would even dare broach such a thing. "Well, you can forget it. No way is that happening. I mean, in case you don't remember, that pretty much results in a one-way ticket to the Shadowland for people like us. And since we did a pretty good job of cleaning up the Shadowland just now, we'd hate to see it resort right back to its old ways. Not to mention how there's no guarantee anyone would even show up to release us like we just released Roman, Drina, Haven, and everyone else." I pause long enough to huff, blow my hair out of my eyes, but not long enough for her to interject. "Also, you should probably know that we have the antidote now—or at least the recipe to make it. Which means we've just been handed a whole new reason for living—a really *good* reason for living. We have each other *forever*. We can live the life we've always dreamed of. And finally, well, the whole dying thing is pretty much moot anyway, since I can't actually die anymore. Back when Haven killed me,

I rose above my weak chakra. I overcame my weakness, made the right decision, and because of it, I came back to join the living. I'm *unkillable* now." I lift my shoulders, knowing it may sound weird, but then, weird is all relative here. "I'm a *true* immortal. Here for the duration. I'm not going anywhere, and I really prefer that Damen doesn't go anywhere either."

"And you?" She turns to Damen, totally unfazed by everything I just said. "Do you agree with this? Do you feel as she does?"

He frowns, glares, teeth gnashing together as he grumbles an unequivocal "Of course I do!" Then he squeezes my hand, eager to leave.

But even though I'm eager to leave too, for the moment, my curiosity's piqued and I want to see where this leads. Wondering if I might already know when I say, "This *way out* that you refer to, is this for us or for *you*?" My eyes narrowing as I recall her earlier words, when she begged me to release her, but from what, she never made clear.

Is she stuck?

A prisoner of the Shadowland but without the glass cage?

The answer coming in the form of her usual riddle when she says, "It is for you, for me, for all of us. Once I learned the truth, I was already too old and frail to make the journey. But now you are here. Returned just for this. I can see it in your eyes, in the light that surrounds you. You are the one. The only one. The fate of many lies in your hands."

"So . . . basically you're saying that my journey isn't even close to being finished? That there's still a heckuva lot more you expect me to do?" My gaze narrows as I try to determine just how I feel about that, mostly veering toward being very much against it.

She nods, her clumpy old eyes never once leaving mine. "You are so close. It is best to keep going from where you now stand. Where destiny is concerned, each step leads to the next."

"Oh, sure," Damen says, the sound of his voice startling me in that it's even gruffer than I would've expected. But to Lotus's credit, she doesn't react, doesn't wince, doesn't flinch, just continues to stand there, observing him with her usual calm. "Sure, we'll get right on that." He shakes his head. "Sorry, Lotus, but you're gonna have to give us a little more to go on. Ever and I have been through the wringer and we came out on top, got the one thing we wanted—the one thing we needed to make our lives complete, and now you think you can just show up, toss another cryptic riddle our way, and steer us out of our much-deserved victory celebration and back into more trouble— trouble that you alone have created?" He glares. "Think again."

"Seriously," I add, encouraged by his argument. "Why should we even consider doing this? Why can't you find someone else, one of the other immortals, maybe? Haven't we been through enough already?"

But instead of answering my question, she tilts her head in Damen's direction and says, "Damen, is it really *I* who created it? Or was that *you*?"

Damen meets her gaze, but clamps his lips shut, refusing to speak. And when it's clear he has no plans to address her, I nudge him with my elbow and say, "What's she talking about? What is it you're not telling me?"

He swallows, squirms, kicks at the ground, puts it off for as long as he can before he takes a deep breath and says, "She claims to be one of the orphans. Claims I saved her from the black plague over six hundred years ago when I made her drink from the elixir."

I balk, eyes practically popping from their sockets as I glance at the two of them. Finally finding enough voice to say, "*And?* Is it *true?*" Wondering why no one saw fit to mention this before. Wondering if this is what she showed him that day when I watched them share a silent communication.

Damen shrugs, swipes a hand over his brow and gazes all around. "No. No way. It's impossible. She's making it up," he says, obviously more flustered than he lets on. Pausing for a moment, long enough to gather his thoughts, sighing loudly as he adds, "Honestly? I don't know. I've been racking my brain since the day she first told me, but I just can't recall. It's her word against my memory and there's no way to know for sure. Usually it's the eyes that give it away, being the window to the soul and all that—but hers are so damaged, they're completely unrecognizable. She's not the least bit familiar to me." He shakes his head, takes a moment to scowl at Lotus, his face softening when he turns back to me. "Ever, you've got to remember we're talking over *six hundred years* since I last saw these people. And the only reason I didn't mention it before is because I didn't want to worry you unnecessarily, especially when there's no way to prove it either way. Besides, my only concern is for you— for us—right here in the present, and well into the future. The past no longer concerns me. Other than Drina and Roman, I have no idea what became of the other orphans. I have no idea where they ended up—"

"But Roman did know," I cut in, remembering what Haven told me, about what Roman told her, the stories he wrote in his journals.

Damen and Drina may have moved on, but Roman stuck around, kept in touch. Eventually discovering a way to re-create the elixir, and when the effects began to wear off, sometime around one hundred and fifty years later, when the immortals began to show the ravages of aging, he tracked them all down and had them drink again, repeating the sequence every century and a half, until now. Now that he's gone, there's no one to look after them. Not to mention there's no telling just how many he decided to turn on his own. If the number of unrecognizable souls we just released from the Shadowland was any indication, it's safe to assume there are many, many more.

I study Lotus, wondering how long it's been since she last drank the elixir. I've never seen anyone as old as her, especially an immortal. All of the immortals I know are young, beautiful, glowing with health and vitality, physically perfect in every imaginable way. Whereas she's just the opposite—old, weathered, her skin so paper-thin, body so frail, it seems as though the slightest hint of a breeze could tip her right over, break her into a million sharp little pieces.

Damen and I are so lost in thought we're both caught by surprise when Lotus springs forward and grabs hold of our hands, her ancient eyes beaming brightly as her mind connects with ours, projecting a slew of images I never would've expected—images that leave me questioning everything.

TWENTY-SIX

Lotus's fingers entwine with ours, the feel of them dry, cool, but surprisingly strong, as her mind projects a series of portraits, like individual sepia prints, one after another, eventually streaming and blending into a moving-picture format. Showing a quick glimpse of the orphans, all lined up in a row, looking as they did back then. Damen and Drina flanking one end, Lotus and Roman on the other, the rest gathered in the middle.

Long before she became Lotus, she was a dark-haired, bright-eyed child named Pia, who, not long after drinking the elixir, fled the orphanage with all the others only to be taken in by a family of modest means, who, mourning the child they lost to the plague, were eager for a replacement.

She lived normally at first, having no idea what she'd become. She grew up, married, but it wasn't long before she realized she was different. Not only could she not bear children, but she couldn't figure out why everyone around her aged while she stayed the same. A realization that soon forced her to do what all immortals must eventually do once the subtle questions and curious inquiries begin to grow into rising suspicion, hysteria, and irrational crowd-driven fear—under the cover of night, she grabbed a few belongings and ran, never to return, or at least not for several centuries.

She wandered. Remarried—more than once. Determined to stay in each place, with each husband, for as long as she could until the constant need to flee became so unbearable she determined it emotionally easier to live on her own. Eventually growing to abhor her immortality, seek ways to reverse it, wanting only to rejoin the natural order of being, to live like everyone else.

She traveled. First to India, then on to Tibet, where she studied with mystics, shamans, gurus, a whole host of spiritual seekers and guides who showed her how to purify her body and cleanse her soul, but couldn't help her reverse the choice she made all those years ago when she was too young to understand the consequences. The irony of her studies being that she'd unknowingly succeeded in strengthening her chakras to the point where she'd rendered herself completely invulnerable, immune to the one thing she sought above everything else—the release that only death can bring about.

Ultimately growing so advanced in her studies, she became known as a celebrated miracle worker, the most sought-after healer. The name she now goes by, Lotus, stemming from her ability to make that beautiful flower bloom right from the center of her palms, simply by closing her eyes and wishing it to be so. An act she was capable of not just in Summerland, but also on the earth plane back home.

Determined to settle into a celibate, solitary existence, but fate had other ideas, and it wasn't long before she met someone and fell in love. Real love. True love. The kind of love which, despite several husbands, she'd never experienced before.

The kind where she built enough trust to confide the truth of her existence, tried to convince her lover to go to Roman, to drink too, to become like her, so they'd never suffer the pain of losing each other.

But he refused. Chose to grow old. And when the day finally came that she knelt beside his deathbed, fretting at the simple gold band he'd placed on her finger, he promised to do everything within his power to *not* reincarnate. To *not* return to the earth plane. Stating he'd much rather wait for her to find a way to reverse her immortality, so that she could someday join him in the great hereafter.

He left her on her own to grow older, then older still. Her body eventually becoming so decrepit, she prayed the sheer exhaustion of keeping it going would ultimately convince her breath to stop coming, her heart to stop beating, so she could meet up with her lover again—but still, she lives on.

She continued her studies, continued to search for a way out, ultimately discovering the solution only after she'd grown too old to make the trip.

Though she refused to give up. With the long-held wish of her reunion finally within reach, she spent the last century tracking down all of the remaining orphans, revealing the truth of what she'd learned, hoping to convince one of them to make the journey—to bring back the chance at a new lease on life.

Life as it was intended to be.

To provide them all with a sort of do-over—a second chance to make a fully informed decision as to whether or not to keep going like they are. Unlike the time when they were too young and scared to realize the consequences—when they all rushed to drink without a second thought.

Drina refused her flat out. Roman laughed in her face. While the others simply shook their heads, gazed upon her with great pity, and told her to go away.

Damen was the last on her list—her last hope.

Until she saw me.

"I thought it was enough that I found a way to release the souls and reverse the Shadowland, but, as it turns out, there's still more you want me to do." I glare, shake my head, and yank free of her grip. My fingers slipping past the thin gold band she wears on her left hand, feeling remorse for the loss of her loved one, but unsure what I'm supposed to do. "You put me through all that hell, when all along that wasn't even the journey you had in mind—you had something else planned for me that whole entire time!"

"Each step leads to the next," she says, her voice far calmer than mine. "Everything you have experienced in this life as well as those prior has prepared you for this moment. Each decision you made has landed you here. And while you have accomplished so much—there is much left to do. The journey is long and arduous—but the reward is too great to miss. There are many who await you—await you to release them. You are the only one who can do so. This is why you keep reincarnating, Ever. You have a destiny to fulfill."

I squint, realizing with a start that's the first time she's ever used my real name, or at least my current real name. Usually she calls me Adelina, or just points as she sings that demented song of hers. And I can't help but wonder what more I could possibly be expected to do after all that I've already been through. Surviving a past life I never realized I'd lived, nearly drowning in the River of Forgetfulness, nearly getting burned alive in the desert of two blazing suns, freeing the lost souls of the Shadowland and restoring it back to the splendor of Summerland.

After all that, I'm just not sure I'm up for any new challenges. Not when everything Damen and I have been striving for all this time is finally well within our reach. All we have to do is head back to the earth plane, collect the ingredients, whip up the antidote, give it a shake and a swig, and the happily ever after is ours.

"Only you can bring back the truth. Only you can find it," Lotus says, the words spoken plainly, simply, bearing no signs of begging or pleading.

"Locate *what* exactly?" Damen asks, making no attempt to hide his exasperation.

But Lotus is immune to our outbursts. From what I can see, she cycles between two moods—veering from slightly forlorn, to calm and serene.

"The Tree of Life," she says, her gaze directed at him. "Only Ever can find it. Only Ever can bring back its fruit. The tree is evergiving. Its fruit provides enlightenment—the knowledge of true immortality—the soul's immortality—to those who seek it—as well as reversing the false, physical immortality of those who've been fooled."

"And if she doesn't go? If she turns her back on you, on all of this, and returns to the earth plane, then what?" Damen's brow rises in challenge.

"Then it's a pity. Then I have misjudged her. Underestimated her. Then she will not realize her destiny and many will suffer. Yet it is her choice entirely. I can only ask, she has the free will to decide on her own." Lotus faces me when she adds, "Do you still have that small pouch that I gave you?"

My eyes narrow, my lips part; I'd forgotten all about the little silk pouch she handed me at the beginning of the journey, and after all that I've been through, I doubt it's still with me.

I snake my fingers into each of my pockets, eventually finding it wedged deep into the corner of the righthand back one, the last one I check. It's crumpled, totally squashed and crinkly, but still I retrieve it and dangle it before me.

Her face lifting into a smile as she says, "Do you remember my words when I gave it to you?"

I squint, searching through the cluttered contents of my mind. "You said, 'Everything you think you need is in here. You decide what that means.' Or something like that."

She nods. Grins. My attention claimed by the large gaps in her teeth when she says, "And so, with that in mind, what is the one thing you desire most—above everything else? Right now, at this very moment, what is it you want?"

I hesitate. Stare at a small patch of grass at my feet. Aware of Damen's gaze weighing heavily upon me, wondering why I won't say it, why the delay.

The same thing I wonder as well.

I wonder why the word won't come—why it feels like such a struggle, when it's the one thing, the only thing, we've sought all this time.

Lifting my gaze to meet Lotus's, I fight to push the words past my tongue. My voice wooden, perfunctory, devoid of emotion, when I say, "The antidote. I—rather *we*, have the recipe, but we still need to collect the ingredients, attend to all the moon phases, and . . . whatnot . . ." I allow the words to trail off. My heart hammering, my stomach jumbled in knots, my fingers twitching wildly as Lotus's eyes travel between Damen and me.

"And so it is." She nods, as though it is done, and when the gesture is met with two skeptical stares, she adds, "Please. Look inside. You will find it contains everything you need to make this antidote of yours. Including a very rare herb that will be difficult to find back on the earth plane. And yes, all of the moon phases have been accounted for."

Content to leave it at that, she starts to shuffle away, stopping only when I call her back to me and say, "You're joking, right?" I dangle the tiny pouch, knowing there's no possible way it could ever contain all the items Roman included in that long grocery list of his. It's too small. A list like that would require a completely stuffed duffle bag, or two.

Lotus stops, steeples her hands at her chest, and says, "Why don't you empty the contents and see?"

I frown, kneel onto the grass, pulling the strings as I tilt the tiny bag on its side. Unable to do anything but gasp when a slew of herbs, crystals, and tiny glass vials of liquids tumble out. Having no idea where they could possibly be coming from—the bag contains far more items than it could ever logically hold.

"It is all there. Everything you need to proceed. Just follow Roman's instructions and the life that you dream of is yours." She stops, looking at me when she adds, "Or is it?"

I gulp. Struggle to breathe. Staring at the bounty all spread out before me—a generous heap of hard-to-find, complex ingredients I've been searching for all of this time—the answer to all of our problems right here for the taking.

And yet, even though I know I should be happy, if not completely ecstatic, I can't seem to stop her words from repeating in my head, can't dampen the doubt she raised when she said: *Or is it?*

"Something wrong?" Her rheumy gaze moves over me. "Have you changed your mind? Is there something else you'd rather have?"

"Ever—" Damen drops to his knees right beside me, willing me to face him, to say something, to offer some sort of explanation.

But I can't.

How can I explain it to him when I can barely make sense of it myself?

He'll only get angry.

Won't understand.

And, on the surface at least, I can't say I blame him.

But this goes so much deeper than that. This harks back to the journey—my destiny—the very reason I keep reincarnating.

And suddenly I know. Suddenly, I'm thoroughly convinced that drinking from the antidote is just another distraction—it's not the answer we've truly been seeking.

In the end, it won't solve a thing.

Won't solve the one thing that needs to be solved more than anything else.

Sure it will allow us to be together in the way that we want—but that's all it allows. It's like slapping a Band-Aid on a big gaping wound—it does nothing to heal the damage of what's already been done.

It does nothing to change the fact that we're on the wrong course.

Once we realize how we've cheated ourselves out of the lives we're meant to live by choosing physical immortality over the immortality of our souls—the antidote is no longer the issue.

If Damen and I are truly going to be together then we'll have to reach far, far deeper than that. We'll have to admit that our problems didn't start the day Roman tricked me—they started several centuries earlier when Alrik couldn't bear to lose Adelina—then culminated when he reincarnated as Damen, perfected the elixir, and changed the course of our souls forever.

If Damen and I are truly going to be together then we'll have to release ourselves from that path, we'll have to reverse the choices he made in the past, we'll have to pay off that huge karmic debt by making this journey to the Tree of Life, obtaining its fruit, and offering all the others a chance to release themselves too.

Only then will we be free to move on.

Only then will we get our *true* happily ever after.

Otherwise, I've no doubt another glaring obstacle will just find a way to present itself, and on it will go, for evermore.

I take a deep breath, but find I don't really need it. It's like I can feel that purple glow radiating inside me once again. I've never felt more sure of myself.

"There is something else I'd rather have." My eyes meet Lotus's, the two of us holding the look for what feels like a very long time. "I want to fulfill my destiny. I want to complete my journey," I say, my voice solid, steady, more certain than ever. "I want to complete the task I was born to do."

I can hear Damen beside me, his sudden intake of breath, and I know without looking that it's partly due to my words, and partly due to the fact that the ingredients have now disappeared.

But I don't look. For the moment anyway, my gaze stays on Lotus. Seeing her standing before me, granting me a curt nod along with a slowly curving smile when she says, "As you wish."

TWENTY-SEVEN

Long after Lotus has left we remain quiet. Damen lost in thoughts of outrage and blame, while I prepare for the moment when I'll have to explain.

The silence broken when he looks at me and says, "Ever, how could you?" Four simple words that cut to the bone, but then, they were meant to. He shakes his head, squints, tries to make sense of it. "How could you do that?" he adds. "How could you just throw it all away? Seriously. You're going to have to explain it to me because it just doesn't make any sense. All this time, you've been blaming yourself for our inability to be together. All this time you've been blaming yourself for Roman's tricking you. Even after I explained, even after I told you that by making me drink you actually ended up saving my life and sparing my soul from getting trapped in the Shadowland, you were still convinced you were at fault, to the point where your sole focus was reserved for obtaining the antidote. So desperate to get your hands on it you were willing to delve into things that put you at great risk. And now, now that you finally succeed in getting the one thing you've been searching for all of this time—you choose to throw it all away so you can go on some crazy old lady's journey to look for some tree that, I'm sorry to say, does not exist!" He looks at me, hands flexing by his sides, gaze filled with all the words he held back. "And so, what I need from you now, what I need from you more than anything, is to answer the *why*. *Why* would you do that? What could you possibly have been thinking?"

I stare at my feet, allowing his words to flow through me, to loop around in my brain, to repeat over and over again, but even though I heard the question, even though I know he waits for an answer, I'm still stuck on the phrase: *Some tree.*

He called it *some tree.*

He questioned its very existence.

And I'm amazed he can't see it. Amazed he can't understand that it's the tree, *not* the antidote that offers real and lasting salvation. That it's the only way to reverse our physical immortality.

The tree is our one and only chance to change *everything.*

But then, maybe he does understand.

Maybe he understands all too well.

And maybe that's why he's so dead set against it.

"You're right." I lift my gaze to find his. "This whole time I *have* felt responsible. I *have* been beating myself up with the guilt. I *have* been so consumed with remorse that I dabbled in magick I had no business dabbling in. I even tried to make deals with people I should've stayed away from. I was so filled with self-loathing and blame, I was so desperate to reverse what I'd done, that I was willing to take whatever risk necessary in order to make it up to you—to make it up to *us*. I was willing to do whatever was needed to ensure that we could be together in the way that we want, until my whole world revolved around getting my hands on the antidote—at the expense of everything else. But now I know just how wrong and misguided that was. Now I know that instead of focusing *solely* on getting the antidote, I should've been focused on sparing our *souls*."

He swallows, squirms, hears the truth of my words, I can see it in the flash in his eyes, but it's gone in an instant. His resolve hardening until he's more unwilling than ever to see my side, which only convinces me to continue.

"Damen, please hear me out. I know that on the surface at least, my decision probably looks pretty crazy, but it goes so much deeper than that. It's like—I finally get it. I finally really and truly get it. If it weren't Roman insisting on keeping us apart, it would've been something else. The reason we can't be together is because the *universe* won't allow it. Our *karma* won't allow it. Or at least not until we do what it takes to right this huge glaring wrong that you've made. Not until we change the course of our lives—the course of our *souls*—by returning them to the way they were always meant to be. You said so yourself, way back before we even started this journey, you freely admitted that what we are isn't natural or right. That we aren't living the lives that nature intended—that we've wrongly chosen physical immortality over the immortality of the soul. Those are your words, Damen, not mine. You also freely admitted that it's cost us both dearly, that it's the reason we keep facing all of these insurmountable obstacles, the reason why we're thwarted at every turn in a way we can't seem to overcome. You said it's why Jude keeps showing up and getting in the way of our happiness. That without his even realizing it, he's playing out his own destiny of trying to keep us from reliving the mistakes of our past." I look at him, determined to make him see it, determined to break through to him, my voice gaining in pitch until it's practically squeaking. "Don't you see what a huge opportunity this is? It's a *very real* chance for us to *truly* be together *forever* in the way we were intended. It's a chance for me to finally seize the destiny I was born for. The same destiny I've been called on for several lives now, and I'm finally ready and willing to embrace it. I just hope you'll find a way to embrace it along with me."

I bite down on my lip, prepared for whatever harsh words he might say, but he just shakes his head and turns away. So overcome with anger he can't even face me. The words ground out between clenched teeth when he says, "The reason we can't be together is because you just disposed of the antidote." He swallows hard, his hands curling and uncurling at his sides. "Ever, I don't get it—don't you want to be with me?"

And when he finally turns, when his gaze finally meets mine, what I find there makes my heart break.

"How can you even think that?" I ask, my voice along with my face completely stunned. "After all that I've gone through in the hopes that I could be with you?" I shut my eyes, take a moment to steady my breath, to collect myself along with my words. "Didn't you hear anything I just said? Of course I want to be with you! I want to be with you more than you'll ever probably realize! But *not* like this. *Not* because of the antidote. There's another way. A *better* way, I'm sure of it now. Damen, we finally have the chance to reverse this huge, glaring wrong—we finally have the chance to live the lives we were meant to live—and once we do, we'll have no need for things like elixirs and antidotes. Don't you realize what this means? Don't you realize how epic this is?"

"Epic?" He practically spits out the word. "Seriously, Ever, do you hear yourself? What could be more *epic* than the love that we share? Isn't that what brings us back together, time and time again?"

I sigh, exhausted by his argument, exhausted by his un- known depths of complete and total stubbornness. Still, I'm determined to make him understand before it's too late, before it's time to leave and he refuses to join me.

"That's only part of the reason," I say. "The other part is because each time I come back, each time I reincarnate, I'm getting yet another chance to realize my destiny. To right the wrong you inadvertently committed all those years ago. And righting that wrong is the only way you and I will ever truly be free to live and love as we want."

He sighs and gazes off into the distance, remaining quiet for so long I'm just about to break the silence when he says, "There's something else you need to know."

I look at him.

"The tree is a myth. It's the stuff of mystical legends. It doesn't really exist. The legends all claim it bears one piece of fruit every one thousand years. One piece of fruit that offers immortality to whoever gets to it first." He smirks. "Tell me, Ever, does that sound even remotely real to you?"

I refuse to react to the faint trace of mocking in his tone when I say, "A year ago, a place like Summerland wouldn't have seemed remotely possible. Neither would psychics, ghosts, chakras, auras, magick, time travel, reincarnation, near-death experiences, mediums, instant manifestation, the power of crys- tals, or magical elixirs that provide immortality." I lift my shoul- ders. "So who's to say this tree doesn't exist too? And imagine that it does, Damen. Do you have any idea what this journey could mean?" My eyes pore over him, willing him to at least meet me halfway. "If it's successful, it could clear your karmic debts. It could allow you to make amends for your past. Begin anew. Wipe the slate clean and all that. Maybe you never forced anyone to drink, well, anyone except me . . ." I pause, press my lips into a thin, grim line, then shaking my head, I add, "Maybe you were far too young and naive and inexperienced to fully understand the far-reaching consequences of what you'd done, the danger you put us all in, heck, the existence of the Shadowland alone, which I know you didn't even know about until you were sent there, but still, anyway, my point is, while you might not have willingly set out to doom a whole host of souls to that horrible abyss—in the end, that's exactly where this leads. And if nothing else, this is your one chance to fix it. Your one chance to present a choice to those you've either changed, or who were changed because of the elixir you made. It's an opportunity that may never come again."

"I never meant to hurt you," he says, voice barely a whisper. "Never meant to hurt anyone." I catch the unmistakable flash of pain and self-recrimination in his eyes before he looks away. "I never anticipated that you would blame me like this—or that you'd view spending an eternity together as a curse. Or 'doomed to a horrible abyss' as I believe you put it."

"I was talking about the Shadowland, Damen, *not* our future together."

"But we're not in the Shadowland. Our future is now. Right now. We still have the recipe for the antidote—it's not too late. All we have to do is head out of here, back to the earth plane, and gather the ingredients. But you'd rather run off on some crazy wild-goose chase in the hopes of reversing this terrible curse that I've put upon you."

"Damen—I didn't mean—"

He holds up a hand, his face as broken as his voice when he says, "It's fine. Really. Believe me, Ever, you haven't said anything I haven't thought of myself a million times before. It's just hearing it from your lips . . . well, it was harder than I ever expected. So, if it's okay with you, I think I'll head back to the earth plane—I need some time to think. And, while I'm at it, I'll gather those ingredients for the antidote. After all, if you're going to be stuck with me for the rest of eternity, at least the antidote will allow for certain . . . *enjoyments* that will make your life infinitely more bearable."

TWENTY-EIGHT

I watch him leave, my thoughts racing through a maze of conflicted feelings. Part of me wanting to crash through the fading corner of that shimmering veil before it's too late—so I can return to the earth plane right alongside him.

But the other part, the bigger part, is determined to get on with the journey.

A journey that is long overdue.

Encouraged by the memory of something Riley said when I'd made a futile attempt to go back in time, only to return to my most current life. It was just before the accident that claimed me again, when she leaned across her seat, looked at me, and said:

Did you ever stop and think that maybe you were supposed to survive? That maybe, it wasn't just Damen who saved you?

And though I had no idea what it meant at the time—now I do.

This is what I came back for.

This journey is my one, and perhaps only chance to seize my destiny.

Which means I can't allow Damen's fears to dissuade me from what I'm meant to do.

Though I do understand his decision—his refusal to search for the tree. He blames himself for giving me the elixir, for altering the course of my life—the journey of my soul—and now I insist on finding the tree so I can reverse those effects, return us to the way we were always meant to be.

Trouble is, if there's no tree, there's no reversal.

Just Damen, me, and his deepest regrets—for the rest of eternity.

But I know something he doesn't. There *is* a tree. I know it in the deepest part of me.

And as soon as I find it, Damen will be freed of his burdensome guilt and self-blame. Guilt that's not even warranted since everything he's done, every choice that he's made, was with the best of intentions. He may have acted out of fear, but the motivation behind it was love.

But since I can't exactly tell him that—I'll have to show him instead.

And so, newly dedicated to what I know in my heart I must do, I steal a moment to manifest a few things I might need before I get too far along and possibly end up in a place where magick no longer works. Manifesting stuff like a flashlight, a sleeping bag, water and food, a light jacket, sturdier shoes, a backpack—then once I have that secured, I busy myself by making a mental list of all that I've learned about the tree so far. Things I've learned from Damen, Lotus, and the few things I've picked up from movies and books and working in Jude's store, repeating this list to myself as I head down the trail.

It's mystical—true.

Some claim it's merely a myth—that remains to be seen.

It's said to bear only one piece of fruit every thousand or so years—if so, then I fervently hope this is the time of the harvest and that I'm the first to arrive (otherwise, I'm in for an awfully long wait).

I stop, close my eyes, and tune into the wisdom of Summerland. Trusting it to guide me in just the right direction as my feet start moving again, seemingly of their own accord, and when I gaze down at the ground, I'm glad I had the foresight to manifest the hiking boots when I start leaving big clumps of grass in my wake. Clumps that soon turn to thick clouds of dust when the grass suddenly gives way to loose dirt, forcing me to rely on the thick treads of my soles to keep my gait steady when the terrain changes again, becoming rougher, littered with sharp rocks and boulders, and so loaded with hairpin curves and switchbacks I'm forced to go slower, and then slower still.

But no matter how treacherous the path may become, I will not cry uncle, I will not give up, and I will not even think about returning to where I came from. Even when it ultimately grows so narrow and steep it falls off into two bottomless chasms that yawn on either side, I'm committed to the journey. There will be no turning back.

I strive to keep my breath even, steady, as I do my best not to look down. Just because I can't die doesn't mean I'm looking for danger. Given the choice, I prefer to play it safe for as long as I can.

The trail soars higher, and then higher still, and when it begins to snow, I can't help but wonder if it has something to do with the altitude. But it's not like it matters. It's not like knowing the reason will keep my feet from slipping precariously close to the craggy abyss that gapes wide far below. It's not like it'll stop my skin from chilling and turning frigid and blue.

Knowing the light jacket I stashed in my bag is hardly equipped to handle a drop in temperature so extreme, I close my eyes and picture a new one—something big and down-filled, something that'll leave me looking like a big shapeless blob but will hopefully get the job done. But when nothing happens, when no coat appears, I know I've reached the part of the journey where magick and manifesting no longer work. I'll have to rely on myself, and the few things I had the fore-sight to manifest before I got to this point.

I slip into the jacket, pulling the sleeves down past my wrists until they cover my numb, frozen fingertips, keeping my eyes on the trail and my mind on my destiny, committed to mak-ing do with what I have, while reminding myself of all the challenges I've already survived—obstacles that wouldn't have seemed possible just one year ago.

But despite all my focus, despite the continuous loop of pep talks and tree facts I repeat in my head, I eventually get to the point where I'm just too cold and exhausted to continue. So I start searching for a place to set up camp, though it's not long before I determine there isn't one. This freezing cold landscape doesn't offer much in the way of rest.

I toss my bag on the icy cold ground and position myself right on top of it, pressing my nose to my knees and wrapping my arms tightly around me in a futile attempt to both warm and steady myself. And though I try to sleep, I can't. Though I try to meditate, my mind won't slow down. So instead, I spend the time convincing myself that I made the right choice. That despite my completely miserable state, all is fine and good and exactly as it should be—but it falls way short of soothing me.

I'm too cold.

Too bone tired and weary.

But mostly, I'm too alone. Too filled with thoughts of missing Damen and the way we used to be.

No matter what I try to convince myself of, no amount of positive thinking could ever replace the very real, very wonderful comfort of having him beside me.

And in the end, that's what gets me through. The memory of him is what allows me to close my eyes for a while and drift off into some other place, some better place. A place where it's just him and me and none of our troubles exist.

I have no idea how long I slept—all I know is that the second I open my eyes and swipe my hand across my face, I see the landscape has morphed. The trail is still impossibly narrow, there's still a huge, gaping chasm on either side, but the season has changed—it's no longer winter, which means I'm no longer forced to huddle against a pounding cold blizzard.

Instead, I'm caught in a downpour, a relentless spring rain that turns the ground to mud and shows no sign of stopping.

I struggle to my feet, quickly slipping my arms out of the sleeves as I haul my jacket up over my head and tie those same sleeves under my chin in an attempt to keep from getting any more drenched than I already am. Tackling the trail one careful step at a time, having given up on inspiring thoughts, reminiscences, or anything else, and reserving my focus for staying upright, staying steady, and not toppling over the side. And when the rain turns to a blazing hot sun that leaves the ground dry and cracked, I don't bat an eye—and when that same sun is cooled by a warm, sultry breeze I know that summer has now turned to fall.

The cycle of seasons repeating itself until it no longer fazes me, until I form a routine. Bundling up and hibernating through winter, dodging the downpour of spring, peeling off my T-shirt 'til I'm down to my tank top when summer comes, then donning it again when summer turns to fall. Through it all, I just keep on keeping on, doing my best to ration my food and water supply, doing my best not to panic, and nearly succeeding with the latter until something happens that shocks me to the core.

Something I've never seen in these parts before.

Not even in the deepest depths of the Shadowland.

It grows dark.

Okay, maybe not pitch-black dark, but still dark. Or at the very least, dim.

Like the beginning of nightfall, or the gloaming as it's called.

That eerie, gloomy moment when everything becomes a silhouette of itself.

That eerie, gloomy moment when it's hard to distinguish individual objects from the shadows they cast.

I stop, my foot slipping, sending a flurry of rocks over the side, knowing that could've been me. My heart hammering furiously as I gather myself, gather my limbs, give myself a quick once-over, and ensure I'm okay.

"I don't like this," I say, my voice breaking the silence until it echoes all around me. Having now officially joined the ranks of all the other crazy people who talk to themselves. "Between the dark and that fog up ahead . . ." I frown, seeing the way the trail abruptly halts into a thick cloud of murky white mist that rises up from seemingly out of nowhere. Giving no indication of what might lie just beyond, and certainly providing no sign of the tree, no hint that I'm even on the right path. "This doesn't look good," I add, my voice so ominous it worsens my unease.

I glance all around, wondering what to do now. Observing the way the fog seems to grow and expand and slither straight toward me, pulsing in a way that makes it seem vital, alive. The sight of it making me wonder if I should maybe backtrack a bit, find a place where it's clear and hang out 'til it lifts. But then I hesitate for so long the next thing I know it's too late.

The mist is already here. Already upon me.

Having crept up so fast I'm swallowed in an instant. Lost in a swirl of white, drizzly haze as my fingers reach, grasp, and claw frantically, trying to get my bearings, to clear even a small bit out of my way.

But it's no use. I'm drowning in a sea of white vapor that presses down all around. Stifling a scream when I lift my hands before me and realize I can't even see my own fingers.

No longer sure which way is forward, which way is back, I reach for my flashlight and set it on low, but it doesn't help. Doesn't make a dent in this fog. And I'm veering dangerously close to succumbing to a raging, full-blown, meltdown panic attack, when I hear him.

A distant voice that drifts toward me, creeping up from behind. The sound of it prompting me to cry out, to shout his name as loud as I can. My tone thready, high-pitched, letting him know that I'm here, that I won't move, that I'll wait until he finds me.

Heaving a huge sob of relief when I feel the grab of his fingers, his hand on my sleeve, gripping tightly, pulling me to him.

I huddle deep into the curve of his arms, bury my face in his chest, and press my forehead tightly to his neck, only to discover too late that it's not Damen who holds me.

TWENTY-NINE

"**Ever.**"

His cheek presses into my hair as his lips seek my ear, and though the voice is certainly male, it's not one I recognize.

The mist continues to gather—rendering it impossible for me to determine just who the voice belongs to. His body pressing, conforming against mine, as I squinch my eyes shut, try to peer inside his head, but get nowhere fast. Whoever this is, he's learned to put up one heck of a shield against such attacks.

I pull back, struggle to break free, but it's no use. He's unfeasibly strong and continues to cling like a drowning man intent on dragging me along.

"Careful," he says, his face shifting, allowing for a gust of cold breath to blast all the way down the length of my neck, as the push of his fingers radiates through my clothes.

Cold breath.

Colder fingers.

Unusual strength.

Thoughts I can't hear.

Can only mean one thing.

"Marco?" I venture, wondering if it means that Misa's here too since I rarely see them without each other.

"Hardly." Chasing the word with a deep, scathing laugh that seems more than a little inappropriate considering the circumstances we find ourselves in.

"Then who . . ." I start, wondering if it's one of the other immortals Roman might've turned, though it's not long before he supplies the answer for me.

"Rafe," he says, his voice low and deep. "You may not remember me, but we've met once or twice. Though always casually, never formally."

I swallow hard, having no idea if that's good news or bad. He's always been a bit of an enigma, though I don't dwell on it long. My main concern is breaking out of his grip. The rest will follow.

"I hope I didn't scare you." He loosens his hold just a little, but only a little, not enough to grant me my freedom. "I lost my footing. Fell deep into the canyon back there. Luckily for me, I didn't hit bottom—assuming there is a bottom. Instead I got hung up on an outcropping of rocks, then spent what seems like just shy of forever finding my way back up the side. Which, by the way, is a lot easier said than done when you can't see a bloody thing. Went through so many seasons, I lost track. Anyway, I was just about to give up, set up camp, or more accurately hang on to what little I could until the fog clears, when I heard footsteps, your voice, and well, it gave me just the incentive I needed to climb faster and find my way to safety. Just knowing I was no longer alone in this godforsaken place made it easier. But, I have to tell you, Ever, I'm a bit surprised to find you here on your own, I thought for sure you'd be with Damen. So who were you talking to anyway? Yourself?"

I narrow my gaze, knowing better than to answer that question, or even to let on that I'm out here on my own. He's mocking me. He's not the least bit sincere. And though the mist does a really good job of obscuring his face, allowing me only a glimpse of the faintest outline of his dark wavy hair, it's not like I need to actually see him to confirm it. The contempt in his voice rings loud and clear.

"If you ask me, we have two choices," he says, as though we're just two good friends pooling our wits, searching for a solution that's mutually beneficial and pleasing. "We can either sit this thing out and wait for the fog to clear, or we can make our way back down and head out of here. I vote for making our way back down, how about you?"

A million retorts rush forth, but I clamp my lips shut before I say something I might live to regret. Even though his proximity is giving me the creeps, even though I'm tempted to pluck his fingers right off my sleeve—I can no longer do that. Not after all that I've learned. Now that I know we're all one—all connected—the old reactions no longer work.

But that doesn't mean I have to engage. I've no doubt his intentions aren't good. I move to push past him, eager to put as much distance between us as I possibly can, careful to silence all thoughts of worry, paranoia, or fear that his mere presence has spawned.

For one thing, I don't want him to overhear my thoughts, and for another, I need to clear my mind so I can reserve my focus for which direction the tree might lie in.

But my mind draws a blank.

Summerland has provided all that it will. What happens from here rests solely on me.

Rafe trudges behind, his stride falling uncomfortably close. But my need for caution precludes me from moving too fast, so I continue along, carefully placing one foot in front of the other, tentatively testing each step before allowing my full weight to fall upon it. Feeling my way along the path like a blind person navigating an unfamiliar room, knowing this may take much longer than necessary, but also knowing it's better to go slow, better to stay safe, than to lose my footing and be eternally sorry.

I just hope I'm headed the right way.

"I still think we should turn back," Rafe says, easily closing the distance between us as he stumbles behind me.

"Then turn back." My eyes sweep the area, on high alert for signs of . . . well, anything, something. "Really. I was doing just fine on my own."

"Wow." Rafe huffs, puffs, makes a big show of letting me know just how offended he is, though his voice sounds far more amused than insulted. "You really know how to make a bloke feel welcome, don'tcha, Ever? You should be happy I'm here. But, then again, Roman did warn me about you."

"Yeah, and just what exactly did Roman say?" I pause, turning to face him, straining to get a better look, but still nothing. The mist is far too thick for me to discern much of anything.

I focus back on the trail, wincing at the way Rafe's bitter, chilled breath frosts the back of my head when he says, "Roman said plenty. Seemed to have a pretty good handle on you. But I'm afraid I can't really expound upon any of that. At the moment, it seems the details have escaped me. I blame the altitude, how 'bout you?"

I roll my eyes, aware that it's wasted since he can't see it, but still, it makes me feel better and at the moment I'll take all the good feeling I can get.

"And speaking of Roman . . ." Rafe pauses dramatically, though it's pretty obvious what's to follow. "Whatever happened to him? Been a while since he and I last caught up. According to the rumor mill, you killed him. But then, I've never been one for secondhand information. Whenever possible, I like to go straight to the source. So, tell me, Ever, is it true? Did you do it? Because even though I don't know you all that well, I have to say, it's definitely got that grim ring of truth. You've got it in you, that's for sure. I knew it the first time I saw you. No offense, of course."

"None taken." I scowl, suddenly feeling very uncomfortable with the fact that he's behind me, but doing my best not to let on. "It's true that Roman's no longer with us," I say, confirming what Rafe already knows, though careful to give no hint of the deep remorse I feel for that loss, nor any indication of who might be to blame. My voice growing bolder when I add, "Turns out he wasn't so immortal after all. But then, you already guessed that, didn't you?"

The breeze quickens, sweeping past us, causing the air to chill to an uncomfortable degree. Becoming so cold my heart sinks, knowing I can't possibly bear another winter again, especially not with Rafe here.

Unwilling to stop long enough to retrieve my jacket from my backpack, I rub my hands up and down my arms in an attempt to warm myself. My ears pricking with interest when a second gust rustles past. Only this time, in addition to the usual crackling of leaves and pattering of rocks tumbling over each other, it carries a whole other sound—one that's either animal or human—I can't be too sure. All I know is that Rafe and I are no longer the only ones here.

My hair lifts, swirling around me as I fight to gather the strands in my fist. Noticing the way the fog thinned just enough to allow for a glimpse of a distant snowcapped mountain, along with the very top branches of what must be a very tall tree (possibly *the* tree?), before thickening again and blotting everything out.

Determined to keep Rafe focused on me, hoping he didn't see what I saw, I turn to him and say, "By the way, what exactly are you doing here? Surely this is no accident? So what is it you're up to? Are you in cahoots with Misa and Marco? Or maybe even a friend of Lotus's, by chance? Or, are you seriously going to try to convince me that you're just out for a day hike?"

I cock a brow, taking in what little I can see of him, his height, his wavy mane of dark hair, but the rest is all white. But when he doesn't answer, when he just moves as though he might try to jump me, I reach for my flashlight and shine it right in his face, the beam cutting through the haze and showing me all that I need to see—which isn't much of anything.

Like all the other rogue immortals I've met this past year, Rafe remains remarkably cool under pressure. His face showing no sign that he's even startled by the sharp beam of light now shining on him. For someone who's just been caught positioning himself to better attack me, he doesn't look even the slightest bit guilty. If anything, he just looks determined.

But there is something else.

Something that really stands out though I try not to let on.

He looks older.

Way older.

Last time I saw him he was just another super-hot, perfect specimen of a gorgeous immortal.

But now, while he's still really good-looking, he's also showing some definite signs of aging and wear—the years catching up with him in the form of graying hair and the fan of wrinkles surrounding his eyes. Even his teeth seem a little yellow, as opposed to what I've come to think of as *bright and shiny immortal white*.

And suddenly I know exactly why he's here.

"Let's cut the crap, shall we?" he says, closing the small gap between us in a handful of seconds. "Neither one of us is on a day hike. You're on Lotus's journey to the Tree of Life. Hoping to get your hands on the one piece of fruit it bears every one thousand years." He stares at me, his voice a perfect match for the glare in his gaze. "One beautiful, perfect piece of fruit that looks like a cross between a pomegranate and a peach. One amazing piece of produce that offers immortality to whoever is lucky enough to pluck it, seize it, taste it. And, as it turns out, the millennium is up. It's time for the harvest. And while I'm sure you consider yourself worthy of a bite, I hate to break it to you, Ever, but this is how it's gonna go down: You're gonna lead me to the tree, and I'll be the one to claim its bounty."

I continue to study him, my flashlight moving over his face, wondering if I should fill him in on the truth that the fruit isn't quite what it's rumored to be. That the story behind its powers was never intended to be taken quite so literally. The tree's fruit grants wisdom and enlightenment to those who seek it—providing the ultimate truth—the knowledge that they are truly immortal beings. For those who've achieved physical immortality, well, it has a reversal effect—returning the body and the soul back to the way it was always intended to be.

Which is not at all the sort of immortality he seeks—though it's definitely the kind that he needs.

But instead I just say, "And why would I agree to do that?"

"Because now that Roman is gone, thanks to *you*, I might add—" he pauses long enough to let that sink in— "the tree is my only hope left. Haven drank what was left of his supply, and since he assumed he'd live forever, he never bothered to share the recipe. Not to mention how he liked having control over us. Liked it almost as much as the party he threw every century and a half, always on the summer solstice, where he'd gather us together, wherever he was living at the time. We'd swap stories, share some good times, and drink a toast to each other, before we said our good-byes and moved on with our lives. Kind of like a high school reunion, but better, if you can imagine. No second-rate hotel ballroom, no need to impress each other with bad plastic surgery and inflated job titles that don't actually mean anything . . ."

I don't say a word. And I definitely don't even try to imagine. I just stand there and let him continue.

"Funny thing was, even though your boyfriend Damen never showed—probably because he was never invited—but still, he was always the most popular topic of conversation." Rafe nods, gaze going inward now, as though he's watching a scene that plays in his head. "For years he was like a legend to me. You should've heard the stories the orphans all told. The first among our kind, the one who turned six, then disappeared, never to be seen or heard from again, or at least not intentionally. Do you realize he never even once thought to track them all down and let them drink again? He *abandoned* them, Ever— did you know that? He left them all to shrivel—to grow old and wither—while he stayed eternally young." He shakes his head and frowns in a way that encourages a whole new set of lines to race across his forehead. "Sorry, but if it sounds as though I don't like him, well, that's because I don't. Still, that has nothing to do with why I can't allow you to reach that tree. It's nothing personal, and I hope you'll understand when I say that the reason you can't get your hands on that fruit is because it's reserved just for me."

I take a deep breath, dimming my flashlight a bit, realizing it's better to try to ease his mind and put him off guard, to convince him to lower his defenses, than to put him on the defensive if I've any hope of regaining the advantage. Fully aware that all it would take to be rid of him is one good shove that sends him over the edge. And as tempting as that might be, I won't do it—and I'm pretty sure he won't do it to me.

He needs me.

Only I can make the journey.

Only I can find the tree.

Which means he needs me to stay healthy, vital, and most importantly, in one piece, if he has any intention of my leading the way.

But what he doesn't realize is that I'm more than happy to do so, as long as I arrive first. And when I do arrive, when I scale that tree and get to the fruit, I have every intention of sharing it. I have every intention of giving him, well, maybe not the eternal life that he seeks, but certainly the one that he needs.

The one that will reverse the effects of the elixir, provide true immortality, and spare him from Lotus's fate.

I look at him, lifting my shoulders casually as I say, "No worries." But if his arched brow and quirked mouth are any indication, he's going to need a little more convincing. "Really. It's not a big deal. For reals."

He looks me over, his gaze narrowed, suspicious, practically spitting the words when he says, "Oh yeah, and I'm supposed to believe that—*for reals*?" He scoffs and shakes his head. "Okay then, so tell me, Ever, if you're not interested in the fruit, then why even bother with this bloody miserable trek? Huh, can you tell me that? Why put yourself through all of this?"

"I'm curious." I shrug. "I heard about the tree and thought I'd go see for myself—didn't even realize it was time for the reaping 'til you just said so." I tilt my head, try to look as though I mean it. "Despite your poor opinion of him, Damen's always been extremely generous. He would've gladly shared his elixir with you if you hadn't already pledged your allegiance to Roman. And anyway, why would I even bother with the fruit when he gives me all the elixir I need?"

"Because the fruit is forever." Rafe's eyes begin to blaze until they resemble two dark flaming pits surrounded by white.

"Damen and I are forever." I glare, knowing in my heart that it's true even though he's not here beside me to prove it. "And, as it so happens, I like the elixir. I like it so much I drink it several times a day. So, why would I want to replace that?"

Rafe continues to study me, his mind weighing, considering, then shaking his head he opens his mouth to speak, when someone else slinks out of the mist and decides to speak for him.

THIRTY

"She's lying."

Rafe spins on his heel so he can see what I already see, know what I already know.

Marco is here.

Though, as always, Misa creeps up right alongside him with her exotic dark eyes, black spiky hair, and multipierced lobes.

My light spills over them as I study them closely, trying to get a read, determine if their showing up is bad for me, bad for Rafe, or just bad in general. Knowing only two things for sure: No matter who it is that they're after (though it's probably safe to assume that it's me) their intentions aren't good. And, just like Rafe, they show signs of aging.

"She's after the fruit." Misa's eyes dart between Rafe and me. "Lotus sent her. Convinced her to go find it just like she tried to convince us all those years ago. But now the ancient one seems to think Ever's the only who can succeed. So Marco and I have been trailing her, which, I'm guessing, is what you're doing too."

Rafe squints but otherwise doesn't move, doesn't give anything away. Too busy assessing the situation, too on guard to supply an answer.

"Lotus has been looking for someone to make this journey for centuries." Misa directs her words right at me as Marco snickers alongside her. "At first we thought she was crazy—well, mostly because she *is* crazy. But now, with Roman dead, and with Haven having drank every last bit of his stash, and with Damen being—well, no need to mince words here is there?—with Damen being as selfish as he is, we had no choice but to befriend her, to learn more about this tree, and to figure out how to find it. She got us to Summerland, but that's it. Claimed she didn't know how to find the tree, said you're the only one who can, that it's your destiny, like you're some kind of chosen one or something." She looks at me, a long, scathing glare that ends in an exaggerated eye roll, wanting me to know just how ridiculous she finds that. "Whatever." She shrugs. "We're just here so you can lead us to it, then we'll take it from there."

"Except I got here first." The threat in Rafe's voice rings loud and clear. "A small detail you've seemed to overlook."

I watch as they tense, square their shoulders, and secure their stances as though they're gonna duke it out right here on this reed-thin trail. Defend their right to use me to get what they want.

"Do you hear yourselves?" My eyes dart between them. "Seriously. You guys are unbelievable! And you call Damen selfish." I shake my head, not even trying to hide my outrage. Though the truth is, while my lips keep moving, spewing forth a slew of similar words, while my features arrange and rearrange to keep up with whatever it is that's being said, my mind is someplace else entirely. Working furiously to find a way out of this mess, knowing I could've taken Rafe while he was still on his own, but now that it's up to three immortals versus my one—I'm no longer sure.

Despite the fact that they can't kill me, they can still do some major damage, or, even worse, they can stop me from getting there first.

"We don't even know for sure if this fruit exists," I say, my eyes darting among them. "But let's just say that it does, let's just say we find it right there, waiting to be plucked. Why can't we just share it? Why can't you each take a bite, then give me whatever's left to take back to Lotus? That way everyone wins. And no one gets hurt."

But instead of the refusal I expected, I'm met with dead silence.

A horrible, lingering silence that's far worse than any argument they could ever wage.

They're no longer interested in me.

Their attention is claimed by something else entirely.

And I know without looking what it is. I can feel it in the way the breeze whispers against the nape of my neck. I can see it in the sudden glow that shines in their eyes.

They *see* it.

The tree.

Which means they no longer need me.

And though I try to move, try my best to flee, it's too late.

There are too many of them, too little of me. And it seems, or at least in this case anyway, they've chosen to work together. Chosen to collaborate.

Misa and Marco grab hold of my arms as Rafe slinks behind

me. His cheek pressed close to mine, his lips chilled, pushing into my flesh when he says, "Remember when I told you earlier that I lost my footing and fell deep into the canyon?"

I swallow hard, steady myself, know all too well what's coming next.

"As it turns out, I lied." He grins, I can feel his lips lifting and curling against me. "Had I been unlucky enough to fall, I never would've made it back up. You see, Ever, it's a sheer drop. A *very* sheer drop that offers no outcroppings of rock—nothing for one to grab onto in order to stop. But then, I should probably let you see for yourself. I mean, no need to wreck the surprise with a bunch of spoilers, right?"

I fight.

I kick.

I scratch, and bite, and claw, and scream, and thrash, and struggle with all of my immortal might.

But despite the fact that I can be satisfied in knowing I did a good bit of damage to each of them, in the end, it's not enough.

I can't beat them.

I'm no match.

And the next thing I know Rafe's pushing me at the exact moment Misa and Marco let go.

Sending me flying.

Soaring.

Hurtling straight over the edge and deep into a bottomless canyon.

THIRTY-ONE

Just like a dream where you find yourself falling and can't seem to stop because there's nothing to grab onto and you've lost all control of your body—that's exactly what this is like.

Except for the fact that usually when I find myself caught in one of those dreams, my body eventually jerks me awake before any grave disaster can take place.

But this time, I'm already awake. And from what I can tell, the disaster is now, and it's about to get worse.

My hair lifts, waving high above my head, as my legs furiously kick, attempting to temper the pace, halt my speed, slow myself down, but it's no use. The effort is as useless as my arms, which continue to flail all around, searching for something to hang onto, but succeeding only in proving Rafe right.

There is nothing to save me.

Nothing to stop me.

The cliff is a sheer solid drop into the void.

The lower I go, the darker it becomes until I can no longer

see in front of me—can no longer see below me—can no longer see where I'm going.

All I know is that the fall seems to quicken, picking up speed, as I race toward an end that may not exist. The awful truth of my existence, the absolute irony of it, is that if I can't find a way to stop this—then this is how I'll spend my eternity.

I can't die—my chakras are so strong they won't let me.

And any injuries sustained won't heal—this part of Summerland won't allow for that sort of thing.

Two horrible thoughts I find too overwhelming to contemplate.

So I don't.

I choose to focus my mind elsewhere instead.

Sifting through the long list of things I've learned this past year—going all the way back to the day when I first died in the car accident that claimed my whole family—to this never-ending crevice where I find myself now. Remembering what Lotus said about knowledge coming when we're most in need of it, and hoping my accumulated knowledge will help me find a way out.

Forgiveness is healing—everything is energy—thoughts create—we are all connected—what you resist persists—true love never dies—the soul's immortality is the only true immortality—

Repeating the words again and again, until it becomes like a mantra, until the words begin to take shape, begin to take hold.

Until my breath begins to steady, my body begins to still, and my heart is able to unload this burden of fear.

Forgiveness is healing—I send a silent thought of forgiveness to Misa, Marco, and Rafe for being so misguided and untrusting they wouldn't even try another way.

What you resist persists—I stop resisting the fact that I'm falling, and start concentrating on a solution instead.

Thoughts create—Even when instant manifestation won't work, our thoughts are still creating on our behalf.

I free my backpack from one shoulder, slide it around to my front, yank the zipper down, and plunge my hand inside. Making sure I've got a good grip on the light jacket I manifested earlier—the one that got me through an excess of repetitive seasons by shielding me from heat, rain, wind, and snow—before I drop the bag, listening as it whizzes down below. I grasp the jacket by either sleeve and lift my arms up high over my head, cutting the wind along with my trajectory, while thrusting my body toward what I can only hope is the side of the cliff. Knowing I've succeeded when I'm left momentarily stunned by the sudden impact of my body bashing into a bed of sharp rocks. My flesh cutting, scraping, as the jagged edges serrate my clothes, grating small chunks of me, as my body continues to fall.

My eyes sear with agony, as my teeth gnash from the excruciating pain of being flayed. Assuring myself that if it won't heal now, it eventually will. Just as soon as I can locate an outcropping of rock, something tangible to hang onto, something to stop this downward descent. Just as soon as I can get to the fruit and make my way back to a better part of Summerland.

My body a toboggan of blood, flesh, and bone that continues to careen down the cliff, and just as I'm sure I can't take another second, something catches—something that juts hard against my foot, stabs me in the knee, and pummels me so hard in the gut it robs me of breath before puncturing me right in the base of my neck where at the very last moment, I reach up, grab ahold of it, stop it from removing my head.

Knowing it's my one and only chance—knowing I can't possibly hold on to both my makeshift parachute and this strange outcropping of sorts—I close my eyes and let go.

My jacket instantly claimed by the airstream as my hands grasp in the dark, putting all of my faith in this odd and pointy protrusion I can't even see.

My fingers circling, curling around it in a death grip, my palms scraped ragged and raw as my weight rappels me down the length of it.

Down.

Down farther still.

Down so far and so fast I can only pray it'll end soon. Knowing that if I lose my grip I'll be right back where I started—free-falling through black, empty space, only this time without my bag, without any tools to help me. Doing all that I can to clear such thoughts from my mind, my body jumps to a stop and I find myself dangling from this strange thing's end.

Caught in midair, my legs flailing crazily beneath me, I grip tighter, reposition myself, using my raw and skinned knees along with this unknown *thing,* to pull myself up.

At first I go slowly. Very, very slowly. Reminding me of the time I had to climb up a rope in my freshman-year gym class. Back when I was just another mortal. Back when, other than being a cheerleader, I had no athletic prowess to speak of. Every inch feeling like a lesson in overcoming unbearable pain in order to put my faith in something I can't even see. My progress measured in inches, not feet, eventually creeping close enough to the summit that I'm rewarded with a tiny spot of light—just enough to reveal exactly what it is that has saved me.

It's a root.

A long and spindly *tree* root.

A long and spindly tree root that belongs to *the* tree—the one I've been searching for. I know it instinctively.

The Tree of Life has saved me.

THIRTY-TWO

The moment after I reach the top—the moment after I heave myself over the ledge and lie facedown, gasping in the dirt—I bolt upright and run like the wind.

Ignoring the searing pain that shoots through my battered legs and feet, I call upon every immortal power I have to help me find my way along the root with some semblance of speed. Sometimes stumbling, sometimes falling, but always picking myself right back up and forging ahead, knowing I need to get there before it's too late, that I'm so far behind I've no time to waste.

Making do without the aid of my flashlight, figuring it's still free-falling in the crevice along with my bag, I push my way through the fog until the trail becomes less treacherous, easier to navigate, until finally, it's just a matter of surviving the climb, pulling myself along, and allowing my body to adjust to the ever-increasing altitude.

An ever-increasing altitude, the kind of which I've never experienced before.

An ever-increasing altitude that leaves me dizzy, short of breath, and that would surely require unlimited use of an oxygen tank if I were back home on the earth plane.

And before I can actually see it, I know that I'm near.

It's in the way the darkened sky begins to glisten and glow.

It's in the way the mist begins to vibrate and pulse.

Throbbing with an entire spectrum of colors—a rainbow of blues and pinks and oranges and deep sparkling purples—all of it shimmering with the finest flecks of silver and gold.

I hurry along the massive root, noting the way it rises and grows. Becoming taller and wider as it mixes with the other roots, tangling and overlapping into a complex system that, from what I can tell, seems to meander for miles and miles before it reaches an enormous trunk I can just now barely see.

I pause for a moment, left breathless as much from the vision that glows before me as I am from the hike. Taking in the whole glorious sight of it—the awe-inducing breadth of it— the branches that reach miles into the sky, the glistening leaves that first appear green and then gold, the vibrant aura that emanates all around it—noting the way the air has grown warmer despite the elevation that should make it anything but.

"So that's it," I whisper to myself, my voice trancelike, laced with wonder, so overcome by the colors, I've momentarily forgotten my enemies, forgotten my pain.

For the moment anyway, I'm a pioneer, a pilgrim, a founder of this glorious frontier. So filled with the wonder of what I witness before me, I'm rendered completely and totally speechless. No words could ever do it justice.

I thought the Great Halls of Learning were amazing, but this—well, I've never seen anything like it. Never seen anything quite so magnificent.

But my awe soon turns, and I'm on guard once again. My initial look of amazement quickly hijacked by suspicion as I glance around the area, study it closely, searching for signs of my fellow travelers.

Remembering the way Rafe's eyes blazed with an unspoken threat when he verbally laid claim to the fruit, and knowing that the best way to overcome them is to surprise them, to catch them off guard. Catch them completely unaware.

Best to keep quiet, move stealthily, to not allow for even the slightest of hints that I've made my return.

I make my way along the long and winding tangle of roots until I've finally progressed far enough to get a clearer view of the enormous trunk. Its width the size of a building—its branches reaching so high it looks like one of nature's skyscrapers. And I've just reached its base, when I see them.

See them looking as battered and bloodied as I probably do—and knowing they did it to one another, that they fought like hell to be the first one to reach it. And despite being outnumbered by Misa and Marco, it appears Rafe has won.

He clings to a branch—one that soars a good few feet from the one Misa and Marco now dangle from.

And if the sight of that wasn't bad enough—if the fact that they've managed to beat me by a long shot isn't completely and totally deflating—what's worse is the fact that Rafe not only beat us all to it—but that he now holds the fruit in his hand.

He succeeded.

Accomplished what we could not.

I can see it in his grin of victory. I can hear it in his triumphant yell.

He's won.

We've lost.

I've lost.

And a thousand years must pass before we get another shot.

But despite the obvious defeat, that doesn't stop me from making a mad scramble up the side, my fingers digging deep into the bark as my feet desperately seek for a foothold. Even though the game is clearly over, even though Rafe is clearly the victor, I refuse to surrender, refuse to forfeit.

He will not rob me of my destiny.

He will not steal my last chance to make things right with the universe.

I will not wait for a thousand more years.

His eyes light upon me. Seemingly amused by my struggle. Lifting the fruit high into the air, high enough for us all to see, he pauses, savoring the moment of victory.

His smile wide, his eyes never once straying from mine as he inserts the fruit between his front teeth, and bites down.

THIRTY-THREE

I cling to my branch, not wanting to watch, yet unable to tear my gaze away. Overcome by the shame and humiliation of having been beaten. Knocked sideways by the horrible realization that I've failed at the one and only thing I was born to do.

My body reduced to a throbbing, bleeding pulp of a mess—my soul mate convinced I've abandoned him—as Rafe makes a show of enjoying the fruit.

And for what?

What was the point of it all?

Why fight so hard? Why succeed at each and every step, only to fail at the one thing that counts more than anything else?

This bitter taste of defeat reminding me of what I once said to Damen after I'd confessed the whole horrible story behind my thwarted bout of time travel:

Sometimes destiny lies just outside of our reach.

And surprised to find that no longer rings true.

My destiny is still very much attainable.

There's no way it ends here.

I leap.

Working past the screaming pain in my body—working past my protesting muscles, my raw and bloody palms. I leap as high as I can, grab hold of the branch just above me, and then the one above that. Swinging like an agile monkey, until I'm just one branch below Misa and Marco, who are now only one branch below Rafe.

And when Rafe surprises us all by leaping from his branch to theirs, I see his face is still aged, still marked by time, and yet there's no denying his glow—he's positively radiant—he has an aura that's beaming—all the proof that I need to know that it worked, his immortality has been reversed. He drops what little remains of the fruit onto Misa's outstretched palms, then scrambles to the ground, as I swing myself up to where they now stand.

I veer toward them. Cringing at the sound of the branch creaking ominously from the stress of our combined weight, though they don't seem to notice, don't seem to care. They're too distracted by the sight of the fruit, and the distant cry of a whooping and hollering Rafe as he makes his way down the roots.

"Don't come any closer," Marco says, taking notice of me.

I freeze. Not because he told me to, but because my eye just caught sight of something unusual, something I never expected to see.

"Stay right where you are." He glances at Misa, gestures for her to proceed and I watch as she shoves the fruit between her lips, her shiny white teeth tearing into the hard, velvety flesh as she closes her eyes, takes a moment to savor the taste before she hands it to Marco, who looks at me and says, "If I was feeling generous, if I had the slightest bit of concern for you, I'd share this last bite. After all, it appears there's enough for both of us, wouldn't you agree?"

I sink my teeth into my lip, hoping he's too involved in taunting me to pay any notice to the miracle that is occuring just a handful of branches away.

Is it?

Could it actually be?

Should I trust in what my gut is telling me?

Should I trust in something that goes against every myth, every bit of wisdom I've ever learned about this tree?

Or shall I tackle Marco right here, right now? Get at that last bit of fruit while I can, knowing they're as bloodied, broken, and weakened as I am?

He holds it before him, teasing, mocking, parting his lips in an exaggerated way. And I know it's time to choose, time to decide between what I've been told and what I see happening before me, when he says, "But, as it turns out, I'm not feeling the least bit generous toward you, so I think I'll just take the opportunity to finish this very last bit."

One step forward, as he shoves the fruit into his mouth.

Another step, closing the gap between us, as he closes his eyes and bites down.

The sight of it blurred by the song of Lotus's voice in my head when she said:

The tree is evergiving.

I stop. Lose my footing. Find myself spiraling backward, back toward the ground. My fall stopped by a tangle of leaves just a few branches down, as Marco towers above me, makes a show of swallowing, wiping the juice from his chin with his sleeve.

I watch, noting how they've transformed much like Rafe did. Though still aged, their auras glow vibrantly, vividly, making them appear positively luminous as they join hands, and make their way down the tree. Paying me no notice as they pass me along the way, but I no longer care. My attention is claimed by something they're too shortsighted to see—something that changes everything.

It's the fruit.

The sheer abundance of fruit.

Turns out the Tree of Life isn't limited to just one single piece per thousand years as the legend claimed; for every piece that's plucked, a new one appears in its place.

And suddenly I understand what my instinct was telling me—suddenly I know what Lotus meant when she said the tree was evergiving.

Suddenly I know what it means when they say the universe is abundant—that it offers us all that we need—that the only shortages that exist are the ones we create in our minds.

I work my way up, finding my way to the place where the fruit hangs ripe and full. Then I yank off my bloodied, tattered T-shirt, exposing the equally bloodied and tattered white cotton tank top beneath, smooth the fabric flat against my lap, and pluck that one lone piece of fruit, place it onto the center, then wait. Hoping I'm not wrong, hoping it really is what I think, and grinning like crazy when a few minutes later another piece of fruit pops right into its place, and I pluck that one too. Repeating the task over and over until my T-shirt is so full it can't hold any more, and I fold the corners, tie 'em all together, and swing it over my shoulder in a makeshift knapsack.

Just about to make my way down when I gaze into the distance and witness the most amazing display of light that breaks through the fog in such a startling, brilliant, colorful way, it's impossible to identify.

"What is that?" I whisper, gaping at the spectacle before me, figuring I'm so high up I must be witnessing some kind of celestial light show or something.

But it's not long before I hear the faint trace of whoops and hollers carried by the wind, a sound that tells me it's either Misa, Marco, or Rafe, or maybe even all three. And suddenly I understand why Lotus sent them after me.

She knew about the tree. Knew that it was evergiving. Knew that no matter what, no matter how hard they'd try to stop me, in the end, I'd succeed.

She may not have been all that forthcoming about the sort of immortality the fruit actually offers, but then, they only told her they were looking for the elixir of life, and so she had every right to send them forward.

And while they may not have realized what they were getting into, from the sound of their excited shouts and yelps, from the way their glow lights up the sky, what they found is even better than what they first sought.

They found enlightenment—*true* immortality.

The kind I now hold in my hands.

And eager for my turn, I make my way down, beginning my own journey back.

THIRTY-FOUR

The first thing I notice when I find myself back in Laguna Beach is that I'm healed.

In all of my excitement, I guess I made my way down the trail and manifested the veil so quickly I didn't even notice my body is no longer battered and bloody, and my clothes are no longer ripped to shreds (though they are pretty filthy).

The second thing I notice is the weather.

It's hot.

Like really, really hot.

Like way too hot for the thick socks and hiking boots I still wear.

I gaze around the crowded narrow streets of downtown, the sun reflecting off the store windows in a way that forces me to shield my eyes until I can manifest a new pair of sunglasses. Part of me hoping that the fact that Summerland temperatures don't really fluctuate, always veering toward cool, is what throws me off now—while the other part fears this isn't just unseasonably warm weather I'm experiencing, but that it is, in fact, all too seasonal.

I've got this horrible, sinking feeling that I've been gone far, far longer than planned.

While there may be no time in Summerland, that certainly doesn't stop it from marching along here, and if the weather is any indication, my winter break has gone way beyond the two-week vacation I was granted from school. In fact, it may have even gone beyond my one-week spring break as well, neither of which can result in anything good.

But even more bizarre than the weather, well, almost more bizarre anyway, is the fact that I can actually *feel* the gravity of the earth plane. I feel heavier, slower, which is just so *weird*. As many trips as I've made back and forth between Summerland and here, I've never really noticed the difference. Or at least not like this. Not in such a profound and obvious way. But then, I've also never spent that much time in Summerland in one continuous stay, so that probably has something to do with it.

Thinking of long continuous stays, I reach for my cell phone, eager to get a peek at the date. Only to remember too late that I didn't bring it, which makes sense since it's not like I can get a signal in a mystical dimension anyway. So then I peer into the nearest store window, looking for some sort of clue as to the day, the time, even the month will suffice. But all I can see is a bunch of high-priced, season-neutral offerings for the home, including a fake-fur cat bed in the shape of a crown, which doesn't tell me much of anything.

I heave my T-shirt knapsack over my shoulder, reassured by its heft that the fruit survived the trip home, knowing how the things that are manifested in Summerland never survive the trip to the earth plane. But then, it's not like I manifested the fruit.

The tree is responsible for that, which is probably the only reason it's with me.

I head for Jude's store, figuring I can drop in, make sure he's okay, and find a subtle way to inquire about the date. But instead of finding Jude, I end up finding pretty much the last person I ever would've expected.

Okay, maybe not *the last* person, because that would actually be Sabine. Still, I'm not gonna lie, the second I see Honor working behind the counter of Mystics and Moonbeams, chatting with a customer as she rings up what looks to be a pretty sizable sale, well, I just stop right then and there, my body stalled in an eye-bugging, jaw-dropping stare.

I was expecting to see Jude, or maybe Ava, or possibly even someone else altogether. But I never expected to see Honor. In fact, she didn't even make the long list of suspects.

She glances up from the register, shoots me a hurried look, then gets right back to number punching, card sliding, and packaging. Her face bearing no sign of how she might feel about seeing me standing before her, which, I gotta say is far more than I can say for my own gaping reaction to her.

The last I'd heard Jude had phased out of teaching the psychic development level one (with a small emphasis on self-empowerment and magick) classes when Honor ended up being his only student. And after a few one-on-one, private tutorials, he'd determined it was best to stop altogether. Which, I have to admit, I was relieved to hear since Honor wasn't exactly using her newfound skills with the best of intentions, or for the best reasons.

I mean, no matter how awful Stacia may be (and believe me, she is really and truly *awful*), I just couldn't allow Haven and Honor's coup against her to continue. It just wasn't right—too many people were getting hurt in the fallout. And it's not like the two of them were doing any better once they'd taken Stacia's place. If anything, they were pretty much mimicking her very worst behavior.

Last I saw, Honor and Stacia had kissed and made up, so to speak, but only because I'd pretty much forced them to do it. And now, after having been gone for who knows how long, I have no idea what's transpired from there. For all I know, they're both right back to being their awful old selves, indulging in their awful old ways. Still, I hope that I'm wrong. I hope they've at least tried to move on to doing something a little more productive with their lives.

The customer grabs her bag and breezes right past me on her way out the door, as Honor takes a moment to handle the receipt. Carefully placing it into the little purple box where Jude keeps them, before settling onto the stool and addressing me.

"Well, well." She shakes her head as her eyes travel the length of me, giving me a very thorough once-over, careful to hide any hints of just how she might feel about my showing up here. "You were pretty much the last person I expected to see."

"Jude around?" I ask, unwilling to play her game, if that's what it is. It's kind of hard to tell just what she's up to, or what her motive might be. "Or even Ava?" I add, making it clear I'm willing to speak to just about anyone but her.

"Ava will be in soon," she says, still peering at me. "Same for Jude." She smiles, an involuntary curving of lips that disappears just as quickly.

I approach the counter, meeting her stare with one of my own. Watching as she lifts her shoulders, leans back against the wall, and continues to study me.

"How long have you been working here?" I ask, as opposed to my real question: *What day, time, and/or month is it?* Knowing they must've hired her to fill in for me, and figuring her answer will give me an indication of just how long I've been gone.

"'Bout six months. Give or take." She shrugs, pushes a chunk of copper-streaked hair back behind her ear, then focuses on the state of her cuticles, while my mind reels with her answer.

Six months.

Six months?

Six months!

The room swimming before me, forcing me to grab hold of the counter in an effort to steady myself.

Six months puts me well into May.

Puts me at the tail end of the second semester of my senior year.

Puts me at great risk of flunking out entirely unless I work some serious manifesting magick back in the school administrator's office!

And I can't help but wonder if it's the same for Damen—if he's in danger of flunking out too. Or if he managed to get back here with plenty of time to spare, while the journey to the Tree of Life put me over the edge, all of those seasons I was forced to find my way through.

But then, Damen's never cared much about school. The only reason he enrolled is the same reason he stayed—because of me. After six centuries of living, he hardly sees the point. And though I've recently taken a similar stance (as evidenced by my poor attendance even before I left on my journey), it's not like I ever intended to flunk out.

It's not like I ever dreamed of being a dropout.

I mean, even if I once believed I had no need for SATs, grade point averages, or college applications, even if I assumed that my being immortal precluded me from having any use for that type of thing, I still never imagined not finishing high school.

Tossing my cap into the air at graduation is pretty much the one normal thing I assumed that I'd do.

And now, apparently I've let that slide by the wayside too.

I sigh and shake my head, try to focus my attention back on the present, to where I now stand, saying, "Wow, that's . . . that's quite a while . . ." Not really knowing what else to say.

"You've been gone a long time." She lifts her shoulders along with her brow. "So, how was it? How is Summerland these days?" She poses the question so casually you'd think we always talked about such things. Barely venturing a glance toward me before she returns to inspecting her cuticles, picking at a hangnail at the edge of her thumb, as I search for a way to reply, but no words will come. "I know about Summerland." She shoves her thumb in her mouth, finishing the job with her teeth before settling her hands on her lap as her gaze lights upon me. "Of course I've never been, though not for lack of trying." She makes a glum face. "But it's tough for a beginner like me. Jude said you're the one who first got him there, and now he's trying to do the same thing for me. Haven't had much luck so far, but I'm not giving up. I've been studying pretty hard, and I've read just about everything I can on the subject. Is it really as magical as Jude says?" She slews her eyes over me, taking a tour of my filthy clothes, but to her credit (and my surprise), she shows no sign of the usual snide judgment I've come to expect from her. "Don't look so shocked. It's not like it's some big juicy secret." She arches her brow high and quirks her mouth to the side. "Well, I guess the fact that you go there all the time is kind of like a big juicy secret, but still, it's not like the place is a secret. Also, it's not like I've told anyone about it, or even about you. Believe me, Jude's already warned me. Fell just shy of threatening me if I so much as breathe a word about you or what you can do. So feel free to take a deep breath and relax now, *k*?"

But even though she assures me that it's okay to relax, I can't. Any relaxing thoughts I might have, have been taken over by the way she said "Jude."

Jude said you're the one who first got him there.

Jude says it's magical.

Jude warned me not to tell.

The word appearing harmless and casual on the surface, unless you heard the way it was spoken: warmly, intimately, bearing a familiarity that goes way beyond a student/teacher/ employee/boss relationship.

Not to mention how often it was spoken, like a girl with the mad-hots who finds any excuse to insert her crush's name into a sentence.

"So, you and Jude, huh?" My gaze meets hers as I try to determine how I feel about that. Searching for signs of jealousy, and relieved when I realize that's not what's niggling me.

I'm feeling protective, not envious. I don't want him to get hurt. Jude has a long history of falling for all the wrong girls— ones who end up hurting him—including me.

And either she's making vast improvements in her psychic skills, or I am wearing my very worst poker face ever, because she looks right at me and says, "Look, Ever, I know you don't like me, or don't trust me, or both, or whatever, but anyway, a lot has happened in the last six months. I think you'd be amazed."

"Yeah, well, last time you said that it turned out to be one of those changes that wasn't even remotely for the better." My eyes level on hers, holding the look for a moment before moving on to the rest of her.

Noticing how her formerly trend-conscious wardrobe has completely transformed, pared down to a yin/yang tee that hangs well past the waistband of her faded old jeans, a malachite ring, or rather, *Jude's* malachite ring, resized with silk thread and shoved onto her middle finger, while a pair of rubber flip-flops dangle from her feet. And I can't help but wonder if she's not just dating Jude, but raiding his closet too.

"You're right," she says, not the least bit fazed by the admission, which alone is a pretty good indication of progress. "But, what I meant was, I think you'd be surprised in a *good* way. I'm no longer working against you, Ever. Seriously. I know you don't believe it, but really, I've changed. My whole outlook has changed. And just so you know, I truly care about Jude. I'm not going to hurt him like you."

I look at her, waiting for her to finish that sentence, sure that what she really meant to say was: "I'm not going to hurt him *like you think*," and that she'll soon correct herself.

But nope, she leaves it at that. Apparently she said what she meant, and it's not like I can deny that it's true.

"And Stacia?" I ask, preferring to change the subject to something just as bad if not worse. "Has she made this change along with you?" Knowing firsthand just how selfish and clueless she is, remembering how hard it was just to convince her to apologize for some of the more horrible things that she'd done. But hey, miracles do occur, and it's never too late to turn your life around and reach for something better—or at least that's what I hear.

Though Honor's pretty realistic where her friend is concerned, which means she just laughs when she says, "What can I say? Stacia's more of a work in progress. But trust me, she's not near as bad as she used to be, and that's saying something, right? Anyway, if Jude sees fit to like me, and Ava sees fit to trust me, well, I was thinking maybe you might try to . . . well, at least tolerate me, then we'll see where that leads."

"And just what is Ava seeing fit to trust you *with*?" I ask. "Other than helping out at the store, I mean?"

Honor stands, her attention momentarily claimed by the bell clanging hard against the door, announcing a new arrival, as she says, "For one thing, she's seen fit to have me track down some rare herbs for Damen. Something to do with some antidote he's making?" She lifts her brow, directs a wave to the browsing customer, then returns to me. "And, as it just so happens, it arrived about an hour ago. Got it right here." She reaches under the counter, grabs a tiny plain-wrapped package, and slaps it down in front of her. "I was gonna call him to come pick it up, but now that you're here, well, maybe you should take it to him? I'm guessing it's been a while since you've last seen him, no?"

I stare at the package, my heart hammering, my throat constricting, aware of her gaze weighing on me.

"What day is it?" I ask.

She shoots me a funny look. "Sunday, why?"

"Sunday . . ."

"Sunday, May twenty-fourth." She slinks around the counter and makes for her customer, as I grab the package, shove it deep inside my front pocket, and make my way out the door.

THIRTY-FIVE

I don't go to Damen's.

I plan to, I have every intention to, but there's something else I need to do first. So after manifesting a car, I head straight for Jude's. Wanting to catch him before he leaves for the store, and nearly crashing right into him when he backs his Jeep out of his drive just as I'm pulling in.

"Ever?" He peers at me from his sideview mirror as his car jumps to a halt and he springs from his seat.

I stare. I can't help it. He looks so completely different from the last time I saw him.

His head is shaved.

And without his trademark tangle of long golden/bronze dreadlocks he's barely recognizable—or at least until his eyes find mine anyway. That brilliant aqua-green gaze is all too familiar, not to mention the wave of cool, calm energy that thrums over me, through me, all around me, in the same way it has for the last several centuries.

He runs a self-conscious hand over his newly shorn head,

his tropical gaze meeting mine when he says, "Figured it was time for a change, but from the look on your face I'm thinking I should start growing it again."

I slip out of my car, trying my best to not overdo it with the staring. Even though he looks great, in fact, better than great, it's still a pretty big visual adjustment to make.

"Nah." I smile brightly and shake my head. "Keep it. I mean, what's the point of going back, when you can go forward instead?"

His eyes graze over me, allowing the words to hang between us until he breaks the silence and says, "You look like you've been through the wringer." He motions toward the sorry state of my clothes. "But you made it, and that's what matters. It's good to see you, Ever." And I can tell by the tone of his voice and the glint in his eye that for the first time in a long time he actually means it. My presence no longer elicits that same brand of longing it used to.

"And you." I chase the words with another smile, wanting him to know that I mean it too.

We stand before each other, allowing the silence to build. But it's not the awkward kind of silence, it's the kind shared by two people who've experienced something so extraordinary there's just no way to put it into words.

"When'd you get back?" I ask, wondering if he was gone a long time too.

He looks at me, squints, and says, "Long time ago. Way before you. I thought about going after you, trying to find you, but Lotus warned me against it, warned me to not get involved." Jude jangles his keys, motions toward his front door. "Do you want to go inside?"

I press my lips together, thinking about *inside*. The kitchen where I once did his dishes, the old chair where I used to sit, the antique door he uses as a coffee table, the brown corduroy couch where he confessed his feelings for me . . .

"No, I—" I look at him, swallow hard, and start again. "I just wanted to make sure you made it back from Summerland. Just wanted to make sure you got through it okay, and . . ." I lift my shoulders, look all around, seeing the peonies back in bloom—big, vibrantly colored puffballs of purple and pink sprouting from the top of sturdy green stems. "And, it seems you did, so . . ."

But he won't let me off that easily. He won't allow me to just brush it away. "Should we talk about it?" he asks, his gaze telling me he's more than willing to do so if I want.

And while we most certainly could, I can't help but think: *What would be the point?*

I mean, what's there left to talk about, really? We know everything now. We relived the actual events for ourselves. So what's the point in rehashing what we already know?

I shake my head and direct my gaze to our feet—he in his usual brown rubber flip-flops, me in my crusty, dirty hiking boots. Then I lift my head and say, "That would just end up being redundant now, wouldn't it?"

He lifts his shoulders, keeps his gaze on me.

"Though, it must be a relief to know you didn't really love me and lose me all those years, right?"

He tilts his head, confused by my statement.

"What I mean is, or at least from what I can tell after stringing it all together, it's pretty clear you were just trying to keep me and Damen apart so he wouldn't make me immortal. You know, so he wouldn't succeed at what he'd failed to do that first life of ours when you were Heath, he was Alrik, and I was Adelina."

"Is that really your take?" He leans toward me, his gaze so piercing it causes me to nod, gulp, scratch my arm. Indulging in all of my nervous tells, one after another, which leaves me wondering why I insisted on saying such a thing if it's only going to result in my own discomfort. But seeing that discomfort, he's quick to let it go, saying, "So, tell me—did you do it? Did you make it to the end of your journey? Did you find the tree you were looking for?"

"Yeah. I did," I tell him, my voice growing hoarse as my mind fills with the whole glorious sight of it. A vision I want him to see too and there's only one way to do that. "Close your eyes," I say, humbled by the speed with which he obeys. "And now open your mind." I place my hands on either side of his face, my palms spanning the sharp planes of his cheekbones that appear even more pronounced with his newly shorn hair, my fingertips seeking the slight inward curve of his temples and pressing lightly against them. Projecting the whole wonderfully radiant scene from my mind to his, showing him the tree exactly as I remember it, in all of its abundance and glory.

"Wow," he says, his voice like a sigh. "That must've been . . . *something*." He looks at me, gaze deeply probing.

I nod, start to remove my hands from his face, only to have him press his palms hard against them, holding me in place.

"I should go." I try to pull away, only to have him hold me even tighter, keep me right there before him.

"Ever . . ." His voice is thick, ragged, a tone I know well.

My eyes graze over him, noting his freshly laundered T-shirt and jeans, the scent of soap, fresh air, and ocean that drifts from his skin—and I know the effort was made for Honor, not me.

"Jude, are you happy?" I ask, fervently hoping he is, that the night star I made granted my wish, or at least that it will soon.

He gives me a long look, one that lingers so long I'm sure he won't answer when he finally drops his hands, shoves them deep into his pockets, and says, "I'm working on it." He shrugs. "I think I'm getting closer. You?"

I start to shoot off some blithe and breezy reply, the kind you toss out when someone asks how you are but you know they're not going to stick around for the answer, but then I stop just as quickly. Jude answered honestly, so the least I can do is answer honestly too. Though it does take a moment to figure out just what that answer might be. I hadn't really considered my own state of happiness—or at least not for a while anyway.

Let's see, I passed every test on my journey and seized my destiny, which makes me completely self-actualized in the deepest sense of the word, and yet, even after all that, there's one thing that's still glaringly missing. Or, make that two things—one huge, one only slightly less huge. But after I leave here, I'll face those things too.

"Same here," I finally say. "I'm working on it too." Chasing the words with a flash of a grin. "But I think I'm making good progress, getting pretty dang close, anyway."

I start to turn, start to head for my car, when he pulls me back to him and says, "Hey, Ever—"

I face him.

"Just so you know, you've got it all wrong."

I narrow my gaze, having no idea what he means.

"That really isn't what I was doing all of those lives, or at least that's only part of it. The other reason I was trying to keep you from Damen is because I wanted you all to myself. Still do." He shrugs, tries to laugh, but it's not the funny kind. It's far too resigned for that. "Remember what you told me—the first day we met?"

I squint. I said a lot of things back then. In fact, I gave him one heck of a palm reading, told him all about his past—or at least his most immediate past.

"You told me I have a serious history of falling for all the wrong girls."

Oh yeah. That.

"Turns out you were right." There's that laugh again, but this time it's lighter, brighter, hinting at a promise of better days to come. "Little did you know it was just one girl in particular—one girl over and over again. Little did you know it was *you.*"

I gulp, my stomach going all twisty and weird.

"It's always been you." He shoots me a rueful grin.

I edge closer to my car, having no idea what to say, what to do, but that's okay, because he cancels the awkwardness for me.

"So, what do you think of Honor?" he asks.

Our eyes meet and hold, until I manage to stammer, "For reals?"

He nods, swipes a hand over his head in the same way he used to back when his hair was long and twisty, only now there's not much to latch onto and his arm falls back to his side. "What did you tell me back then? If I'm fool enough to ask, then you're fool enough to tell?" He laughs, adding, "So yeah, what the heck? Have at it. What do you think of Honor? Or, better yet, what do you see for our future? Do we even have a future?"

He offers his palm, wanting me to take it, to tell him all that I see. And I stand there before him, knowing all I have to do is lower my psychic shield, press my finger to his skin, and everything he wants to know, including stuff he most likely does not, will be revealed.

I inch toward him, just about to do it, when I remember what Damen once said, and decide to quote him instead.

"Life is not meant to be an open-book test," I say, turning back toward my car and driving away.

THIRTY-SIX

My next stop is Sabine's.

I figure since it's late on a Sunday afternoon there's a good chance I'll find her at home.

Maybe even at home with Munoz.

And the closer I get to her street, the more I start hoping Munoz will be there, if for no other reason than he seems to be on my side—or at least for the most part. Which means he just might be able to help me convince her of the truth.

The startling, mind-blowing, world-rocking truth that proves everything she so vehemently denies is actually real.

The truth she'll most likely fight like hell to refuse no matter how much evidence I put before her.

And even though I'm fully prepared to pull out all the stops, do whatever's required to make her believe (knowing that may require no less than a judge, a carefully selected twelve-man jury, and possibly even a handful of alternates thrown in for good measure), it'll still be good to have Munoz around to help build my case.

You know, two against one.

Power in numbers.

That sort of thing.

I drive up to the gate, feeling even more guilty about my extra-long absence when I see the way the security guard looks at me, openly gawking as she does a triple take before waving me in. And when I pull into the driveway, see the way the yard has changed, having transitioned right out of a season I pretty much missed, and going headfirst into a new one I hope to stick around long enough to enjoy, the guilty feeling goes into overdrive.

Still, that's nothing compared to the way I feel when I stand at the door and ring the bell only to watch Sabine's features tumble through a series of almost cartoonish expressions. Beginning with an initial reaction of surprised recognition, before making their way through utter shock, to complete and total disbelief, to a quick glint of hope, to absolute defiance, and then settling on grave concern when she takes in the sad and sorry state of my scuffed-up hiking boots, dirty jeans, and the filthy white tank top I keep forgetting to manifest myself out of.

"Where've you been?" she asks, her voice a strange combination of anger and curiosity, as her blue eyes continue the inventory.

"Trust me, you wouldn't believe me if I told you," I say, knowing the words are far truer than she could ever realize.

She folds her arms across her chest as her lips press together in a thin, grim line. Transitioning right back to her stern side, the one that's all too easy to recognize, saying, "Try me."

It's the angry Sabine.

The self-righteous Sabine.

The Sabine who gave me the ultimatum that ultimately convinced me to leave.

I peer over her shoulder, knowing Munoz is here somewhere since I saw his silver Prius in the drive. Heaving a huge sigh of relief when I see him coming out of the den, his face pretty much exhibiting all the same expressions as hers, minus the defiance and grave concern, which I take as a good sign.

"I'd love to explain." I fight to keep my voice calm, nonconfrontational, knowing the only way to get through to her is to keep the emotion at bay. "In fact, that's why I'm here. I plan to tell you all about it. I *want* to tell you all about it. But it's kind of involved, so I thought maybe I could come in and sit down and we can take it from there."

Her cheeks flush in indignation. She can hardly believe my audacity. Expecting to be let in after showing up on her doorstep, completely unannounced, after months of no communication whatsoever. I can practically hear the thoughts as they swirl through her head even though I promised myself I wouldn't eavesdrop. Though it's not like I need to eavesdrop when I can see the way her energy radiates all around her, flashing and sparking in a rising tide of anger.

Still, she swings the door wide and motions me in, following me into the den, where I claim one of the overstuffed chairs and watch as she and Munoz place themselves side by side on the couch that sits opposite.

"Would you like something to drink?" she asks, her voice stiff as she jumps to her feet once again. Unable to contain her own nervous energy, unsure how to handle my sudden presence, she goes straight into hostess mode, a role she knows well.

"Water," I say, seeing the way her brows draw together, knowing she's unused to seeing me drink anything other than the elixir, not realizing it's been around six months since my last sip. "Water would be great, thanks." I edge back in my chair, crossing my legs at the ankle as she heads into the kitchen and Munoz settles back on the couch, his arms spread wide across the cushions in the comfortable, relaxed way of a man who's fully at home.

"We didn't expect to see you." His voice is cautious, unsure what to make of my presence, worried about my motives, what brings me here.

I gaze around the den, relieved to find it exactly the same after so many other things have changed. Then I gaze down at my filthy clothes and quickly manifest some clean ones in their place.

"Ever—" Munoz keeps his voice lowered so Sabine can't overhear. "I don't think that's such a good idea . . ."

I gaze down at my newly manifested blue dress and beige leather sandals and shrug. Drumming my fingers against the upholstered arms of my chair when I say, "Listen, I may need your help on this one, so please, just try to trust me. I'm not here to continue the argument, or make anything worse. I just want to clear up a few things before it's too late and I no longer can."

He looks at me, face full of alarm, about to ask for an explanation when Sabine comes back into the room, hands me a glass of water, and takes her place next to him.

I cross and uncross my legs, brush my hands over the skirt of my dress until the hem falls just shy of my knees. A series of gestures greatly lacking in subtlety, a series of gestures that practically beg her to take notice, to inquire how I managed to change clothes so quickly, to say something, anything, but a denial as deeply rooted as hers is hard to defeat.

Hard, but not impossible.

I can't allow myself to believe it's impossible. Otherwise there's no point in my being here.

Knowing it's best to just take the lead and jump in, I look at her and say, "I missed you."

She squirms, nods, leans closer to Munoz, who welcomes her into the crook of his arm and gives her shoulder a reassuring squeeze. But all she can manage in reply is, "So, are you going to tell me where you've been?"

I press my lips together, a little stunned by her response, but I guess she figures the emotional cost is too high for her to admit that she missed me too. But that's okay. Even if she won't admit it, I know she *did* miss me. I can see it in the way her aura flashes with just the slimmest hint of pink in the midst of all that still raging red.

Auras never lie. Only people do.

"I was in Summerland," I say, my gaze traveling between her and Munoz.

"In Santa Barbara?" She shoots me a skeptical look but I'm quick to deflect it.

"No. Not the beach town in Santa Barbara, the *real* Summerland. The *first* Summerland. The mystical dimension that exists between this one and the one just beyond."

Munoz tenses, his body on full-scale alert, prepared for the worst. While Sabine's mouth grows grim, her gaze narrowing as she says, "I don't understand."

I lean forward, scooting to the very edge of my seat, saying, "I know. Believe me, I totally get it. It's a lot to take in. Especially the first time you hear it. It was the same way for me. I chose to deny it for a really long time. Pretty much until I no longer could. I also know this will be even more difficult for you because of your reluctance to believe in anything that falls outside of your comfort zone, and how you prefer to dismiss anything you can't see happening directly in front of you. But the reason I've decided to confide in you anyway, despite the uphill battle I face, is because I've grown tired of the game. I've grown tired of lying to you all the time. I've grown tired of hiding things from you. But mostly, I've grown tired of having to work so ridiculously hard at being this totally manufactured, false version of me just so you can continue to believe what's most comfortable for you to believe." I pause for a moment, giving her a chance to respond, but she just looks as cold and stone-faced as ever, so I quickly press on. "The first two weeks I was gone, I was at Damen's. And I know you know that because I know he told you. But what you probably don't know is that I was fully committed to never coming back. I'd vowed to move far away after graduation and to never see you again. And it's not because I was being vindictive or trying to punish you—despite what you may think, I truly bore you no ill will. The reason I'd planned to leave you forever is because I truly believed it would make both our lives easier. But now things have changed, or at least they're about to change in a really big way . . ." I swallow hard, chance a glance at Munoz and see him nod, encouraging me to go on, and I do. "But before that really big change can take place, I wanted to come clean with you. I wanted to take one last stab to try to make you believe."

"And just what is it that I'm supposed to *believe*?" she asks, but I can tell by the defiant arch of her brow and the challenge in her tone that she already knows.

"I need you to believe that I'm not just some crazy, sad, attention-starved teen who's so scarred and damaged by the loss of her family that she pretends to have psychic powers. I need you to believe that I'm not some con-artist charlatan who rips people off for a living. And the reason I need you to believe that is because it's the truth. I *am* psychic. I can and do hear other people's thoughts. I can also see a person's entire life story with merely a touch, just as I can see auras and communicate with all the ghostly spirits who choose to hang around the earth plane long after they should've moved on. And, in addition to that, I'm also immortal." I stop, allowing enough time for my words to sink in, for my confession to take full effect. Knowing it has when her aura begins to flare and rage so bright, I'm surprised by the absence of smoke I thought for sure would be shooting out of her nose and ears.

"That red juice I always drink?" I tilt my head and look at her. "As it just so happens, it's the elixir of eternal life. The one man has sought through the ages—only Damen is one of the few who actually succeeded in discovering the secret formula just over six hundred years ago."

"Ever, if you think that I'm . . ." She shakes her head, far too furious to even complete her own sentence, though she does manage to think it, and this time I tune in. If for no other reason, it might help prove my point.

My eyes meet hers, watching her closely as I slowly repeat her unspoken words. "No, I really don't think you're *willing to consider something so ludicrous, so ridiculous, so far-fetched, so . . . sad—for even one second.*" Seeing her eyes widen in shock, but she's just as quick to dismiss it, assuring herself it was obvious what she was thinking. And though it was, I'm not about to stop there.

"And if that didn't convince you, then maybe this will. Though I have to warn you, I'm going to pull out all the stops to prove to you I'm not lying, I'm not crazy, and I'm not some attention-starved phony. I'm going to show you exactly what

I'm capable of, which is something I probably should've done long before. And the only reason I didn't is because neither of us was quite ready. But now we are. Or at least I am, and I'm pretty sure you are too. And as for Munoz"—I switch my gaze to him—"he already knows. In fact, he's known for some time."

Sabine turns to Munoz, her eyes imploring. But he just takes a deep breath and nods, directing her attention back to me when he says, "It's true. Sabine, honey, Ever's not lying. She possesses powers that are nothing short of astonishing. All I ask is that you give her a chance. Just try to watch and listen with an open mind, and I think you'll be amazed at what you see. And if not, if you still choose not to believe . . ." He looks at her, clearly hoping that won't be the case. "Well, then, that's your choice. But for now, why not just try to broaden your world to a whole new set of ideas you may have never considered."

She crosses her arms and legs, which, as far as body language goes, is a pretty discouraging display. Her eyes warily focused on me, when I say, "For starters, what was I wearing when you opened the door?" She squints, her eyes moving over me, engaged in a full inspection, and when she refuses to answer, when she just wraps herself up even tighter, I say, "Is it the same thing I'm wearing now?"

She shifts, squirms, but refuses to reply, which as far as I'm concerned is answer enough.

"Or was it this?" I manifest the filthy clothes I was wearing when I first got here, the sight of which garners no response from her. "Or maybe it was this?" I manifest a dark green silk gown just like the one I wear in the pavilion when Damen and I revisit scenes from my London life, back when I was the spoiled little rich girl named Chloe. Choosing to remain like that, sitting before her in a bright and shiny display of centuries-old finery. Willing her to say something, anything, but she won't. She's completely unwilling to budge from the ideas she's clung to for so long.

"My powers aren't just relegated to rapid wardrobe changes," I say. "I can manifest an elephant just as easily." Then I close my eyes and do just that. Choking back a laugh when I see just how much effort she puts into maintaining her cool. So completely dedicated to her rigid set of views, she refuses to react in any way whatsoever when an elephant appears right beside her and swings his trunk in her face. "I can manifest flowers as well," I add, covering the coffee table with a huge pile of bright yellow daffodils. "I can also manifest jewels." I close my eyes and when I open them again Sabine is dripping in diamonds and rubies and emeralds and yet, all it does is make her even more stone-faced. "I can even manifest cars and boats and houses and, well, basically whatever you can imagine. Virtually nothing is off-limits—well, except for people. You can't manifest a person because you can't manifest a soul—though you can manifest their image as I once did with Orlando Bloom." I smile briefly at the memory and Damen's reaction that followed when he saw what I'd done. "But what I can't manifest, no matter how hard I try, is your willingness to stop denying what you see right in front of you. That's called free will, and it belongs only to you."

She tilts her chin and narrows her eyes, looking angry, defiant, though her voice easily betrays the fear that's behind it. "I don't know what you're up to, Ever, but you need to stop! You need to stop with the . . ." She looks around, searches for the right word. "You need to stop with the magic tricks, now!"

Her demeanor so shaken, so stricken, I'm quick to comply. Nodding and blinking until every last trace of it's gone—until it's all returned to normal again, including my clothes, which are back to the far more comfortable, though far less impressive blue dress and beige sandals.

My eyes meet hers, and I can't help but think this is going even worse than I'd thought. Still, I refuse to give up. I can't allow myself to stop now when I still have a few more tricks up my sleeve.

"There's more." I nod, instantly manifesting a jewel-handled knife I position right over my flattened, raised palm. "I know you're squeamish, I know how you hate the sight of blood, but I promise it'll be over soon."

I jab the tip into the center of my palm, and drag the sharp blade all the way across. Hearing the gasp Sabine is unable to stifle, and seeing her horrified face as she watches the blood pouring out of me—the way it splashes over my dress and pools onto the carpet—until—until—it no longer is.

The knife is gone.

My palm is healed.

And there's absolutely no sign of the blood I just shed.

And even though it was a pretty impressive display, I have to admit I'm starting to feel a little ashamed, starting to feel like the world's creepiest circus act.

"Listen." I glance back and forth between her and Munoz, who's not even trying to hide his shock over what he just saw. "I could go on for hours. I could show you every trick that I'm capable of. And I will, if that's what it takes. But really, all you need to know is that everything you just saw is real. And though it may make you uncomfortable, while it may make you long to turn your back and pretend you didn't see it, that won't stop it from being real. I'm sorry, Sabine. I'm sorry to have to do this to you. And while I get that it's your choice whether or not you choose to believe, and while I get that there's a good chance that no matter what I do I won't be able to change your mind, here's the thing: Whether or not you choose to believe is entirely up to you—but if you ever want to see me again, if you want to have any kind of a relationship with me, then you're going to have to move past your own deeply rooted prejudices and learn to accept me. All of me. Even the parts you don't like. Even the parts that scare you. Because that's exactly what I've chosen to do with you. Your tendency toward self-righteousness and bullheadedness, your penchant for shunning me instead of trying to understand me, well, it scares me just as much as my display of immortal party tricks just scared you. Yet I still prefer to accept you as you are, rather than face a future of never seeing you again. I guess I was just hoping that by doing all this, we could find a place to meet in the middle. But again, it's your choice. Either way, I'll accept your decision."

I sit back, watching as the steam seeps right out of her, watching as her aura deflates and settles like a week-old helium balloon.

"How long have you been like this?" she finally asks.

And when my eyes meet hers, I realize she thinks I've always been like this—that I was born a freak. Figuring it must be the reason I survived the accident when the rest of my family didn't. Though I'm quick to deflect that.

"I *did* die in the accident," I say. "I had what's called a near-death experience, though I think the term's a little wonky since there was nothing *near* about it. Anyway, Munoz probably knows more about all that than I do. He's read up on it quite a bit." I look at them, seeing her shoot him an inquiring glance, which he answers with a nod and a shrug. "Anyway, instead of crossing the bridge to the other side along with Mom and Dad and Buttercup, I chose to linger in Summerland, in this amazingly beautiful field. And that's what my soul was doing when Damen found my body by the car and made me drink the elixir that brought me to life."

"And Riley?" Sabine leans forward, her eyes wide, assuming the worst.

"Riley got stuck for a while." I squirm.

"Stuck?"

I sigh. "Stuck between here and Summerland. She started visiting me back when I was in the hospital. Then, when we moved here, she used to drop by the house nearly every day until I convinced her to cross the bridge and move on. And though I think she might visit me in my dreams every now and then, I haven't been able to see her since. I can't see the ones who've crossed over. Their energy vibrates too fast. Though a friend of mine used to see her . . ." I pause, remembering how Jude tried to teach me to see her too, but to no avail. "And he says she says she's just fine. Actually, he says she's better than fine. She's happy. Mom and Dad and Buttercup are happy too. Apparently they feel more alive than ever." I look at her. "You know, just because you can't see them, doesn't mean they no longer exist. The soul is eternal. It's the only true immortality there is."

I don't know which part of my speech finally got to her, but the next thing I know Sabine is sobbing into Munoz's T-shirt. Her shoulders violently shaking as he rubs his hand over her chin-length blond hair and down the back of her blouse, whispering softly, providing comfort, assurance, until she starts to collect herself and is ready to face me again.

I sit quietly, knowing exactly how she feels. Remembering all too well how I first reacted when I saw my ghostly little sister standing before me—how I denied it was real. And how

I treated Damen that day in the parking lot at school when he first told me the truth of my existence—how I chose to banish him from my life, to send him away with cruel, fear-driven words rather than face a truth I felt so completely unprepared to handle.

We're not so different, Sabine and me.

I know what it's like to have everything you believe turned upside down.

So after a while I say, "I'm really sorry to just spring this on you. I know it's a lot to digest. But I just wanted you to know before—"

She lifts her head, her eyes bleary, teary, as she turns to face me.

"—I just wanted you to know before I return to normal again."

She blinks, shakes her head, and mumbles, "What?" Swiping a sleeve across her face when she adds, "I don't understand."

I take a deep breath and gaze down at my feet, stalling for a moment, gathering my words, before I return my gaze to hers. "To be honest, I'm not sure that I understand either. It's such a long story, and there's so much to explain . . . but it's not like the details are all that important anyway. I just thought, well, I just hoped that if I came clean about who I am now, then maybe, when I'm no longer like this, we can still hang out together. You know, without all the yelling and fighting and name-calling. I mean, if you want. It's pretty much up to you. I promise to respect whatever you decide."

Sabine rises from the couch, her arms outstretched as she starts to move toward me, but I'm faster than she is—so much faster that I'm huddled against her well before she can even clear the corner of the coffee table.

And it feels so good to be back that I can't help but cry too. The two of us turning into a wet, soggy, over-apologetic mess until I remember Munoz and swipe my hand across my eyes as I say, "Hey, is there anything you guys want?" I glance between them, adding, "I mean, you saw what I can do, all the things I'm capable of. So, with that in mind, what'll it be? A new car? A vacation house in some exotic location? Backstage passes to Bruce Springsteen?" I wiggle my brows at Munoz, knowing what a big fan he is.

But they both shake their heads.

"Are you sure?" I frown, desperately wanting to give them something. "I mean, I'm not sure if I'll still be capable of all this once I . . . after I go back to how I was before. I may lose all of my powers, or at least some of my powers. Which means this could be your last chance."

Sabine returns to Munoz and I watch as she places her hand on his shoulder and says, "What more could I possibly want when I have everything I could ever dream of right here?"

And that's when I see it.

That's when I see the brand-new sparkling engagement ring she wears on her left ring finger.

"Family's the only thing that ever meant anything to me," she says, pulling me back into their circle. "And now that you've returned, I have everything. I have all that I need."

THIRTY-SEVEN

I had every intention of heading to Damen's.

I had every intention of saying good night to Sabine and Munoz and heading right over there.

Only it didn't quite go as planned.

Sabine and I stayed up late. Like, way late. Like, well past the time Munoz bid us good night and headed back to his place.

The two of us hanging on the couch until the wee hours of the morning, picking at a box of leftover pizza (yes, I had a piece, or two, and I could hardly believe what I'd been missing all this time!), while getting ourselves all caught up on each other's news—and the next thing I knew there were only a few hours left until I had to be at school.

According to Munoz, I absolutely, positively, had no choice whatsoever but to show up at school and either work some serious manifesting magick in the administrator's office, or put in a superhuman effort at making up all that I missed, or both, if I had any hopes at all of graduating with my class.

So, instead of going to Damen's, I chose to grab a few hours of much-needed sleep in my old room, wanting to be fully rested and recharged when I dropped by his house, since I didn't know how he'd react upon seeing me again, fruit at the ready. But I knew I'd need to bring my A-game.

The second I spy his black BMW in the student lot, I realize I won't have to wait all that long. Apparently he's still showing up every day, attending his classes, going through the much-dreaded motions, even though, for the life of me, I can't imagine why.

"Because I made you a promise," he says, answering the question in my mind when he appears by my side. Holding my door open, waiting for me to climb out and join him, but for the moment anyway, I remain frozen in place.

My eyes travel over him, savoring the look of him, the feel of his presence next to mine, while the deep, aching pang in my gut reminds me of just how much I've missed being with him.

Despite the thrill of my recent accomplishments—despite the triumph of seizing my destiny—without Damen by my side, it all dims—it all feels so hollow and empty.

"I searched for you." His eyes pore over me, thirsty, drinking me in—telling me he missed me as much as I missed him. "Searched all over Summerland. And though I was unable to find you, I could still sense you. That's how I knew you were okay. Far away—in a place I couldn't fathom—but still okay. And it's that comfort that kept me going, waiting for the day when you'd find your way back to me."

I swallow hard, swallow past the huge lump that's now lodged in my throat. Knowing I should say something, anything, but I can't. Staring at him is pretty much all that I'm capable of.

"So, when'd you get back?" His gaze remains steady, and though he strives to maintain a calm, casual vibe, I'm afraid the way I react is pretty much the opposite.

His question sets me in motion—horrible, nervous-making motion. Grabbing my bag, fooling with my hair, scratching my arm, and shifting in my seat until I finally maneuver past the offer of his hand and haul myself out of my car. My eyes darting crazily, searching for a safe place to land, which ends up being pretty much anywhere and everywhere but him.

My breath coming ragged, too fast, when I say, "Yesterday." A truth so horrible I can't help but cringe.

Knowing exactly how he chooses to interpret it—the only way it can be interpreted. And as much as I'd love to deny it, I can't. There's just no getting around the fact that I've been back from my journey for an entire day and yet I never found the time to see him until he just now approached me.

No way to get around the fact that I put other people before him.

A whole host of other people, including Jude.

Damen stands by my car, carefully weighing that one single word until it becomes permanent, irreversible, like an accidental footprint left in a square of fresh cement I make no attempt to smooth over, no attempt to erase its permanent imprint.

And even though I know I need to say something, I have no idea what that something might be.

He looks at me, clearly torn between feeling even more hurt and even more confused, and settling on somewhere in the middle.

"I was afraid to see you," I tell him. "Mostly because I don't want to fight with you again. I can't bear to fight with you again. And yet, I think we both know that's exactly where this is headed. But before we get there, I need you to know that just because I delayed this moment doesn't mean I didn't miss you—" My voice cracks, becoming so choked up I'm forced to clear my throat a few times before I continue. "Please, don't ever think I didn't miss you." My gaze grows watery, bleary, pleading with his.

But instead of admitting he missed me too, instead of moving to comfort me like I'd hoped, he says, "Why is it you think an argument is so inevitable?"

His dark eyes graze over me, widening in shocked disbelief when I reach into my bag, find the package Honor gave me, and hand it over to him, saying, "Because of this."

He studies the small, plain-wrapped parcel, examining it as he flips it back and forth in his hands.

"It's the herb." I look at him. "It's the hard-to-find, special-order, rare herb that you need to finish your antidote. The antidote that will allow us to be together in the way that we want, so we can continue our lives as immortals."

His fingers curl, causing the paper to crinkle in protest, his gaze lighting on mine, the weight of it causing me to suck in a lungful of air. The first bell ringing, the sound of it sending all of our classmates into a flurry as they race toward the building, while Damen and I stay rooted in place. As much as I need to get to class and start making up for all the damage my extended absence has done, we need to finish this first. We need to reach some sort of conclusion, before I can go anywhere, do anything else.

"But I still cling to my belief that this life is cosmically wrong. And even if we take the antidote, something else will crop up to keep us apart. The only true way to achieve our destiny—to be together forever—is to reverse our immortality. To eat the fruit." I gaze down at our feet, gaze at the dark shine of his car, gaze toward the soon-to-be-locked gate, hearing the final bell ring just as I gaze into his eyes. "Damen, I have the means to do that now. I found the tree. It's real."

He doesn't react, doesn't move, doesn't flinch.

"I journeyed there. Saw it for myself. I scaled its enormous trunk, swung from its mile-long branches—" I pause, wanting to ensure I have his full attention before I continue, "I picked its fruit."

My gaze stays on his, but still nothing. No indication he's heard.

"That's why I was away for so long. It was a long, arduous, treacherous, lonely, scary, and yet completely wondrous journey. I passed through a rush of seasons to get there, made it through a winter so brutal I was sure I'd turn into a frozen-solid mass, got so rained on I was sure I'd never dry, and yet, even though I wasn't always convinced I would make it, I *did* make it. I succeeded in what I set out to do. And now I'm here to say that it's not a myth like you think. In fact, it's even better than the myth. Remember when Lotus said the tree was ever-giving? She was right. The tree just keeps giving and giving and giving. There's no truth to the one-fruit-every-thousand-years rumor. From what I experienced there are no shortages of any kind. There is only abundance. The Tree of Life is the very definition of abundance. And I brought back an entire bag full of its fruit with which to prove it."

"You brought it *back*?" His face takes on an expression that's impossible to read. "Why would you do that? Why wouldn't you just hand it over to Lotus and let her handle it?"

"Because I'm taking over for Roman," I say, nodding as I confirm it for myself. And now that I've said it, an entire plan begins to form in my head.

But Damen just looks at me, not comprehending.

"The party he throws every century and a half?" I suppress a smile, but I can't seem to suppress my rising excitement. "This time I'm going to host it. I'm going to gather all of the immortals he's made, and give them a choice between physical immortality—or *real* immortality."

"And if they refuse you?" he asks, clearly convinced that they will since he pretty much has.

"Then they refuse me." I shrug. "Though after I explain it to them, after they see the effects, I don't think they will."

Damen's eyes widen, his face grows pale, ashen, and it takes me a moment to figure out why. He misread my words. Assumed I've already tried it.

"Did you—?" he starts, but I'm quick to wave it away.

"No." I shake my head, as my eyes fix on his. "I wanted to wait for you. I want us to reverse our immortality together. I don't know what I'll do if you deny me—whether I'll choose this life with you, or a mortal life on my own—I honestly don't know. But I really hope you won't make me choose. I hope you'll think it over and share the fruit with me. It's the only way we can have the future we want."

I gaze at him, my eyes pleading with his. But finding only regret, I turn and head for the gate.

THIRTY-EIGHT

I stand before the big iron gate Damen unlocked with his mind, watching as he beckons for me to join him on its other side. And as tempted as I am to do just that (and believe me, I'm extremely tempted) if I'm going to start living normally then I'm going to have to start here.

Now.

If I'm going to start living normally then I'll have to stop relying on magick to free myself from all of my messes.

I shake my head, move past his bewildered gaze, and make my way toward the office, where I send the secretary into a complete frenzy of activity the second I approach her desk and say, "Hi. I'm Ever Bloom. I'm a senior here. And not only am I tardy, but I've pretty much skipped out on the last six months and I'm wondering how I might go about making that up."

Her eyes grow wide as she looks me up and down, then she points toward a chair by the wall, tells me to sit, to not move an inch, while she turns, simultaneously reaching for her computer and the phone. The hand piece wedged between her shoulder and ear as her fingers pound hard on the keyboard, alerting the principal, the vice principal, my teachers, and Sabine, who was well aware of my plan and was waiting for this very call. The fate of my diploma being decided with little to no input from me, and when my previous suspension is mentioned, I'm sure that I'm doomed, but then luckily, thanks to Sabine's finely honed negotiation skills they allow me to attempt what I'm sure they all consider to be the impossible: telling me that if I make up everything that I've missed—every single test—every last assignment—within the next two weeks, then they'll let me graduate.

Six months of neglected work that needs to be completed in just fourteen days in order to wear the cap and gown along with the rest of my classmates. Otherwise, I won't be getting anywhere near it until the same time next year, if then.

With great emphasis on the *if*.

Clearly if there was ever a time for magick, and manifesting, and trips to the Great Halls of Learning, it's now. But, while I refuse to rely on my powers, that doesn't stop me from relying on my friends—including a few people I didn't even realize were my friends.

So when classmates I've barely even spoken to offer to lend me their notes, and when Stacia and Honor (prompted by Miles, but still) offer to help me catch up on all I missed in physics, I'm so shocked by the offer, I say yes. And for someone who's avoided doing any form of studying or schoolwork for over a year, it's a little hard to get back into the groove of doing so now.

It's also impossible to stop myself from just automatically intuiting the contents the second I touch the cover of my huge stack of textbooks. Mind reading I can control, all I have to do is lower my psychic shield or use my quantum remote, but tapping into the universal consciousness of just *intuiting* things is something I have no control over. So, instead of fighting it, I decide to use it to my advantage to get through a pile of reading assignments that would be pretty much impossible without it. Besides, I still have to write the papers, and I still have to solve all the equations and memorize the formulas, so it's not like I'm totally cheating. Though, I admit, when it comes to the makeup tests, well, yeah, all the right answers just automatically appear. But then, there's nothing I can do about that either.

Still, even with the help of my friends, along with my psychic powers, it's a lot to tackle in such a short amount of time. So while I'm busy with schoolwork, Jude and Ava offer to do their part by reading through Roman's old journals in an attempt to track down all the far-flung immortals—the orphans Damen turned as well as the ones Roman deemed worthy enough to change through the years. While Romy and Rayne pool their twin talents by crafting handmade party invitations they mail out pretty much all over the globe, as Sabine handles my college applications that are so late it looks like I'll be forced to take a year off. Which is probably for the best since it's been so long since I even thought about having a normal future, I don't even know where to start.

Not to mention how I always assumed that wherever I ended up, Damen would be right there beside me.

I always assumed we'd head off together, just the two of us.

I never once considered I might end up going it alone.

But not having seen him since the day I left him standing at the gate, I have to admit it's a real possibility. He's avoiding school. Avoiding me. And while I'm willing to give him the space that he figures he needs—I hope in the end, he'll decide to come join me.

Despite all the evidence pointing against it—I hope in the end, he'll make the right choice.

If he doesn't, I don't know what I'll do. And maybe that's part of the reason I've welcomed the overwhelming volume of schoolwork—it's distracted me from the terrible, unavoidable fact that if Damen chooses against the fruit, I'll be forced to make an impossible choice. Choosing between a misguided life as an immortal—where the universe will conspire to keep us apart at every turn—and a life without Damen, which is just too horrible to contemplate.

So in the midst of all the studying, and reading, and exam taking, and essay writing, and getting next to no sleep in order to fit it all in, I finally take a little time out to visit Summerland.

Partly because I'm eager to find Lotus so I can tell her just how much I accomplished, and partly because, well, I'm also eager to visit it while I still can, while it's just a simple matter of envisioning that shimmering golden veil and stepping through to its other side. I mean, even though I know plenty of mortals who can get there, I have no way of knowing if I'll still be able to get there once I become mortal again, and so I'm determined to enjoy it while I can.

After spending a few wonderful moments in the vast fragrant field where I land, after a visit to the Great Halls of Learning, where I stand before its ever-changing façade and re-experience the thrill of being admitted inside, after visiting all of Damen's and my favorite places—the replica of Versailles he once manifested expressly for me, the field full of tulips that surrounds the pavilion he made for my seventeenth birthday—

after returning to the place where the grass once turned to mud and where the trees were all barren—the former entrance to the Shadowland—after finding my way to the beautiful pond still blooming with hundreds of the loveliest lotus blossoms—after all that, when I still can't locate Lotus, I decide to tuck one of Romy and Rayne's handmade pink-and-black party invitation envelopes under a large rock I'd seen her lean against, in the hope that she'll find it.

Then I return to the earth plane, bury myself in my studies, and wait.

Wait to hear from Lotus.

Wait for the RSVPs from all the other immortals to come pouring in.

Wait to hear from Misa, Marco, and Rafe.

Wait to see if they'll let me graduate.

Wait to see which direction my future might take.

The days ticking past with small bits of news trickling in—but not the news that I want.

There is no word from Damen.

THIRTY-NINE

Maybe I bought into the hype.

Maybe I built it up way too much in my head.

But in the end, I'm sorry to say that graduation is, well, a little anticlimactic.

Don't get me wrong, it's well organized, flowing along just fine. In fact, it's a lot like you see in movies and on TV with all the caps, and gowns, and speeches, and laughter, and tears, and reminiscing, and fervent promises to stay in touch. But despite Sabine and Munoz perched in the crowd smiling and waving every time I look their way (and even when I don't), despite Miles and Honor and (still shocking to me but I'm starting to get used to it) Stacia, catcalling and clapping and cheering me on when it's my turn to head for the stage—there's no Haven. No Damen.

And it's those two glaring absences that pretty much eclipse everything else.

So when I throw my cap in the air, I seize the chance to work a bit of magick. Making it sail way up high into the sky, much higher than anyone else's, and watching as it loops first into the shape of a tulip and then into the shape of an infinity symbol, before I let it go, watching it free-fall back to the ground.

And I'm just making my way toward Sabine and Munoz when Stacia finds me in the crowd, places her hand on my arm, and says, "So, see you at the party?" She flips her fingers through her long, blond-streaked hair and settles her eyes on mine.

I squint, taking in her bright yellow aura, amazed to see she's sincere.

And before I can answer, Honor catches up and says, "We figured we'd stop by a little early, help you set up."

I look at her and Stacia, wondering when I'm ever going to get used to this new side of them. Despite their combined efforts to help me get to this point, every kind gesture they make still comes as a great shock to me, and I know that's not at all fair. They're working so hard to improve the least I can do is let them.

Stacia cocks her head, waiting for me to respond, while Honor fidgets with her finger, twisting Jude's malachite ring back and forth.

"Um, that's really sweet and all, but you guys don't have to come. Really." I nod, hoping they won't take it the wrong way, but I'm not sure I want them there. "I mean, I'm sure you have better things to do, better parties to go to, so . . ."

"Better than this party? Doubtful!" Stacia shoots me one of her old *You're crazy* looks, then remembering she doesn't do that anymore, she quickly clears her face. "Besides, we already have our costumes and everything!" She glances at Honor standing beside her, nodding in agreement. "After all we've done to help you graduate—you can't disinvite us now!"

I gape, surprised she would say that since I don't exactly remember ever inviting them. But then, I also wasn't in charge of the invitations, the twins were. Nor did I know there'd be costumes. In fact, I have no idea how this happened, how they even know about it, how it got so blown out of proportion. I mean, originally, this was just supposed to be a nice small gathering. Immortals only. I had no idea it'd turned into the grad night to end all grad nights. The year's most anticipated event.

"I worked really, really hard on my costume," Stacia says, her voice accusing. "So no way will you keep me from wearing it. Everyone's gonna flip when they see it!"

"Jude's is a surprise," Honor says. "Though he says it won't be a surprise to you, since you've already seen it." She looks at me in a way that lets me know she pretty much knows everything there is to know about Jude and me and still isn't sure how she feels about it. "But I've got a little surprise of my own. Something Romy and Rayne helped me come up with; I'm pretty excited about it. Trust me, Ever, this party is going to be epic. And you're crazy if you think either one of us would miss it!"

Costumes?

Epic?

And here I thought it was all about convincing a bunch of eternals to eat the fruit.

"You saw the invites, right?" Stacia asks, her eyes moving over me.

I shake my head, realizing too late that I didn't. All I saw was the pink-and-black envelope I left near the pond. It never occurred to me to peek inside. I've been so overwhelmed with all the catching up I had to do to get to this point that I never thought to ask questions. I never offered to pitch in with the planning, or even inquired into how it was going. Everyone seemed so happy to take over that I happily left it to them. Thinking that all I had to do was to show up on time with the fruit—but now apparently I need a costume too.

"Okay, well, just so you know, it's a 'Come As You Were' party. You know, like who you were in a past life?" Stacia says. "And just so you know, we're going, whether you like it or not." She shoots me a challenging look, the kind that reminds me of the old days, back when I first got here and she went after me in the most relentless way.

The only difference is, unlike back then, this time I deserve it. She's worked pretty hard to help me turn things around, giving generously of her time, the least I could do is acknowledge her efforts and the long way she's come.

"Is it still at Ava's?" I ask, wondering how we're all going to fit into her snug little bungalow now that the guest list has multiplied.

"No." Miles grins, stopping beside Honor and inserting himself into the conversation. "It's at your house. And trust me, Sabine and Munoz are going all out—no expense spared. It's totally gonna outdo that Halloween party of yours." He nods. "So if I were you, I'd get myself home and manifest a good costume like, pronto, because the party starts at seven."

FORTY

For once, Miles didn't exaggerate. Sabine and Munoz really did go above and beyond with the decorations.

From the moment we pull into the drive, all I can do is gape in astonishment at how they've taken this semicustom, faux Tuscan McMansion and turned it into something that looks like it's straight out of the old country.

"Wait 'til you see the inside!" Sabine's eyes light on mine. "I know you wanted a small gathering, but I thought it might be nice to throw a big party with all of your friends. You've worked so hard, Ever. You deserve a little fun, and, quite frankly, so do Paul and I!"

When she leads me into the house with Munoz hot on our trail, well, let's just say that if the outside was astonishing, then the inside is amazing.

"Again, just the beginning," Munoz says, face widening into a grin. "Each room has its own theme."

"How did you—?" I start to ask how they managed it all without my even being aware, but then I see—there are decorators, caterers, bartenders, all manner of helpers roaming the place. This isn't just a party. It's a huge high school graduation blowout bash.

"There's a lot to celebrate," Sabine says. "So we figured we'd go all out. Think of it as a welcome home slash happy graduation slash engagement party. Oh, and we haven't had a chance to tell you yet, but a major publisher just made an offer to buy Paul's book—so it's a book deal party too!" She gazes up at him, her face flushed with the pride of his success, and I take a moment to steal a quick glance at him too, catching his smile and wink, and knowing he's remembering the day when I prophesized that very thing. "We're expecting a lot of people, I hope you don't mind. I know it's not at all what you'd planned, but we thought it might be fun. Miles came up with the theme and it just took off from there."

I nod, trying to match her smile with one of my own, but all I can think about is the fruit—the real reason behind this get-together—and how it's pretty clear that's been lost along the way.

But just as soon as I've thought it, Sabine looks at me and says, "Don't worry, it's covered. I've left the den off your bed-room free for you to do whatever you need. I just hope you'll take a little time out to enjoy yourself as well."

I look at her, unsure what to say. I never expected any-thing even remotely like this, and I'm left feeling a little over-whelmed.

But Sabine just places her hand on my shoulder and says, "Now go. Go upstairs and manifest yourself a costume while Paul and I get into ours. Just make sure you're ready by seven to greet everyone."

I do as she says. It's easier that way. After tackling the stairs

I head straight for my room, where I plop myself onto my bed, feeling more than a little stunned by it all. Remembering the very first day I arrived, when Sabine picked me up at the airport and drove me to my new home, my new life. I was so lost in my grief I couldn't appreciate all the trouble she'd gone to in an effort to make my life comfortable. All I could do was throw myself facedown and cry—or at least until Riley appeared and set me straight, made me see things through her eyes.

Riley.

I close my eyes, attempting to ward off the sting, the tears, and the lumpy throat that always accompany any and all thoughts of her. Though I'm surprised by how fleeting it is— the symptoms here and gone in a matter of seconds. And I know it's because of the fruit.

Even though I still miss her, even though I long to see her again—now, for the first time in a long time, I know for a fact that I will. And knowing that goes a long way in lessening the pain of missing her, of missing all of them, Buttercup included.

With just one taste of that fruit my body will cease to be immortal. It'll revert right back to the usual procession of aging and withering until it ultimately dies and my soul reverts back to its true eternal, infinite state—free to cross the bridge to where my family now lives.

No matter what becomes of me, my soul will live on, allowing my family and me to be reunited again.

I just hope Damen and I will be reunited too.

I just hope I can find a way to convince him of what we both need to do.

But first, I need to come up with some kind of "Come As You Were" costume, and for someone with seven previous lives to choose from, you'd think the choice would be easy.

I mean, should I go as Adelina—the life I just learned about? Evaline—the Parisian servant? Abigail—the daughter of a Puritan? Chloe—the spoiled young socialite? Fleur—the artist's muse? Emala—the sad little slave girl?

Or should I go as all of them?

Find a way to stitch together all of the pieces of my various lives, like a sort of karma quilt, if you will?

I ponder for a while, liking the concept, but having no idea how I might go about it, and then, just like that, I know exactly what I'll do.

I glance at my bedside clock, seeing I have very little time and some serious manifesting magick to get to. So I jump to my feet and get started, hoping it'll turn out just like the image I hold in my head.

Hoping it'll serve as more than just a costume. That it'll provide the evidence, all the proof that I'll need.

FORTY-ONE

When I'm finished, I stand before the mirror and take inventory. Going over my mental checklist and making sure everything is present and accounted for. Hearing Damen's voice in my head, the exact words he used when he explained it to me—assuring me that every piece, from my fiery red hair to my elaborate dress, from my flirtatious gaze to my inner strength and humility, found its origins in the past, while my eyes themselves remain unchanged, eternal, no matter what guise my soul decides to wear. And knowing I've come as close as I can to replicating the painting he made (including a few new references to Emala and Adelina, whom I didn't know about then), until I remember one last thing. One last thing I'm not sure I can go through with.

The gossamer wings.

The moment I manifest them onto my back, I feel silly.

Silly and embarrassed and, well, a tiny bit mortified.

There's no way I can face my guests like this. They won't understand. They'll take it the wrong way. Think that I think I'm so special I've actually descended from angels in order to walk among them. When nothing could be further from the truth.

I press my lips together, about to close my eyes and make them disappear, when I remember that I'm not doing it for them. I'm doing it for Damen. Well, for Damen and me.

The night he painted my portrait in the Getty Museum he claimed they were there—claimed he alone could see them. Claimed that just because I couldn't see them didn't mean they weren't real. And while I'm sure no one will understand what I'm up to, all that matters is that Damen does. That the sight of my costume will help to convince him of what we must do.

I just hope that he still sees me this way.

I just hope that I'm not trying to reclaim something that no longer exists.

I fool with my hair, unused to seeing myself as a redhead other than when I'm in the pavilion as Fleur, but liking the change in this life as well. Then running my hands over my long, filmy gown, I take one final look and head out the door before I lose all my nerve.

The full effects of what Sabine and Munoz and their talented team of decorators envisioned, now realized. Making me feel as though I'm drifting into a magical, mystical world, taking a trip back in time, noting how each room differs from the next, and yet all of it's themed to the very last detail.

The kitchen is ancient Greece, the den is the Italian Renaissance, the powder room the Middle Ages (except the sink and toilet both work!), the dining room the Dark Ages, the living room harks back to Victorian times, while the backyard is pure 1960s—and as the house begins to fill with lots and lots of costumed people, I'm pretty amazed by what a fun idea it turned out to be.

So far, the party just started and yet all the usual past-life favorites are already present and accounted for. Cleopatra is mingling not just with Marc Antony, but also with Marie Antoinette, and Joan of Arc, and Janis Joplin, and Alexander the Great, and Napoleon, and Einstein, along with some guy in a robe with a long wispy mustache and beard who I think is meant to be Confucius, and someone with a long gray beard who keeps shouting out prophecies who I think is meant to be Nostradamus, and I can't help but think how funny it is how everyone always assumes they were someone famous. No one ever imagines themselves as having been a chambermaid or a slave like I was.

Miles finds me first, walking hand in hand with Holt. And before I can even ask, he points to himself and says, "Leonardo da Vinci. Gorgeous, gifted, and totally and completely genius—makes perfect sense, right?"

I nod in agreement, narrowing my gaze on Holt, taking in his shock of silver hair and severe black turtleneck, and saying, "Okay, you're either Andy Warhol or Albert Einstein—"

But before he can answer, Stacia appears as Marilyn Monroe (big surprise), alongside Honor, who's dressed as Pocahontas (which really is a big surprise).

"Wow, great costumes." I nod at each of them.

Stacia runs her hands over her white halter dress, as Honor swings her long black braids and says, "Okay, I wasn't exactly Pocahontas, but I did see a life as a Native American."

I squint, wondering if that means she made it to Summerland.

But she's quick to correct it when she says, "Romy and Rayne hypnotized me."

My gaze narrows further. I have no idea what she's talking about.

"You know, they did a past-life regression on me. They're pretty good; we're talking about offering them at the store, with Ava's help of course."

"Wow." I squint. "I had no idea." And I can't help but feel a little bit bummed about all that I missed, how easily they moved on without me. Then I shake my head, clear the thought from my mind and look right at Miles, and say, "So, did you get hypnotized too? Does this mean you really were Leonardo da Vinci?"

But just as he's about to answer, Jude, who came as the artist otherwise known (well, otherwise known to me anyway) as Bastiaan de Kool, stops right before me. Taking his time taking me in as he tries to make sense of my costume. Studying me for so long I can't help but squirm. Can't help but feel nervous and uncomfortable enough to sneak a quick peek at Honor, knowing she won't be thrilled with all this attention.

"I get it," he says, eyes still narrowed. "You've taken a piece from each of them." He shakes his head in wonder, his gaze traveling over me again when he adds, "What a great idea. Wish I'd thought of it."

"Wish I'd thought of it too." I glance across the room, waving at Sabine and Munoz, who are dressed as a Viking princess and William Shakespeare respectively, then back to Jude when I add, "It was Damen's idea."

"Is he here?" Stacia asks, her cheeks flushing crimson when she realizes how I might take that, how after all that we've been through I could easily misinterpret her interest. "I mean, not that I care." She pauses, realizes that might've sounded even worse, and hastily adds, "I mean, I care—I just don't care in the way that you, um, think that I care."

I place my hand on her arm, wanting to comfort, tell her it's okay, only to be overcome by a rush of energy so strong I feel like I'm caught in the eye of her own personal tornado. And though I'm quick to pull away, it's not long before I realize it wasn't all bad. If anything, I got an inside peek at just how far she's come, and how she sincerely meant what she said.

I look at her, trying to sound more positive than I feel when I say, "Honestly? I have no idea if he'll show, but I'm hopeful."

Ava waves at me from across the room, beckoning me to join her in the den, where she's dressed as John Lennon, standing next to Rayne, who's dressed in the pillbox hat, pristine white gloves, perfect little suit, and flippy hairdo of Jackie O, while Romy is dressed as Jimi Hendrix, complete with an electric guitar strapped to her chest. Which is totally the opposite of what I would've thought, but then, even after all this time I've never really been able to get a good handle on them.

And I'm just about to thank them for doing such a great job, and for all the help they've provided this last year, when someone sneaks up from behind me and says, "And so it is done."

I turn, instantly recognizing the voice.

She looks older. So delicate and frail I can't help but worry for her health. The cane I once saw her with is now back. Though it's not long before I realize why—it's the first time I've seen her on the earth plane. And after spending so much time in Summerland, the gravity here starts to weigh pretty heavily.

"From the moment I first saw your glow, I knew."

I look at her, noticing she's the only one not in costume, and yet, in her cotton tunic and matching pants, most people probably assume that she is.

"But I don't glow," I say, my eyes still poring over her, realizing how odd she appears now that she's here. How out of context she seems. "I don't have an aura," I add. "No immortals do."

But she ignores that. "Auras are a reflection of the soul," she says. "And yours is lovely. You have been made aware of its presence, caught a glimpse of it, no?"

I gaze down at my hands, remember the way I saw them glow a gorgeous shade of purple back when I was in Summerland, back when I was still on my journey. I remember the way I'd felt the color thrumming from somewhere deep inside—the intensity of feeling convincing me of just how to proceed. Then I remember how Drina saw it too, how she'd commented on it just after I'd freed her soul from the Shadowland, and now Lotus sees it as well. Which makes me wonder if it might actually be real, and if it'll still be with me even after I've tasted the fruit?

Which of course gets me thinking about Damen, wondering if he'll agree to taste the fruit with me.

"He needs time," Lotus says, tuning in to my thoughts. "Unlike me. I have waited too long."

I nod, offering my hand as I lead her up the stairs, but she just shakes her head and relies on her cane.

Figuring I'll give it to her first, serve her privately before I gather the others, I'm surprised when she tunes in to my thoughts once again, saying, "You will find them already gathered. They are waiting for you."

True enough, when we enter the den off my room we're greeted by a startling collection of the eternally young and beautiful. The eternally young and beautiful with the best collection of costumes I've ever seen. Some of them choosing to interpret the theme literally by dressing as actual people, and some choosing to interpret it figuratively by dressing as objects like flowers and trees—there's even a shooting star standing off in the corner. And, I guess if it's true that everything is energy, if it's true that we're all connected, then there's really nothing that divides us from nature—we are all a part of the whole.

They turn to face me, over fifty people whom Roman deemed worthy, making for approximately three people every century—a much smaller group than I would've imagined, but still a much bigger group than I'd hoped.

And honestly, when I really start to take them all in, I mean each and every one, I start to feel a little ridiculous about what I'm about to propose.

I mean, these people have traveled far and wide for the sole purpose of maintaining the very life they've grown used to. These people are so advanced in every conceivable way, so well traveled, so experienced, so worldly—well, they're intimidating to say the least. And I can't help but wonder why they would even think to listen to me—a seventeen-year-old girl whose biggest worldly accomplishment so far (other than locating the tree) is having barely gotten through high school.

Why should they even think to consider giving up everything they've known and loved for so many years for some unknown, completely esoteric idea, which I can easily explain but have no way to prove?

But then I look at Lotus, see the way she nods encouragingly, those rheumy old eyes cheering me on, and it prompts me to gulp down my fears, addressing them all when I say, "I know you're expecting to see Roman, but Roman's no longer here, and so you get me. And while I'm sure I can't even come close to competing with him, now that you're here, I hope you'll at least consider hearing me out."

This is met by mumbling. Lots and lots of mumbling. With a good amount of grumbling thrown in as well. The roar growing so loud I've no choice but to shove two fingers into my mouth and let off a long loud whistle to quiet them down.

"When I said that Roman is no longer with us—I meant it in the physical way. His body has perished, though his soul still lives on. And I happen to know this because I've seen it. I've communicated with him. The soul never dies. He's *truly* immortal now." I pause, expecting more outbursts and surprised by the quiet that greets me instead.

"And so, while I know you were expecting the elixir, I'm going to offer you something else." I shift my gaze, my eyes taking in the multiple bottles of red juice left to chill in my mini-fridge, and suddenly changing my tack when I say, "No, actually I'm going to give you a choice." My eyes meet Lotus's, afraid of what she might think, but find her nodding encouragement, not the slightest bit disturbed by my words. "It only seems fair that you get a real choice. But I want you to consider the choice very carefully, because after today this choice may never come again. So, in short, I'm going to offer you a drink from the elixir that'll extend your life as you know it—preserving your youth and beauty and vitality for another one hundred and fifty years—but you should know that it comes at a price. You can still die. If one of your weak chakras is targeted your body will disintegrate and your soul will be trapped in the Shadowland—a terrible place you don't want to visit. *Or . . .*" I pause, knowing how important this next part is, and wanting to get it just right, to stress its full importance, before I lose them completely. "Or, you can taste from the fruit I picked from the Tree of Life—the fruit that offers true immortality—the immortality of the soul. And just so you know, eating it will reverse everything you are now. Your body will age, and grow old, and yes, you'll eventually die. But your being, your true essence, your soul, will realize eternity as it was always intended to be." I bite down on my lip as my hands fidget by my sides, knowing I've said all I can. The choice is now theirs. And though I think it's an obvious choice, it's still a pretty big decision to make.

There's much murmuring, much questioning, much suspicion, and since everyone already thinks Lotus is crazy, and since everyone equates me as the girlfriend of the one person they've been trained to hate, it's pretty clear that my little speech was not nearly as well received as I'd hoped.

But just as I'm sure I've only convinced them to embrace another one hundred and fifty years of what they've come to know and love—the flower, the shooting star, and the tree step forward, step right out of the crowd, making their way to where I now stand. And I blink in astonishment when I realize it's Misa, Marco, and Rafe.

They're glowing.

Absolutely, positively glowing.

Their auras beaming bright, glistening in the most unmistakable way, just like they did upon leaving the tree.

They pick up right where I left off, talking excitedly, voices overlapping, explaining about the miraculous transformation they made the moment they tasted the fruit.

Telling the crowd what I already sensed to be true—all of that whooping and hollering they engaged in just after having eaten the fruit wasn't because they believed they'd ensured

their physical immortality, but because they felt their souls'
immortality being restored.

Experienced the thrill of their karma righting itself with
the universe.

While they're talking, Lotus looks at me, steeples her hands
against her chest in a silent blessing, and goes about placing
small bits of fruit into little paper cups, ensuring there's enough
for everyone, before she plucks one for herself, looks at me,
and says, "Please. Come with me."

I hesitate. Wanting to witness the moment when the immortals, convinced by what they've heard, all step forward as
one, and choose their new path.

But Lotus just shakes her head and says, "You've done all
you can. The rest is left to them."

I glance over my shoulder, see the way the crowd moves
closer to Misa, Marco, and Rafe, then I follow Lotus down the
stairs and through the house, collecting Ava, the twins, Jude,
Stacia, Honor, Miles, Holt, even Sabine and Munoz along the
way, wanting to take this final journey with those who've helped
her to get to this point.

She leads us into the backyard, where she kicks off her
shoes, closes her eyes, and sighs as she sinks her toes deep into
the grass. Then lifting her head, she glances at each of us, her
gaze settling on me when she says, "You have released me. And
while my gratitude knows no bounds, your trust in me has been
at your own great, personal expense. For that I am sorry."

She nods, bows ever so slightly, and I wait for her to say
something more, to tell me not to worry, that it all gets better
from here, but instead she brings the cup to her lips and in-
gests. Shuttering her eyes as her hands swiftly rise, her fingers
uncurling, her palms flattening—the yard falling quiet as

Lotus begins to glow the most beautiful golden color that can't be ignored.

Her face radiant, beaming, her cane all but forgotten, abandoned by her side—a witness to something miraculous, something viewable only to her. And I can't help but gasp when instead of the ash I've grown so used to seeing, two perfect lotus blossoms bloom forth from her palms.

She turns toward me, places one behind my ear and the other in my hand, gently closing my fingers around it as she says, "This one is for Damen. You must go to him now."

I nod, eager to do just that, but also wanting to see this thing through.

Torn between leaving and staying when Jude leans toward me and says, "He's here."

I look at him, my heart leaping into my throat, thinking he's referring to Damen, but soon realizing he meant someone else.

"Her husband. He's come to escort her to the other side." He motions toward the space beside Lotus, a space that appears empty to me.

I watch as Lotus steps forward, once, twice, before she simply disappears. Her body so old, so worn, its immortality so suddenly reversed, it could no longer withstand the gravity of the earth plane. And yet, she got exactly what she wanted, what she sought all this time. Leaving nothing more than a glittering pile of gold dust behind.

Everyone remains quiet, reluctant to mar it with words.

Everyone but Stacia, who says, "O-*kay* . . . now that that's done, can someone *please* tell me where to find that super-hot guy who's dressed as a gladiator?"

Miles and Holt burst out laughing and lead her into the

house, while Ava and the twins hang back with Sabine and
Munoz, going over the details about the upcoming wedding,
as Romy and Rayne beg to be bridesmaids.

Then Honor looks back and forth between Jude and me
and says, "Okay, here's the deal: I'm taking my Pocahontas-
costumed self back inside so that you two can settle whatever
it is you need to get settled. Seriously, have your little powwow,
get it all out of your system, and then, Jude, when you're ready,
when you're ready to put your full attention on me, and only
me, well, you know where to find me."

I start to reach toward her, start to say that there's nothing
to settle, nothing to get out of our systems, that we've been
through it all, that there's no more to be said. But she turns,
shoots me a look that shows she means business, so I let her go,
turning my focus to Jude.

"So, Bastiaan de Kool." I smile, hoping if I hold the look long
enough, it will start to feel real. Wondering how it's possible to
feel so bleak after having accomplished so much. But I know
why, and I intend to deal with that soon enough. "Out of all of
your lives, was Bastiaan your favorite?" My gaze settles on his
filmy white cotton shirt and paint-splattered pants.

Jude laughs, his aqua gaze on mine when he says, "Well, he
is the one who got all the girls. Well, all except one."

I look toward the window, catching Honor peering at us.
Her face betraying just how anxious and worried she is at the
thought of losing him to me. And while I have no way of knowing if they're truly meant to be together for the long haul, they
seem to really enjoy each other, seem to be good for each other,
good to each other, and that's all that really matters right now.

"Give her a chance," I say, returning to Jude. And when he
starts to cut in, I flash my palm, adding, "Last time, when you

asked me what I thought of her, it's no accident I didn't answer. At the time, I really wasn't sure. But now I am, and I think you should give her a real, genuine, full-blown, honest-to-goodness chance. She's come a long way since I first met her, and she's crazy about you." I meet his gaze. "And honestly, I think you deserve someone to be crazy about you. I think you deserve all the happiness you can possibly handle. Besides," I shrug, "you're no longer Bastiaan, and, despite my red hair," I point toward my head, "I'm no longer Fleur. Nor am I Adelina, or Evaline, or Emala, or Chloe, or Abigail, or any of them. Those were just roles we played until it was time to move on to the next. And while we'll always carry a part of them with us, we have so many more roles still to play. When you think about it, in the big scheme of things, our time together is like a dash of spice in a big cosmic soup—important for richness of flavor, but still, not quite the main ingredient. The past is over. It can't and shouldn't be reclaimed. All we ever have is now anyway." I nod toward the window where Honor is waiting. "Don't you think it's time we embrace it?"

Jude stands before me, gives me a long lingering look, then nods in agreement. "And you?" he asks, remaining there even after I turn to walk away. "Is that what you plan to do?"

I glance over my shoulder, first at him, then down at the lotus blossom in my hand, saying, "Yeah. Starting right now."

FORTY-TWO

On my way to Damen's I make a quick detour.

Just one quick stop to utilize my manifesting powers while I still can.

Just one brief diversion that I hope will amount to something that Damen and I can enjoy together.

If not, then I can only assume that someone else will enjoy it for us.

But I can't allow myself to think like that.

Can't allow even the slightest bit of negativity to slip in.

I'm sure Damen will bear enough for the both of us, so it's not like I need to add to it.

I wave at Sheila the gate guard, who surprisingly, considering how long I've been gone, just waves me right in. Then I make my way up the hill and around the series of turns, until I'm pulling onto his street. Remembering the very first time I came here—back when I was uninvited and forced to climb through an open kitchen window—only to find the place devoid of all furnishings in a way that wasn't just empty, but eerily empty. Well, eerily empty except for the room upstairs where he kept all of his most cherished mementos from his past—a room that took me some time to learn to appreciate.

I leave my car in the drive and head for the door. Not bothering to ring the bell or knock, I just let myself in. Charging right through his enormous foyer and straight toward the stairs, knowing just where to find him, just where he goes when he's feeling troubled like he is.

He stands at the window, his back turned to me, his gaze fixed on some faraway place, when he says, "There was a time when you thought this room was creepy. When you thought *I* was creepy."

I pause by the old velvet settee, making no attempt to deny what he said. Taking in his collection of handwoven tapestries, crystal chandeliers, golden candelabras, gilt-framed master-pieces—a visual reminder of a very long, adventure-filled life—a visual reminder that what I'm about to ask of him is no small request.

"There was a time when you held great resentment toward me for what I'd done to you—for what I'd *made* you."

I nod, there's no use denying that either, we both know it's true. And though I wish he would face me, though I beg him with my mind to turn so he can see me, he remains where he is, rooted in place.

"And it's clear you still cling to that resentment. It's why we find ourselves here. Divided like we are."

"I don't resent you," I say, gaze glued to his back. "I know everything you've done, you've done out of love. How could I possibly resent you for that?" My voice cushioned by antique rugs, heavy drapes, piles of silk pillows, but still managing to echo right back at me, sounding much smaller than I would've anticipated.

"But we are now at a crossroads." He nods, his finger playing at something he holds against the windowsill, something he keeps just out of view. "You want to erase what I've done and go back to the old way of being, while I want to stay as I am, hold on to the life I've grown used to living." He sighs. "And, I'm afraid in light of all that, there's really no way to compromise. We've come to a juncture—a place where we either have to find a way to agree on a shared destination, or head off in separate directions, and live separate lives."

I stay quiet, still, hating the sound of his words—the way they cause my gut to clench and stir—yet knowing it's true. A choice must be made, and it must be made soon.

"You must understand, Ever, that even though you've built a very strong and valid case, even though my choice is wrong in many, if not every, way—for the last six hundred years this all that I've known. This is the life I've become accustomed to. And, as much as I hate to admit it, I'm just not sure I'm cut out to be mortal. While it was easy to give up on my extravagant ways when I thought my karma was to blame for our problems— while it was extremely easy to trade in my handmade motorcycle boots for rubber flip-flops—what you ask of me now, well, it's another thing entirely. And I know how incredibly hypocritical I probably sound. On the one hand, I claim to be so concerned with the karmic state of my soul, and yet, on the other, so fervently resistant to the one and only real solution that's presented to fix it, but still, there it is. Stated plainly, I'm not willing to give up my eternal youth and physical perfection in order to watch my body grow old and decay and eventually die. I'm not willing to give up my access to magick and manifesting and easy trips to Summerland. I'm just not. Perhaps it's easier for you, having only been immortal for a year versus my six hundred. But, Ever, please, try to understand that my immortality has defined me for so long, I'm not sure who I'll be if I choose a life without it. I'm not sure who I'll be if I'm no longer the man you now see. Will you still love me? Will I even like me? I'm just not willing to take the chance to find out."

I balk. Seriously, balk. But it's not like it matters. It's not like he sees me. I mean, I knew he was fearful, I knew he was afraid of making such a huge change, but I never once considered he might be fearful of losing me once his physical immortality is stripped away.

Finally finding my voice enough to say, "You honestly think I won't love you anymore? You honestly think that all of your experiences and talents and beliefs—all of the things that have shaped you into the amazing person I know you to be—will somehow vanish and leave you a dull, empty, unlovable shell, the minute you choose to eat the fruit? Damen, seriously, you must know I don't love you because you're immortal, I love you because you're *you*." But even though my words are impassioned, spoken straight from the heart, they fall short.

"Let's not kid ourselves, Ever. First you fell in love with the magical me—the fancy car, the tulips, the mystery. It was only later when you got to know the real me. And even then, it's hard to separate the two. And, if I remember correctly, you weren't so wild about what you once referred to as my 'monk phase.'"

He makes a good point, but I'm quick to refute it. "It's true that I fell fast and hard for the magical, manifesting, mysterious you—but that was infatuation, *not* love. Once I got to know you, once I got to know your heart, and soul, and the truly wonderful being that you are, well, that's when that infatuation grew much deeper and turned into love. And yeah, while it's also true that I didn't exactly love it when you chose to give up all the fancy stuff, I never stopped loving you. Besides, aren't you the one who once told me that everything that can be done in Summerland can be done in the earth plane too? Didn't you claim that it might take a little longer to see it come to fruition but that it works all the same?"

I move toward him, stopping just a few inches shy, wishing he'd turn and face me, but knowing he's not ready.

"In the end," I say, my voice softly coaxing, "it all comes down to what you already know to be true. You know how the universe works. You know that everything is energy, that thoughts create, that we can work our own magick right here on the earth plane by keeping our intentions positive and clear. So now it's just a matter of putting all that we know into practice. Now it's just a matter of having faith in all that you've taught me. Now it's just a matter of trusting the universe enough, trusting me enough, and trusting yourself enough, to *believe*. Damen, don't you want to slow down? Don't you want to stay in one place for more than a few years? Don't you want to build lasting friendships, maybe even, I don't know, but maybe even have a family someday? Heck, don't you want to see your own family again?"

He takes a deep breath, takes several deep breaths, then he turns, his dark eyes going impossibly wide when he sees me— sees how I'm dressed.

"You're a vision," he says, his voice edged with wonder. "You're just like the painting. *Enchantment*. Isn't that what we called it?"

But while his eyes are busy roaming me, mine are fixed on what he holds in his hand.

The thing he'd kept hidden when he was facing the windowsill now plainly in view.

The sight of it reminding me of Roman's last night, when he sat before me on his rumpled bed—a gleaming glass vial filled with sparkling green liquid pinched between his finger and thumb.

Much like Damen stands now.

He catches me looking, grips the glass tighter, causing the green liquid to splash up the sides, swishing just shy of the lip.

And I know that all we have to do to be together in the way that we want is to drink it.

Just one small sip from each of us is all it'll take.

One small sip and all of our problems disappear.

Only that's what I used to think. Now I know that it's no longer true.

While the antidote may be a sure thing, the bigger solution, the real solution, offers no guarantee. It requires a leap of faith—a pretty big leap for sure—but still one I'm willing to take.

Though from what I can see, with the way Damen lifts the vial before him, I'm clearly the only one feeling that way.

Still, I can't help but be transfixed by the sight of it. Transfixed by the realization that I'm ready to turn my back on the one thing I sought for so long.

I lift my hands before me, the lotus blossom cupped between my palms as I say, "I saw Lotus—just before she crossed over. She wanted you to have this." My eyes meet his, noting how he's absorbed by the sight of me, as the antidote continues to swirl in his grip.

And while he doesn't reach for the flower, he does manage to say, "I always figured it was the stuff of myth. I had no idea it really exists."

I edge closer to him, edge past an ancient marble-topped table covered with stacks of very impressive, first-edition signed books that would easily fetch hundreds of thousands of dollars at auction.

"The *actual* Tree of Life!" He flicks his gaze between me, the lotus blossom, and the antidote he holds in his hand, softly shaking his head when he says, "It's amazing to me that you not only found it, but that you brought back enough fruit for all of our kind. While I can't bring myself to taste it, I'm impressed and amazed that you managed to do such a thing."

Despite the warmth in his eyes, all I can hear is: *I can't bring myself to taste it.*

The words resonating in a way that robs me of breath, makes my knees threaten to crumple.

We gaze at each other, the silence gathering, building between us. And if I could, I'd encourage the moment to stretch and grow and linger forever, but I know it must end. Everything does. I also know what needs to be said, so it may as well come from me.

"So, I guess this is it then?" I try not to sound as broken as I feel but don't come close to succeeding.

He looks at me, his expression standing in for any words he might say, so I heave a deep sigh, curl my fingers around the lotus blossom, and start to haul myself out of his room, out of his life.

We've reached the crossroads.

The juncture.

There is no turning back.

This is where we go our separate ways.

Aware of the *almost* feel of his hand on my arm when he pulls me back to him and says, "Yes."

I look at him, unsure what he's saying *yes* to.

"The questions you asked earlier, about wanting to settle down, start a family, see my family? Yes. Yes to all of it."

I try to swallow but can't, try to speak but the words just won't come.

His hands sliding around me, grasping me to him, he lets go of the vial, allows it to fall, to crash to the ground. The sparkling green liquid seeping out all around as he says, "But mostly yes to you."

FORTY-THREE

Even though he's agreed to do it, he still hesitates.

His hand shaking, his gaze so full of trouble and worry it prompts me to say, "Look at me."

He takes a deep breath, but does as I ask.

"Let this be the proof."

He cocks his head, not quite understanding.

"Let this costume be the proof of how I'll always come back to you. No matter what happens, we'll always be together, always find a way to locate each other. Whether I'm Adelina, Evaline, Abigail, Chloe, Fleur, Emala, Ever, or, eventually, someone else entirely." I smile. "No matter which guise my soul decides to wear, I will always return to you. Just like I always have returned to you."

He nods, holds my gaze, lifting the cup to his lips as I do the same.

Surprised to learn it's not at all sweet like I thought, but still, I hardly notice its bitterness—the way it doesn't sit so well on the tongue. I just urge the fruit down. Encourage it to flow through my system as though it's the sweetest ambrosia any god could create, while Damen does the same.

And when I see the way the room sparkles and glows, when I see the way the furniture vibrates and all the paintings come to life—I understand exactly what made Misa, Marco, and Rafe whoop and holler and carry on like they did.

Everything is alive.

Everything is bursting with color, throbbing with energy, and it's all connected to us.

We are part of each other, part of everything that surrounds us.

There are no boundaries of any kind.

The world appearing just as it did when I died as Adelina. When I soared through the sky and gazed down on creation.

Only I'm not dead. In fact, it's just the opposite. I've never felt so alive.

My eyes meet Damen's, wondering if he'll change, if I'll change. But other than my hair returning from the red that I manifested to its natural state of blond, other than the purple aura that surrounds me, and the indigo blue that surrounds him, there doesn't seem to be much change at all.

I reach toward him, just as he reaches toward me. Tentative, our fingertips just about to touch, when he flinches, pulls away, causing me to look at him and say, "Even if it doesn't work, even if we discover our DNA is still cursed, even if one of us should die trying, we'll find each other again. And again. And again. Same way we always have. Same way we always will from this point on. No matter what happens, we'll never be apart. We're truly immortal now. It's like when we're in the pavilion, right when we're about to enter the scene and I always freeze— what is it you always say to me?"

He looks at me, face softening when he says, *"Believe."*

And so we do.

We take that big leap of faith and believe.

The silence pierced by twin intakes of breath the moment we reach forward, make contact.

Our fingertips touching, meeting, pressing solidly together, seeming almost to merge into each other, until it's impossible to tell us apart, determine where he ends and I begin. And I can't help but marvel at the warmth of him—the surge of pure tingle and heat that he brings. And soon, no longer content with just that, longing for something much deeper, we slip into each other's arms.

My hands at his neck, his at my waist, clutching me tightly, pulling me close, and then closer still. Exploring the path of my spine before threading his fingers through my thick mane of hair, he steers me toward him, expertly angling my lips to meet his. The soft pillowy firmness of his mouth reminding me of the first time I tasted him—in this life and all the others as well. Our whole world shrinking until there's nothing but *this*.

One perfect everlasting kiss.

Bodies pressed together, we sink down to an antique rug that some of history's most illustrious figures have walked upon, Damen lying beside me, curled all around me, the two of us completely overcome by the wonder of each other, the wonder of being together. Hardly believing this moment has come after having waited so long.

The curse finally broken.

The universe no longer working against us.

Damen pulls away, gaze drinking me in as his fingers rediscover the feel of my skin. Exploring the expanse of flesh between my temple, my cheek, my lips, my chin, down around my neck, and then lower still, as my lips swell in anticipation of his, eagerly tasting, taking small nips at his hand, his shoulder, his chest, whatever comes near. I can't get enough of him. Can't help but want more of him.

All of him.

Now.

"Ever," he whispers, gazing at me in the same way that Alrik once did, only this time it's better, happening in real time.

I lift my face to his, capture his lips, and pull him back to me. My body heating, thrumming, wanting nothing more than to deepen this feeling—discover just how far it might go.

"Ever." His voice is thick, hoarse, the words requiring great effort, when he adds, "Ever, not here. Not like this."

I blink. Rub my lips together, as though awakening from a dream. Realizing we're still on the floor, when there are far more comfortable places we could be, including one that I manifested just before I came here.

I rise to my feet, and lead him downstairs, out to my car, and onto the curving, winding expanse of Coast Highway, until I pull up to the most beautiful, old, weathered stone manse perched up high on a cliff, with floor-to-ceiling windows that look down upon a swiftly churning sea—a dwelling that wasn't there just an hour before.

"Did you make this?" He turns to me.

I nod, grinning. "What can I say? I was hoping we'd come to an agreement. I was going to book us that room at the Montage, but I thought this was better, more private, more romantic. I hope it's okay?"

He grasps my hand in his and we both hurry toward it. Scaling a long, winding, seemingly never-ending series of stairs until we reach the top, breathless for sure, but more with anticipation than the climb.

I swing the door open and motion him inside, seeing the way he laughs when he steps onto the old limestone floor and sees that despite the size of this place, despite its massive square footage, it only consists of one very large bedroom with a wood-burning fireplace, a beautiful four-poster bed, a gorgeous old woven rug, a well-appointed bathroom, and nothing more.

I flush. I can't help it. Quickly mumbling something about having not had much time, how we can always add to it if we decide to hang out for a while.

But he just smiles, stops the flow of excuses with a gently pressed finger he soon replaces with his lips, turning my suddenly hushed silence into a nice, long, deeply soulful kiss. Pulling me toward him, toward the bed, voice softly whispering, "You are all that I want. All that I need. I couldn't ask for anything more."

He kisses me gently but thoroughly, taking his time, making a great effort to handle me with care. But even though I know our time together is infinite, that we'll always be together, I'm eager for more.

I tug at the hem of his sweater, yank it up high over his head and toss it aside. Pausing to explore the landscape of his chest— the curving hills of his shoulders, the rippled valley of his abs— before my fingers dip lower, working a button, a zipper, an elastic waistband. And even though it's not the first time I've seen him, I still can't stop the gasp from escaping my throat. Still can't stop myself from drinking in the astonishing sight of him.

He removes my clothes too. Fingers moving deftly, expertly, far more practiced than mine. And it's not long before there's nothing left between us—neither physical, nor mystical.

There is only he and I.

No barriers of any kind.

He anchors his leg over me, around me, until his body covers mine. My insides quivering with tingle and heat as I shutter my eyes to the warmth of him, the feel of him, then lazily lifting my lids to find his gaze burning into me. The two of us pulled into the hypnotic lull and sway of each other, and it's not long before he reaches down and joins us together.

Joins us in the way of Alrik and Adelina.

Joins us in the way we've dreamed of all this time.

But it's so much better than anything that went before.

Because this is real.

This is right.

A final confirmation that we're made for each other.

Meant to be together.

Always and forever.

Our bodies rising, lifting, soaring high, then higher still—the moment growing, expanding, holding for as long as it will . . . until we collapse into the warmth of each other, and the ceiling bursts open, and a deluge of beautiful red tulips comes raining down.

FORTY-FOUR

I roll onto my side, edge closer to him, allowing my fingers to follow the trail from his chest to his abdomen and down lower still. Amazed by the actual feel of him, his warm and wonderful being—wondering how I managed without it so long.

"What are you thinking?" he asks, his lips nipping the lobe of my ear.

"Oh, you know . . ." I smile flirtatiously, my pinkie inching back up, finding his navel and navigating the perimeter, as he laughs and pulls me onto his chest. Planting a kiss on the top of my head as my mind fills with one single word: *Content.*

I am totally and completely content.

I'm also happy, relaxed, and at peace.

I have everything I could ever want.

My life is complete.

I gaze up at him, wishing we could linger, drag this out for as long as we can, but Damen has other plans, claims we've got somewhere important to be.

"I'll miss this place," he says, getting to his feet and stepping over the carpet of tulip petals that kept raining down until they covered the floor.

"Don't sound so final. It's not like it's going anywhere." I smile. "Unless, we're going somewhere? Are we going somewhere?" I peer at him, hoping for a clue. But he's wearing his very best poker face, which means there is no getting through.

I shrug, slip into the dress I was smart enough to manifest earlier, since it's not like I'm willing to wear that winged costume again.

Then as soon as we're dressed, he grabs my hand and leads me to the window, the two of us watching the waves crash against the rocks far below.

"Do you still see it?" He glances at me.

I nod, then, trying something I was too nervous (not to mention too preoccupied) to try earlier, I think: *Do you?*

He looks at me, smiles, and thinks: *Yes. And, even better, we can still hear each other!*

I lean against him, wondering how long it will last. Knowing the vibrating colors, the lyrical hum of the universe will eventually fade. Even when Misa and Marco and Rafe raved about the experience, it was in the past tense. Still, though it may fade from sight, it'll never fade from my mind. Now that we know the truth of everything, the way the universe works, the world will continue to be as magical and amazing as ever, even for mortals like us.

"Ready?" he asks, hand grasped with mine, the blur of our combined energy all the proof that I need that we are one with each other—one with everything.

I nod, walking alongside him as we make our way to my car. Experiencing a moment of panic when I try to start it with my mind like I usually do, then relaxing once I remember I'd had the foresight to bring the key along, since from what I can tell, that sort of mental magick no longer works.

And when Damen tries to manifest a tulip for me, sadly, it never makes it past the vision he holds in his head. But before he can really start to feel bad, I'm quick to remind him that if it's true what they say about the universe, that thoughts truly do create, then that tulip will show up eventually.

When we arrive at my house, I dash up the stairs and head straight for my closet, busying myself with throwing a bag together, while Damen heads for the den, calling out, "What should I do with all this?"

I zip the duffle closed and swing it over my shoulder, glad to see I've still got at least some of my immortal strength and stamina since I basically threw in everything that would fit.

I go to where he stands, seeing him point toward the bottles of elixir still stored in my mini-fridge. Only their numbers have greatly diminished from the last time I looked.

I slip around the counter, dropping to my knees as I conduct a quick mental count. A count I repeat again and again—each time coming to the same startling conclusion: Not all of the immortals went for the fruit.

"I was thinking we should destroy them, or at least keep them under lock and key. I'd hate for them to get in the wrong hands, or even unsuspecting hands, you know?" Damen turns to face me. "Hey, what's wrong?" he asks, alerted by my expression.

"It used to be full." I look at him. "When I left the party, it was full. And now . . ." I shake my head, place my hand against my stomach, starting to feel a little ill. "I was really hoping to convince them—all of them. But maybe I left too early? Maybe I should've stuck around a little longer?"

I grip my knees, preparing to stand, when Damen says, "How can you be sure it was an immortal?"

My eyes meet his, and suddenly the room begins to swirl, forcing me to grab hold of the counter to steady myself.

But just as quickly, it's passed.

In the end, it's just like Lotus said—I did all I could—the rest was up to them.

There's such a thing as free will, and from the looks of it, someone has decided to exercise theirs.

"Toss it," I say. "Toss all of it. I've reserved plenty of leftover fruit for any immortals who find themselves trapped. But as for the elixir, we've no need of it—it's time to wash our hands of it."

We get to work, me removing the tops, then handing him the bottles, which he empties down the drain. And when we're finished, he turns to me, grasps my hands in his, and tells me to envision a shimmering golden veil.

"Summerland?" I quirk my brow, wondering why I need to pack a bag for Summerland when you can just manifest anything you want, and wondering if we'll still be able to get there. Knowing I'll be crushed if it turns out we can't.

But he just shakes his head and says, *"Believe."*

So I do.

And a moment later, we're stepping through the light, stepping right into that vast fragrant field, feeling happy, satisfied, pleased to know it's still within the realm of possibilities.

Damen looks at me, as relieved as I am when he says, "And now for part two . . ."

I wait, hold my breath, having no idea what that might be.

"Remember when Miles used to talk about us all backpacking around Europe after high school?"

I nod, growing even more perplexed.

"Well, I thought it sounded like a great idea. And since we never went on that vacation because of the journey to the tree and all, and since you got a late college admission, I figured we'd take him up on it."

"But Miles isn't going to Europe," I say, knowing for a fact that he's on his way to a big audition in New York City and that Holt's going with him. And, if memory serves, I prophesized that he'd get that audition—he's going to be a huge Broadway star, and Holt's going to be by his side for a very long time.

"I know. But then I figured that doesn't mean we can't go, right? So, if it's okay with you, I thought we'd start in Italy. I can't wait to show you around my old haunts—Firenze is a beautiful city, I know you'll love it. And the food!" He looks at me, grinning when he says, "Well, I hear it's vastly improved over the last six hundred years."

"So . . . we're going to the Summerland version of Italy?" I say, trying not to sound as disappointed as I feel.

But Damen just laughs. "No. I had two reasons for coming here—one, to see if we could—and two, because I wanted to beat the traffic. We're departing out of LAX. Our plane leaves at—" He glances at his watch, then at me. "Our plane leaves in fifteen minutes."

"But we have to go through security! And get to the gate, and—"

My words stopped by his own when he says, "*Shhh* . . . just close your eyes and picture yourself in seat three-A with me sitting right there beside you . . ."

FORTY-FIVE

We land in our seats. And despite my fears, there's so much preflight commotion no one seems to notice how we just suddenly appear. And when Damen busies himself with placing my bag in the overhead bin, that's when I notice how he failed to bring one of his own.

"What about you?" I watch as he takes the seat beside me. "I know it's going to be an adjustment, but you can't just manifest new stuff whenever you need it, you know? You're going to have to actually go to the store and buy it. You're gonna need money and credit cards and passports and—oh my gawd, did you remember to bring money and credit cards and passports? And why are we even flying? Why didn't we just make it so we landed in Italy?"

Damen grins, stops the flow of words with his lips. Instantly dissolving my worries, reminding me of what matters most.

He pulls away, brushes his hand across my cheek, tucking some stray strands back behind my ear when he says, "No worries. I've got it covered. Everything's handled. We're good. Oh, and as far as the plane goes, you wanted to be normal . . ."

"First class is normal?" I glance around the spacious, well-appointed cabin, then back at him.

"It is with me." He laughs.

I nod, enjoying the warmth of his hand in mine, gazing out the window as the plane makes for the runway. Unable to stop marveling at how far we've come—how far we've yet still to go. Realizing I feel happier than I have in a very long time—perhaps maybe, ever.

Just about to direct my attention to the safety video (now that I'm no longer immortal I'm forced to worry about mundane things like that), when I see her.

Standing on the wing, jumping up and down and waving at me.

Riley.

My adorably sassy, ghostly little sister—and from what I can see, Buttercup is right there beside her.

I gasp in amazement, press my hand to the window. Wondering if the vision is real, if I'm truly able to see her now, or if it's just wishful thinking. Then Buttercup barks and wags his tail, as Riley looks all around, as though she's expecting to see somebody, as though she was followed.

I turn to Damen and yank on his sleeve, wanting him to see what I see. But by the time we turn, she's gone. And try as I might, I can't bring her back.

But I saw her.

I know for a fact it was her.

I also know that I'll see her again. If not lolling on airplane wings, then on the other side of that bridge.

I just hope that one doesn't come anytime soon.

The plane pitches down the runway, gaining in speed, so I lean into Damen. My head just meeting his shoulder when a beautiful red tulip drifts down out of nowhere and lands on my lap.

The same tulip Damen tried to manifest earlier.

We look at each other, our eyes wide with wonder, having all the proof that we need that it really is true.

Everything that can be done in Summerland, can be done on the earth plane too—it just takes a little longer, that's all.

I place my hand on the stem, as Damen places his hand over mine. The two of us leaning into each other, feeling happy, content, eager to embrace whatever comes next, as the plane lifts into the sky.

ACKNOWLEDGMENTS

Writing this series was an incredible journey, and I'm grateful to have had such an amazing team of Sherpas to show me the way! Big, sparkly, glitter-strewn thanks go to: Matthew Shear, Rose Hilliard, Anne Marie Tallberg, Katy Hershberger, Angela Goddard, Brittney Kleinfelter, Bill Contardi, and Marianne Merola—you guys ROCK!

Also a special thanks to my foreign publishers and editors: Thank you for bringing The Immortals to readers across the globe!

And, of course, to Sandy: Always.